The Madman Theory

Harvey Simon

ROSE
MOOR
PRESS

ROSE
MOOR

PRESS

Rosemoor Press, LLC
10421 Motor City Drive
#34056
Bethesda, MD 20827
info@rosemoorpress.com

THE MADMAN THEORY

Publisher's Cataloging-in-Publication Data

Simon, Harvey.
    The madman theory / Harvey Simon.
      p. cm.
    ISBN: 978-0-9855166-0-4
    1. Cuban Missile Crisis, 1962—Fiction. 2. Nixon,
Richard M. (Richard Milhous), 1913-1994—Fiction.
3. Presidents—Fiction. 4. Alternative histories (Fiction),
American. I. Title.
PS3619.I5475 M33 2012
813–dc23   2012906909

Library of Congress Control Number: 2012906909

ISBN: 978-0-9855166-0-4

Printed in the United States of America

12 11 10 9 8 7 6 5 4 3 2 1   12 13 14 15 16 17 18 19

For my mother
and in memory of my father,
Saul Simon,
1916–2007

"Under the prevailing system, John F. Kennedy
was inaugurated, but it is not at all clear that
this was really the will of the people..."

—Tom Wicker, foreword to *The People's President,* by Neal R. Peirce.

"It must be God's will."

—Hannah Nixon, on learning of her son's loss to John F. Kennedy in 1960.

Author's Note

I N OCTOBER 1962 the world stood on the brink of war. American spy planes had discovered a Soviet nuclear missile base in Cuba, just ninety miles off the Florida coast. The United States demanded the missiles be withdrawn. As history had it, President John F. Kennedy and Soviet Premier Nikita Khrushchev negotiated a peaceful resolution.

But how would this crisis have played out if John Kennedy had not been president?

As much as we may think of Kennedy as personifying the American presidency of the early 1960s, he nearly didn't. Kennedy won the presidential election by the slimmest margin and, many have argued, by fraud. The shift of a small number of votes in a few key states would have made another young man, Richard M. Nixon, president of the United States at the most dangerous moment in history, leaving Kennedy to watch from the sidelines as the junior senator from Massachusetts.

Because the margin of victory in 1960 was so narrow, any of a number of minor decisions could have reversed the election outcome. For example: In the months leading up to the November contest, President Dwight Eisenhower had become angered by Kennedy's attacks on his administration. As a consequence, the president, who maintained an enormous well of popular support in the nation, wanted to do more as November 8 approached to help Nixon, his vice president. Nixon declined Eisenhower's offer and asked the president to limit his final campaign appearances. Eisenhower, unaware of his vice president's concern for his health, was livid, but grudgingly agreed to a very modest schedule of public addresses.

What if Eisenhower, who was known for his stubbornness, had insisted on campaigning full-out on Nixon's behalf? The president would certainly have gotten his way and Nixon might well have succeeded him in the White House.

We live in the actual world, of course. But there also exist—in some weird, abstract way—an infinite number of possible worlds that are just like our own. Until they diverge. In one, your parents never meet. In another, the Japanese decide not to bomb Pearl Harbor. This novel describes one such world—the one in which Richard Milhous Nixon is elected president in 1960.

Cast of Characters
1962

Jacob Beam, United States ambassador to the Soviet Union, from 1961–

Fidel Castro, prime minister of Cuba, from 1959–

Anatoly Dobrynin, Soviet ambassador to the United States, from 1962–

Helene Drown, friend of Pat Nixon, from 1940–

Allen W. Dulles, director of Central Intelligence, from 1953–

John Foster Dulles, United States secretary of state, from 1953–1959 (died 1959)

Dwight David "Ike" Eisenhower, 34th president of the United States, from 1953–1961

Robert Finch, chief of staff to the president, from 1961–

Thomas S. Gates, Jr., United States secretary of defense, from 1959–

Andrei Andreyevich Gromyko, minister of foreign affairs of the Soviet Union, from 1957–

Leonard W. Hall, United States attorney general, from 1961–

Leo A. Hoegh, director of the Office of Civil and Defense Mobilization, from 1958–

John F. Kennedy, United States senator from Massachusetts, from 1953–

Nikita Sergeyevich Khrushchev, first secretary of the Communist party of the Soviet Union, from 1953–

Sergei Khrushchev, elder son of Nikita Khrushchev and Nina Petrovna Kukharchuk

Herbert G. Klein, presidential press secretary, from 1961–

General Curtis LeMay, air force chief of staff, from 1957–

General Lyman Lemnitzer, chairman of the Joint Chiefs of Staff, from 1960–

Henry Cabot Lodge, Jr., 37th vice president of the United States, from 1961–

Arthur Lundahl, lead CIA photo interpreter, from 1953–

Rodion Malinovsky, defense minister of the Soviet Union, from 1957–

John Jay McCloy, United States secretary of state, from 1961–

Anastas Mikoyan, first deputy premier of the Soviet Union, from 1946–

Julie Nixon, younger daughter of Richard and Pat Nixon

Pat Nixon, First Lady of the United States, from 1961–

Richard M. Nixon, 35th president of the United States, from 1961–

Tricia Nixon, elder daughter of Richard and Pat Nixon

William Pawley, Florida businessman and former ambassador to Peru and Brazil

General Issa Alexandrovich Pliyev, commander-in-chief of Soviet forces in Cuba, from 1962–

Joseph Quinn, Los Angeles civil defense director, from 1961–

Admiral Arthur W. Radford, U.S. Navy (retired); special assistant to the president for national security, from 1961–

Charles "Bebe" Rebozo, confidant to Richard Nixon, from 1950–

Jack Sherwood, Secret Service agent, assigned to Richard Nixon, from 1953–

Oleg Troyanovsky, interpreter and foreign policy aide to Nikita Khrushchev, from c. 1954–

Rose Mary Woods, secretary to the president of the United States, from 1961–

Chapter 1

Thursday, November 17, 1960

THE PRESIDENT-ELECT STRODE ONTO the stage of the Embassy Ballroom to a deafening, pulsing roar, thrust his arms into the air above his head, hands in the V-for-victory sign he stole from Eisenhower, buttoned suit-jacket straining, and made them roar louder still. He did not have to remember to flash a smile. This afternoon it came unbidden, sincerely. He couldn't have quit smiling now if he had wanted to.

And then the sound stopped. All the yells and whoops and hollers stopped and there was nothing but a soundless thumping echoing from the crowd.

He looked over at his wife and his two girls by his side as they smiled into the storm of applause and yelling and foot-stomping and horn-blowing rushing at them from the sea of bodies below. The vast room was filled to the corners and the doorways, crowded with the clean-cut Republican youth, with the middle-aged, with working people and professionals both, and with the graying heads of the retired, all of them gathered here after months of knocking on doors, the lady of the house interrupting her afternoon cleaning to accept a brochure extolling their candidate's superior experience—all of them together now in victory, clutching with both hands the cardboard signs that bore his name, thrusting them forward, again and again, waving them wildly, their mouths open in wide, wild contortions. NIXON! NIXON!

It had been a full week since he had watched Kennedy on the television in his hotel suite upstairs—Kennedy taking the stage at the Armory in Hyannis, Massachusetts, Kennedy standing before his supporters, so calm and collected, speaking of the still-inconclusive election results with tentativeness and yet managing with the same words to grab the mantle of the presidency for himself.

In a flash—everything seemed to happen so fast these days with television—the news men, high and holy and ready for the kill, were at his door, eager to phone in their stories for the afternoon edition. First they needed a quote from the forty-seven-year-old vice president who had, despite all the advantages of his office and his fame, lost to the unknown senator. In their simple judgment the race had all but been decided in Kennedy's favor.

On the basis of what? he had demanded to know from the aides who had stayed with him since the election in one continuous weeklong meeting. They came and went, sometimes only two of them at the long table that had been set up in his suite, sometimes all of them there, and always the same questions. What should they do next? they asked, once again revising their calculations when the latest news came in over the telephone or a news flash interrupted the day's regularly scheduled programming on the radio. Could they continue to hold off the calls for recounts in the states where they had won by the slimmest of margins? What if the count in California did not go their way? How could they turn events to their favor? What should they say to the press? How should they respond to Kennedy's most recent statement? And again he asked: On the basis of what?

Until that afternoon.

The press had declared him the loser, with only the most perfunctory nod toward the possibility of reversal, except now the results *had* been reversed. He *was* the winner.

His own election night prediction had been right: Illinois, Missouri, and Michigan were all critical wins, though in the end it had come down to California, just as he had said it would. With California's absentee votes duly counted, a crowd of bug-eyed reporters crowded about as election officials signed the certification documents transferring the state to the Republican column and giving him 279 electoral votes to Kennedy's 243.

And with that the helicopter and the limousines and the Secret Service detail headed for his new transition headquarters at Los Angeles's Ambassador Hotel, where gaiety reigned and the ballroom crowd, reassembled after their week of uncertainty, called out for their candidate-in-residence upstairs to make his appearance.

And still he had waited to appear before them, waited to accept what had rightfully been his all along, waited for Kennedy, on the other side of the country, to say he was wrong, waited to hear Kennedy say he'd mistakenly crowned himself Eisenhower's successor. Kennedy had been careful never to come straight out and say he had won. He didn't have to. His manner said it for him. He had the swagger of a winner. That and an interpretation of a trend and a wish that it could be so were all it had taken for the press to find the excuse they needed, the excuse they'd wanted all along, to rush to Jack's side. He longed to hear the words, longed to hear Kennedy say, "I owe President-elect Nixon an apology." If the shoe were on the other foot, that's what he would do, he told himself.

He knew that a single decision could have turned the election. Less than a month ago he lied to the president, told Eisenhower he'd already done enough campaigning on his behalf. Mamie was afraid her husband would have another heart attack if he went through with his plans to go all out for the Republican ticket and the president's doctor agreed. "Ike won't listen to me," Dr. Snyder said. "It's up to you to stop him, Mr. Vice President." What if Ike had gone along, instead of throwing him out of the Oval Office, to campaign nonstop on his behalf anyway? Ike attracted huge crowds and plenty of press coverage lambasting Kennedy as a "young genius" in Michigan and downstate Illinois, even generating great enthusiasm in eastern Missouri. If Eisenhower had listened, it would be Dick Nixon, not Jack Kennedy, who was now conceding the week-old election.

If it were him, not Kennedy, standing there now before a crowd of disappointed supporters, he would turn to the camera and, drawing on lessons he had learned about how to perform for a crowd that went back to his days in amateur theater, apologize for declaring himself the winner before all the votes had been counted. Always look gracious in defeat, he liked to say, though he had never lost an election.

This last week, with Jack pretending to the crown and the results looking as though they could go either way, he began to see on himself the ugly face of a loser, of someone who had screwed up, who had humiliated himself, the sour taste of defeat in his mouth for the first time. But never did he have to swallow, never did he feel the lump in his throat, trying to choke it down.

And so he had sat in his hotel room, his supporters chanting for him in the ballroom many floors below. He watched the television and waited. He refused the entreaties of his aides to go downstairs. He waited to see Kennedy swallow.

Instead he saw the senator leave the stage, smiling. Why was he smiling? Kennedy had just conceded defeat, acknowledged to the country that he was not the president-elect, and yet there were those big, white teeth of his. The man refused to swallow.

Nixon punched the knob on the Zenith. "Tell Pat to be ready in fifteen minutes," he said to his campaign manager, Bob Finch, as Kennedy's image shrunk to a small white dot in the center of the screen. "We're going downstairs."

Without bothering to look at himself in the bathroom mirror he prepared his razor and shaving cream. His beard had come in early and even then it had been heavy. He was a typical "black Irishman," his mother had told him. Not until he entered politics after returning from his service in the Pacific during the war did he begin shaving twice a day, on Pat's advice. When the political cartoonists started drawing him for their papers, after he became famous as a young congressman, he ripped the caricatures from the paper and threw them in the rubbish, even banned the *Post* from being delivered to his house so the girls wouldn't see that filthy trash. What they did to his nose, transforming a slight upward tilt into a veritable ski jump, was bad enough. Then they made him look as though he hadn't shaved for an entire day and it was only a short step from there to showing him in any sinister pose they pleased, not least of all climbing out of the sewer. Right from the beginning they were ready to use his very beard—what control did he have over his damn beard?—against him, to have him play the devil, if that was the easy way out. The cartoonists were just as bad as the reporters, just as lazy and just as ready to destroy him if it would boost their circulation for a few days.

As he shaved he thought about the call from Kennedy that morning, before the senator went on television, and how they had talked amicably for a few minutes about the election and the odd events of the last week, Kennedy congratulating him and saying to please call on him if he could be of assistance. They had agreed on the importance of presenting a united front to the Communists and concluded that both parties would support a strong foreign policy.

He wondered if Kennedy had been trying to erase some of the damage the election had done to their friendship, which had gotten its start on the train ride back from their first debate, in McKeesport, Pennsylvania. It was 1947 and the two of them, who'd entered Congress together as freshmen that year, had gone to Pennsylvania to present their opposing views on the Taft-Hartley bill as a favor for a colleague. Lying on his back on the upper bunk in the dark, Jack directly below, he lamented the long road to seniority in the House. Maybe someday, if he were lucky, he could make a run for the Senate. That would be a good life, he thought, and Jack agreed.

He did not speak of the presidency that night, though it had been on his mind. He'd already confided in Pat that it was his dream to live with her in the White House one day. On the train back from McKeesport he was afraid Jack would look up at the bunk above where this freshman congressman from a poor family, who had gone to all the wrong schools, was dreaming of being president of the United States, and laugh at him. If Jack, who sometimes acted as though he were the rightful heir to the men who carried the world on their shoulders, if this son of privilege, so handsome and intelligent, was content to leave the presidency to the giants of their time, to Dewey and Taft and Stassen, then he would not dare speak with such grandiosity.

It was not many years later, talking into the early morning hours after dinner at the house of Jack's older sister, Eunice, talking about the Communist threat and deciding their views were pretty similar, when, without any discernable pause, they were speaking again of what the future might hold for them and this time Jack was talking openly of his ambition. By then everyone in Congress knew Jack for his many long absences and it was no secret among the men there that Kennedy preferred occupying himself with young ladies to attending to the important business of governing.

Jack's reputation as a lightweight who was riding high at his father's expense had fooled them into underestimating Jack's intelligence. He knew as well that Jack was capable of the greatest things, glimpsing even then his friend's glowing promise.

The two of them were a pair of unmatched bookends, he liked to say. But underneath it all he believed they were really not that different. They were of the same generation, of course, Jack just four years his junior. It went much deeper though. He thought that Jack, despite the glib charm, shared his shyness. He believed that beneath Jack's barely concealed philandering was a private man who concealed his emotions. This even after Jack gave him the names of the women in Paris he might like to meet as he prepared to travel to Europe in '47, forgetting how embarrassed he'd felt and forgetting that charm came naturally to Kennedy while he tried to learn charm as he had learned everything else, through hard work.

Perhaps they did share one thing, at least: Each man, in his own way, understood the pain of being an outsider, for all of Jack's money wasn't enough to buy a Catholic admission to the innermost circles of power.

And so listening that night at Eunice's house to Jack's open talk, the sun threatening to rise, he was able to speak openly to his friend of his own desire, without fear of ridicule.

The thought of losing that friendship was with him as he left the hospital in '54 after visiting Jack, who'd just had surgery on his spine, tears coming from his eyes as he got into his vice-presidential limousine. Jack, by then a senator, was close to death and the priest had been called to administer the last rites. "That poor young man is going to die," he said over and over again to Jack Sherwood, his Secret Service agent. "Poor brave Jack is going to die. Oh God, don't let him die."

When he returned to his office he found his copy of Kennedy's "Why England Slept." Opening it to the title page he read the inscription, "To Dick, from his friend John F. Kennedy," and cried again. He remembered receiving the invitation to Kennedy's wedding to Jacqueline the year before, remembered Jack privately handing him an envelope full of cash from his father for his '50 California Senate race against his Democratic opponent, Helen Douglas, and remembered Jack later congratulating him on his victory, remembered the note from Jack wishing him "all kinds of good luck" after Eisenhower picked him for his running mate in '52.

Somewhere here he had the note he'd received afterward from Jackie. Jack had fooled death and Nixon returned to Bethesda Naval Hospital, hoping to lift his friend's spirits. "If you could only know the load you took off his mind," she wrote. "He has been feeling so much better since then and I can never thank you enough for being so kind and generous and thoughtful... I don't think there is anyone in the world he thinks more highly of than he does you... and this is just another proof of how incredible you are."

When finally Jack was well enough to return to the Senate, there was a basket of fruit on his desk and a "Welcome Home!" message from "your friend, Dick." Kennedy would always use crutches after that, hiding them only for the cameras, but in these first weeks of his recuperation, struggling to walk, the vice president wanted to spare him the frequent trips between the Senate Office Building and the Senate Floor. "When you return, I want you to know that my formal office will be available for you to use anytime you have to stay near the Floor," he wrote Kennedy. "I think you will find it very convenient to handle your appointments or any other business which you have to take care of when you find it necessary to attend a session."

Friends they were. And so when it became clear he and Jack were on a collision course for the 1960 presidential election, two friends forced to play the role of political foes, he made up his mind to run a clean campaign. For the first time he pulled his punches. No dirty tricks. Not that there wasn't plenty of dirt to dig, not the least of which the documentation his aides found of Jack's secret first marriage and, of course, his day-in, day-out cheating on his wife, the time he openly appeared before the press with that Smith College student he was sleeping with being only the most egregious case. With another man he would have given Finch the nod to leak it all to the press and that would most certainly have ended Kennedy's presidential campaign, and probably his entire political career.

Out of deference to Jack he held back. And what did he get in return? A blatant attempt to steal the election, that's what. Out and out vote fraud. If half the stories he'd heard in the last week were true, he had good reason never to speak with Jack again. They said it was Jack's father, old Joe, Sr., who was behind it all, paying off Mafia bosses and politicians right and left to steal votes for his son; the truth, he knew, was that sort of thing didn't go on without the candidate's tacit consent. With all that vote-buying it was a miracle Jack *hadn't* won. If he had—if Kennedy had succeeded in stealing the election from him—no one could say what the consequences would be, for the country and for himself. He liked to think he would recover from the defeat, perhaps challenging Kennedy to a rematch in '64, this time with the gloves off. Without hesitation he would ruin him.

Let it go, he told himself, rinsing the lather from his blade and returning the razor to the base of his neck. With his head tilted up he carefully guided the blade toward his jaw. You won, it's over.

It wasn't that simple, and yet by the time he had finished shaving and had put on a freshly pressed suit, he was thinking instead of what lay ahead. With the Negroes restless in the South to end segregation he'd have to walk a fine line, pushing his Southern supporters only so far before they began to get the idea that he was no better than those nigger-loving Democrats, while trying to give the Negroes some hope that the future would be better for their children. Most importantly, he wished to rob America's enemies of the charge that we were a racist nation.

Still, it was the fragile balance of power between the United States and the Soviet Union that was foremost in his mind as he considered his new responsibilities. Allow that delicate balance between East and West to tip toward the Soviets and the Cold War peace resting so delicately in the middle would collapse. Meanwhile, this crazy man in the Kremlin, Nikita Khrushchev, was jumping up and down on his end of the seesaw.

For all he had to be grateful to Eisenhower for—gritting-through-his-teeth grateful, but grateful nonetheless—it was the president's acquiescence when he asked if he could go to Moscow two years ago, in '59, to meet Khrushchev for which he was perhaps most indebted. The publicity shots of him poking at Khrushchev's chest had surely won him tens of thousands of votes. When the American people went to their local fire station or school to vote they knew the world needed an experienced leader in this modern era, a man who had stood on the world stage, and they remembered the pictures flashed back from Moscow when they pulled the lever for Richard M. Nixon.

In his own mind it was his chance during that trip to size up the Soviet leader firsthand—to look into his eyes and know how he must deal with this man who had directed the worst barnyard epitaphs at him during their impromptu debates in a mocked-up American kitchen—that would prove most valuable as they fought for the respect of millions of people in dozens of countries who would either be duped into following the Communist line or reject those false promises for the American way.

On his return from Moscow there had been great interest in what the vice president had learned in his historic meetings and he willingly accepted requests to appear on television to speak to his countrymen of what he had seen, to share his insights into the strange ways of our dangerous foe. There was an old Russian proverb, he said with a wry little smile at the camera, that it is better to see once than to hear a hundred times.

And this is what he had seen: The strength of a great military economy that left little for the workingman. He had spotted few automobiles on Moscow's grand boulevards. American women should be glad they did not live in Russia, he told his audience. There, difficult economic conditions forced a full 30 percent of women to leave the home and become part of the workforce.

Make no mistake about it—he had been very firm with Mr. Khrushchev and careful to make this point—neither of our great nations could escape indescribable ruin in a war and certainly neither of us want to see that, he said. Mr. Khrushchev calls us the downtrodden masses, which is funny, isn't it, since, as I told the premier, we have the highest living standard of any country in history. And let me say this, we must always stay on the offensive. But we must also be willing to talk with them, or eventually we're going to fight with them.

Privately he doubted it would ever be possible to talk with Khrushchev. He had tried to get through to him that the American people were willing to fight to defend their way of life; Khrushchev, he thought, didn't believe him.

And that was the real danger. If Khrushchev believes we won't fight, war is inevitable. The one path to deterring war in the nuclear age is to erase all doubt about our strength and our willingness to use it. Only by standing up to the Communists as we did in Korea, demonstrating our resolve to use every weapon in our arsenal rather than accept defeat—only then will we avoid World War III.

He would use every opportunity to make that clear, starting today, and with that decision the roar of the crowded ballroom returned.

"Some of you may remember this," he said, after his repeated pleas for calm had been heeded, only an occasional boisterous supporter breaking through the low hum of voices. "After I received the party's nomination in Chicago this summer, a bunch of you reporter fellows"—an upward motion of his right arm in their direction—"got me on the couch, ha!—no, not that couch." A big, quick smile, then serious again. "This was in the Blackstone Hotel. Julie was there, Tricia, Pat, and my mother, too." A motion of the hand in acknowledgment of his family. Mother, he hoped, was watching on television. "One of the reporters asked me a question about the election. Was it you, Paul?" Another smile at the reporters. "I answered at the time that I thought this would be the closest election of the twentieth century. What I can say now is this. We're being told that the popular vote is so close it's still too early to say which of the two candidates will gain a majority." With this, the crowd murmured a note of discontent. He put up his hands. "Now, there are some people who will try to say that the Constitution should be changed so that the popular vote decides who will be president. But I would say this, the founding fathers understood something that was very important about this great nation of ours. They did not say, 'The United States is.' They used the plural. They said, 'The United States are.'" Then, with his voice raised, speaking faster and louder as he went: "We are a collection of individual states, each state has its vote, and a majority of the states' votes are for Nixon!"

When the room grew quiet again, he thanked his tireless campaign workers, thanked the voters, thanked his staff and his family, his running mate, Henry Cabot Lodge, and everyone else he could think of, even Eisenhower. Must thank Eisenhower. Should have probably mentioned him first. The old man didn't really want me to win, he thought. A good thing Ike hated Kennedy so much. That left him no alternative except to support me. Treated me like shit for eight years, though. "Let's hear it for President Eisenhower, a truly great man!" The expected cheers.

Next he read a telegram of congratulations from his opponent and thanked Kennedy for his kind and thoughtful words. A few in the crowd booed at the mention of the Kennedy name and he said, No, no, we won't have any of that here.

"Now let me say this. I pledge to you this afternoon that we will never become complacent in the struggle against Communist slavery." He paused for the applause that had greeted similar statements during the campaign, even in Democratic strongholds. "The Nixon administration will oppose the spread of Communism in Asia, in Latin America, and elsewhere. And to the Communists who say their goal is a Communist America, we answer that our goal is nothing less than a free Russia, a free China, a free Eastern Europe, and a free Cuba."

Chapter 2

Saturday, October 20, 1962

T HE WHITE HOUSE GROUNDSKEEPERS, optimistic for Indian Summer, had yet to remove the outdoor furniture from the patio outside the Oval Office. Pausing here on his way to meet with a carefully chosen group of Cabinet members, military men, and staff, the only sound President Nixon could hear was the light traffic along Pennsylvania Avenue and Seventeenth Street as the janitors, cashiers, waitresses, and others who had pulled the Saturday morning shift made their way to work. When they unfolded the *Washington Post* on the breakfast table this morning, or listened now to the hourly news on their push-button car radios, they learned of his return yesterday to the White House from South Dakota where he had campaigned for Senator Joseph Bottum, who was in a tight reelection contest against a two-term former congressman, George McGovern. The president had taken the time to travel to South Dakota hoping his popularity and the glamour of a presidential visit would tip the balance in favor of the Republican candidate.

Bob had suggested the White House put out a story that the president had developed a head cold so he could cancel that long-scheduled trip to devote all his energy to preparing tomorrow night's television address. The important thing, he'd emphasized to Bob, was to keep up the appearance of normalcy for as long as possible to avoid any inkling that the United States was preparing for war. Only a very small group of men in his administration were aware of what had occurred and what he was planning to announce and they understood the potentially deadly consequences if word were to get out prematurely about his plans. Soon, though, he would have to brief members of Congress and there would be others with a need to know in advance, significantly increasing the likelihood of a leak. By the time this morning's commuters started home for the evening, he predicted, picking up his briefcase from the white wrought-iron chair and beginning the short outdoor walk to the double-glass doors of the Cabinet Room, the press would already be buzzing with speculation about the massive movement of troops over the past few days to Florida.

"Please be seated," he said, taking the tall chair at the center of the long conference table, his back to the high, east-facing windows that looked out on the Rose Garden. "Today I've asked the attorney general," he said, gesturing toward Len Hall on the opposite side of the table, "to join our discussions. There will be many matters of civil law that may arise in the coming days and General Hall will be critical to that process. I would therefore ask Secretary Gates," Nixon said, pausing for a half smile and a gesture to his left at Defense Secretary Thomas Gates, Jr., "to provide a brief overview of the situation at this point."

"Thank you, Mr. President." Gates was a tall Philadelphia patrician. Normally easygoing, this morning his voice was tense. "On 15 October, U.S. air assets conducting surveillance over Cuba photographed what CIA analysts have conclusively determined to be Soviet medium-range ballistic missiles. Four to five of these MRBM sites are under construction, with four launchers at each site and more on the way."

"By ship?"

"That's right, Mr. Attorney General. Now these MRBMs carry nuclear warheads of up to 700 kilotons—35 times larger than the bomb dropped on Hiroshima—and can travel in excess of 1,000 nautical miles, as you can see on this map," he said, pointing to a poster board on an easel at the south end of the room. The map displayed the Western Hemisphere. Two large circles had been drawn on the map, each with Cuba at its center. "The inner circle there, that represents the range of the MRBMs." The circle's arc reached from Texas around to the East Coast. "That puts them in striking distance of any city in the southeastern United States, as far north as Washington. New York City is safely out of range."

The president felt Hall turn to look at him. What could he say? What expression would be appropriate? Better to keep his head down and pretend to be taking notes.

"The MRBMs—R-12s, the Soviets call them—threaten an area that includes 58 cities with a population of more than 100,000, with a total of 92 million people."

"Jesus," Hall said, looking back at the map.

"I'm afraid they're the real McCoy, Len," said CIA Director Allen Dulles, who was in the last chair to the right of the president. At sixty-nine the burly, barrel-chested director suffered chronic gout that often forced him to wear slippers. This morning he wore dress shoes that were dull and scuffed.

"When will these things be ready to fire?"

Gates slid two large U-2 spy-plane photographs across the wide table toward Hall. The high-altitude plane had snapped sharp, detailed black-and-white photographs of the island below. These were the modern era's crown jewels, the wonders of a secret military technology program. The CIA's photo interpretation center had enlarged the pictures, identifying the missile sites with white lettering. "The two sites circled there at Sagua la Grande are already operational," Gates said. "The remaining MRBMs should become operational in about one week. In addition, we have discovered larger intermediate-range ballistic missiles—the R-14—with a range of 2,200 nautical miles. As you can see from the larger circle on the map, that encompasses almost all of the continental United States." The northwest corner of the United States stood alone, outside the perimeter. "The two IRBM sites could be operational as soon as 15 December."

Hall wiped his forehead with a monogrammed handkerchief as the other men at the table listened to the now-familiar facts they had reviewed so many times in the last five days. "Didn't Khrushchev say he was only sending arms to Cuba to defend against attack? But these are clearly, I mean aren't they clearly offensive weapons?"

"The only purpose of these missiles is to launch a nuclear attack against the U.S.," Gates said, "or to threaten to launch them."

Nixon looked up from his notes. Len needed to know the full extent of the Communist double cross, just as the nation would soon know. From his very start in politics he had warned that all Americans should be on the watch for Soviet duplicity of the worst kind. Soon they would all know, even the commie-lovers—everyone would know Nixon had been right. "Ambassador Dobrynin told me yesterday, when I met with him, Len, that his country was not sending Cuba any weapons that could be used to attack the U.S."

"He lied to your face," Hall said.

"Which is just what I expected he would do." He had thought until now that nothing the Communists could do would surprise him. The missiles, though, were different. Even he had not predicted Khrushchev would try to pull off such an audacious stunt. In thousands of speeches warning of Communist aggression and their quest for world domination, he had never thought to warn of this. Though it came out of the blue and could not have been predicted, he was sure his enemies would say he should have seen it coming. "Here's what we've worked out. Tomorrow night I'll go on nationwide television to announce that we've discovered these missiles and that the Air Force has begun to destroy the missile sites."

"First, Mr. President, we'll go after the SAMs, the MiGs, and the IL-28s," the Air Force Chief of Staff, General Curtis LeMay, said in a gruff voice.

"I'm not clear on all of these terms—not my usual bailiwick," Hall said, looking to Gates.

"MiGs are Soviet fighters, IL-28s are their bombers, SAMs are surface-to-air missiles," Gates explained.

"What's the latest intelligence on those, Tom?" the president wanted to know.

"We've spotted 20 to 25 MiG-21 fighters and 10 IL-28 bombers."

"These would carry conventional explosives, isn't that right?" Nixon asked.

"Yes, sir, though we have to assume they have been modified to carry nuclear warheads as well. They are certainly capable of penetrating our coastal air defense. We're very vulnerable to attack in the Florida area. Our air defenses would have a hard time spotting them coming in low over the water," Gates said, looking toward LeMay, to the president's right, to elaborate.

The general squashed his cigar stub in a porcelain White House ashtray. "As soon as we clean out their whole air complex, we'll go after the missile installations and the nuclear storage sites," he said.

Nixon drew a curved line on his pad to represent Cuba and, an inch above it, a large U-shape for Florida, then an arrow pointing at Miami. "What's the range of those Russian aircraft?"

"The bombers, four jet engines, 1950 vintage, have a cruising radius of about 740 miles," LeMay said. "The MiG fighters—the 21s are the latest Soviet model—have a short range, about half that of the bombers."

"Won't this mean war?" Hall asked.

"As you can probably imagine, Len, we've looked at this thing from every angle over the last few days and we don't think the Soviets will want to start a nuclear war over Cuba," Nixon said.

Secretary of State John McCloy leaned forward to look past the men sitting between him and the attorney general. "I just want to emphasize, Len, that everyone here today is in agreement with the president's analysis."

"Of course, precautionary measures are being taken," added National Security Adviser Arthur Radford.

"Thank you, admiral," Nixon said, nodding at Radford to his immediate right, a smile masking his anger with himself at not having gotten together with Gates, Radford, and anyone else who might speak up to warn them against giving out any more information than necessary. He worried that too much emphasis on the possibility for war and Hall would go to mush. Len, a balding, round-faced man with a hefty second chin, didn't have experience with these kinds of issues. At the Justice Department he was where he belonged. Born into politics at Theodore Roosevelt's Long Island manor house, his father had driven Roosevelt about in the future president's horse-drawn carriage and had later become White House librarian. As a result, Len had practically learned to count by counting votes. He'd become a lawyer at age nineteen and started his career in politics at twenty-six, when he was elected to the New York State Assembly. His influence and power before becoming attorney general stemmed from his four-year term, ending in '57, as head of the Republican Party.

"There are presumably Soviet soldiers on the island who will perish," Hall said, with an intonation somewhere between a question and a statement.

"We estimate eight thousand to ten thousand Soviet troops in Cuba," Gates said.

"What we're most concerned about is this," Nixon said, hoping to divert Hall's attention from the missiles in the photographs the attorney general was still studying and the destruction they could wreak on their targets in the United States. "Khrushchev may make a move against West Berlin." If there was one place the Soviets had Uncle Sam by the balls it was West Berlin; Khrushchev had only to squeeze, to move tanks, trucks, and soldiers across the line to enslave the last free people in East Germany. In his first trip abroad as president he'd stood with Pat in front of the Brandenburg Gate—oh how they'd loved Pat in Berlin—stood with tears welling in his eyes from the sight of the enormous crowd there to welcome him and promised the Germans living in both the East and West halves of that strange city deep within Soviet-controlled East Germany that they would always be free.

"Our Berlin defense plan is based on defending our sector with tactical nuclear weapons," Gates said.

The president looked at his notes, holding the bridge of his nose between two fingers.

"Maybe I don't understand," Hall said, "but doesn't that just land us in the same situation? I mean, aren't we ultimately fighting a nuclear war with the Soviets in either case?"

"Not really, Mr. Attorney General," Gates said. "The tactical weapons we're prepared to use to defend West Berlin are much smaller than the warheads atop the Soviet missiles in Cuba. Tactical weapons have more of a Hiroshima-sized explosive."

"The other difference," Nixon said, brightening, "is that we'd be using nuclear weapons in Germany in self-defense. It wouldn't be an act of aggression where we fire the first shot."

"That's right," said General Lyman Lemnitzer, chairman of the Joint Chiefs of Staff, who was seated between Radford and LeMay. "And again, in a similar decision calculus with Cuba, Khrushchev would have to decide whether he's going to go to general thermonuclear war with the United States just to take over West Berlin. We don't think he will—"

"No," Nixon said.

"Because if he uses nuclear weapons against the U.S., whether it's against our armed forces or an attack on our territory," Lemnitzer said, "our plans call for going to general war."

"Have you given consideration to a blockade of some kind to keep more missiles from coming in—trying that before using force?" Hall asked, looking beseechingly around the table.

"That would lead right into war," answered LeMay. "It would be almost as bad as Chamberlain's appeasement of the Nazis at Munich. The Soviets' MiGs would fly, the IL-28s would fly against us. And we'd just gradually drift into a war under conditions that are at a great disadvantage to us, with missiles staring us in the face that can knock out our airfields in the southeastern portion of the U.S. and if they use nuclear weapons, it's the population down there. We would just drift into a war under conditions that we don't like. There's no other solution except the course we're on."

"There's another important aspect to this, Len," Nixon said, eager now to conclude Hall's briefing but with no way to avoid dropping the other shoe. "Five days after the bombing starts in Cuba we'll begin a general invasion of the island. The Joint Chiefs unanimously recommended bombing the missiles and fully support the invasion," Nixon said. How could a president overrule the Joint Chiefs? Could you, Len?

"I'm coming to this late, I know," Hall said, "but what exactly do we gain by invading? The bombing I can understand may be necessary, though I'd like to see a diplomatic track explored further. But if we destroy the missiles, the threat has been removed and the question arises: Is there a firm legal justification for further action?"

"What we're saying is, the reason for the invasion is to make sure all the offensive weapons on the island have been destroyed," Lemnitzer said. "And that is a legitimate rationale. These missiles are mobile and can easily be moved, so there's a chance our bombers will miss some, meaning they could still be used against us. We want to take as few risks as possible."

"As long as any missiles might be on the island, there's a risk," Radford added. "There's always the chance for an accident, or a Soviet officer might act without authority from Moscow."

"That's right," Lemnitzer said, nodding his acknowledgment to Radford. "And a full U.S. military presence on the island and in the surrounding waters will allow us to ensure that no additional ships reach the island to offload more missiles."

"Aren't there also risks involved in direct combat with Red Army soldiers in Cuba?" Hall asked.

"On D-Day we expect to encounter very few Sino-Soviet troops on island," Lemnitzer said, speaking as the most vociferous advocate in the administration's ongoing discussions over the last two years about getting rid of the Cuban regime. "Most are technicians there to assist with equipment setup and operation, so we do not expect they'll be a major concern. We'll primarily encounter Cuban forces as we come ashore at Red Beach."

⊸∞∞⊷

The cut facets of Khrushchev's crystal cognac glass, raised in another predinner toast, sparkled beneath the Empire-style chandelier hanging from the dacha's high dining room ceiling. "To bright future."

"To bright future," echoed Defense Minister Rodion Malinovsky, who raised his glass without putting a wrinkle in his buttoned double-breasted uniform.

"Now that we've put hedgehog down Uncle Sam's trousers, Nixon will learn to see things our way," Khrushchev said. "They will have to treat us with respect."

Malinovsky raised his glass again, puffing up a chest covered in medals. "To Communist West Berlin!"

Khrushchev emptied his glass in a single gulp and wiped his broad mouth with the back of his pudgy hand. "Americans are going to get surprise of their lives when we tell them about missiles pointing at them from Cuba." The premier lowered his short, stocky frame into the wide, intricately carved mahogany chair and Malinovsky followed suit across the wide table. "They will learn what it is like to have their land and their people threatened, just as we have American missiles pointing at us from Turkey." In the war against the invading Germans two decades earlier, he had seen death's reign, its victims as common as the living, fleeing if they could the rubble that had been their homes and their shops, and he was determined that no people, wherever they might live, should ever suffer such a fate again. Malinovsky, whose military leadership had turned the tide against the Germans, would surely agree. "Americans have not had war on their soil for long time. Maybe missiles pointing at them from Cuba will help them remember."

Malinovsky offered another toast. "To peace."

"Our Cuban missiles will also save Cuban revolution from Nixon's plots. If not for our boldness, it would only be matter of time—and not much time—before Americans would try again to invade. This time, Nixon would not make same mistakes he made when invading at Trinidad. But once we let Americans know about our missiles, it will be different story. Our dear Cuba will be safe from capitalists."

"You were right not to inform Dobrynin of missiles. Our ambassador has many fine qualities but he is not expert liar."

"Dobrynin would never have been able to answer like Gypsy caught stealing horse: 'It's not me and it's not my horse. I don't know anything.' He might have inadvertently given Nixon clue about our missiles. Instead, he repeated what I told him, that only weapons we sent to Cuba are ones it can use to defend itself—nothing that could be used to attack United States."

Malinovsky asked, "Have you chosen day to inform Americans that we are now their equals?"

"I will wait until after they have their elections next month. Then I will attend United Nations General Assembly session in New York in November and reveal to Nixon that we have nuclear missiles in Cuba that are pointing at U.S. cities. He will shit in pants."

"There will be nothing he can do about it," Malinovsky said.

Khrushchev carved another portion from the whole trout on the platter between them. "It will be too late. U.S. will be impotent, like old pensioner." His smile showed all his white teeth.

"Hedgehog will eat Nixon's nuts! But why wait until imperialists hold elections to share our good news, Nikita Sergeyevich?"

"Our announcement will create big upheaval that rightest forces in United States could use in election to get more power."

"Premier is very perceptive about Americans—if only comrade Mikoyan was so wise. Mikoyan still insists United States will try to destroy what we have accomplished when we tell world about our missiles."

"Our first deputy premier has traveled to Cuba and to United States, but I've been to United States as well, so let us not fall into trap of believing Anastas Ivanovich is so smart." Khrushchev pulled a long, hair-thin trout bone from between his teeth and threw it on the floor. "He was right when he said in Presidium that our plan hinges on taking Americans by surprise, but we see he was wrong to say Americans would uncover our plot before missiles reached Cuba. Mikoyan also showed how stupid he is when he predicted Castro would object to accepting our missiles on his soil."

With the palms of both hands Malinovsky smoothed his mostly gray hair, already neatly combed in straight lines, front to back. "I will tell you why Americans did not find our missiles. It is because they underestimate premier's cunning."

Khrushchev silently accepted the compliment as his due. "There is another reason to keep our mouths quiet for now about missiles. Once all missiles are operational and we have forty-five thousand soldiers on island it will be too late for devil Nixon to stop us. He could destroy some of our missiles, but some would remain—enough to destroy New York and Washington. That's a minimum. There won't be much left of those cities. An awful lot of people will be wiped out. But that will never happen, comrade. That prospect will be too frightening for imperialists. And that's why they won't attack Cuba when we tell them of our missiles."

Khrushchev had already warned the United States three years ago to keep its hands off Cuba, telling them he was prepared to use rockets in the Soviet Union to protect Cuba. "Soviet artillerymen can support Cuban people with their rocket fire, should aggressive forces in Pentagon dare to start intervention against Cuba," he'd warned. It was a bluff, of course. He had too few rockets that could reach the U.S. for that. Things would be different now with the missiles in Cuba. And as extra insurance he would travel directly from the U.N. to Havana to sign a new defense agreement with Castro, pledging that Soviet soldiers would fight alongside their Cuban comrades to do whatever is necessary to repel an American invasion. This was a fight he was sure he could win.

In this very room at his Zhukovka dacha on Moscow's western outskirts he had shared his optimism about his Cuba plan with members of a delegation about to travel to the island to convince Castro to accept the missiles. The weapons, he told them, have one purpose—to scare the Americans, to restrain them, to give them back some of their medicine. "And of course it will be wonderful for us to swat America's ass."

But the missiles also had another purpose—to win America's respect and forge better relations with the West. Once the U.S. feared Soviet strength it would have to accept Soviet terms for better relations and treat the Soviet Union as an equal by acknowledging legitimate Soviet interests and heeding demands to get out of West Berlin and close the N.A.T.O. military bases that surround the U.S.S.R. Nixon would have to stop acting like a bully and treating the Soviet Union as a second-rate power.

Khrushchev looked forward to returning to the efforts he had begun with Eisenhower to forge a détente with America that could bring the Cold War to an end. The constant threat of nuclear war was too dangerous for both sides for it to be allowed to continue. As it was, whenever he offered a plan to improve relations, such as his proposal for nuclear disarmament, the U.S. all but ignored him. He desperately wanted to renew this initiative. It would not only reduce the risk of nuclear conflagration; by radically reducing defense spending he would be able to live up to his pledge to improve the standard of living for Soviet citizens. The cost of building enough rockets capable of reaching the U.S. from the U.S.S.R. would forever make this improvement impossible. On a good day, forty-two ICBMs might make it to their destinations in the United States. If the United States struck first, only twenty-six—those in underground silos—had a chance to survive the American strike. By moving existing short-range missiles to Cuba he had about doubled the number of Soviet warheads targeted at U.S. cities while avoiding the cost of building more ICBMs.

Once he went to America and announced the new balance of power, Nixon would have no choice but to accept better relations between the two nations.

Outside the Cabinet Room, the president motioned for the chairman of the Joint Chiefs. "Walk with me to my office, if you would, general." Nixon led the way past the ground-floor staircase and into the narrow Cabinet Room corridor. "I have to meet with Commander Schirra in a few minutes."

"Jesus."

"His wife and two kids will be there." It had been the same ordeal with the astronauts who had preceded Schirra into space.

"I think we can say everything turned out for the best— Schirra and the others made it safely into orbit *and* we have the pretext we were looking for, thanks to Khrushchev," Lemnitzer said in a whisper directed to the president's ear. "You could almost call it the best of all possible worlds."

The president spoke emphatically yet quietly. "I want every last copy of those plans burned." If anyone found out about Operation Northwoods, it would be all over.

Everything had been in place on February 20, as Lieutenant Colonel John Glenn, Jr. waited in his small Friendship 7 space capsule atop a giant Atlas missile for his epic blastoff from Cape Canaveral. The United States broadcast the event live for everyone to watch on their televisions, no matter what happened. The Soviet Union might have beat us into space, but when Yuri Gagarin took off the year before, the launch was conducted with the utmost secrecy, typical of Communist rule. If his rocket had exploded, no one might ever know. If Glenn's rocket exploded, they'd instantly know that and in short order they'd learn who had been responsible and how the United States would retaliate.

He had sat in the middle chair, close to the Zenith brought in to the Oval Office for the occasion, with Dulles on one side and Finch on the other. They would either cheer the success of the country's first man in space, or he would reach for the phone and place the call to put Operation Northwoods into effect. First, he would order an immediate investigation of the disaster, under the direction of a special panel, to be led by Lemnitzer. The evidence had all been prepared and it clearly pointed to a Cuban plot.

Once the results were announced, the public outrage against Cuba would provide all the political cover he would need to order an invasion in retaliation for the death of America's greatest hero. Even Richard Nixon, the most careful and critical student of the cold and calculating Communist mind, never imagined the Reds were capable of such a despicable act, he would tell the nation in announcing the invasion. Still, we really shouldn't have been surprised, he would say. They're capable of anything, aren't they?

Whatever happened, Glenn would be a hero, either the first American to circle the Earth or, if his rocket exploded, unknowingly responsible for ridding the Western Hemisphere of the pernicious influence of a Red Communist outpost close enough to America's Florida space center to allow such evil to be perpetrated on U.S. shores.

Three months after Glenn's successful Earth orbit, the television was set up for Scott Carpenter's launch into space and, again, just a few weeks ago for Walter Schirra's flight. They were all brave men and he cheered their historic feats in the vastness of outer space. He was also satisfied he had made the proper preparations to assure that if their missions went tragically awry, they would not die in vain.

"I know who you are," the Schirras's youngest daughter said.

"Who am I?"

"Can I pet the dog?" she asked, looking at the cocker spaniel sitting at her feet.

"Yeah, sure. You know who I am?"

"You're the president," she said, her small hand on a big black spot on Checkers's head.

"You're awfully smart for a such a pretty young girl. Now, just how old are you?"

Suzanne held up the five fingers of her left hand.

The astronaut and his wife proudly nodded, smiling.

The president opened a drawer in the bureau behind his desk and, with his back turned to his guests, held out a handful of commemorative tie clips, cufflinks, and pens. With what he was about to say it was easier to face the Rose Garden than his guests. "Your father's a real hero, Suzanne. He was ready to give his life for a cause we all believe in."

⸺∞⸺

President Nixon used the short break in his schedule before his next meeting to review the material in the thick binder Gates had handed him this morning in the Cabinet Room, choosing a comfortable chair in the small study off the Oval Office. The binder listed U.S. cities, military installations, seaports, and factories, estimating the probability each would be targeted in a war with the Soviets. The grim statistics of loss had only changed for the worse since the briefing he had received in a windowless room deep inside the Pentagon a few days after his swearing-in ceremony. The generals talked that day of the great advances in atomic weaponry, of hydrogen superseding atomic, of megaton replacing kiloton, and told him in the military's sanitized way that everything he thought he knew about the horror of nuclear weapons was, in this modern age, quaintly outdated. The black-and-white images flickering on their rollup movie screen looked nothing like the pictures he'd carried in his mind, formed and frozen there by newsreel images of Hiroshima and Nagasaki. Superimposed on Washington, he imagined the White House and the Capitol Building in Romanesque ruin, columns lying in repose, toppled and broken, dazed survivors with ash-streaked cheeks wandering downtown, unable to start their cars. They had achieved so much more, the generals said, a modern miracle, really. No toppled columns, no cars, no people, no sounds.

In Moscow, Khrushchev must have received a similar briefing from his generals. For the Soviets, the tally of loss could
only have been more unimaginable, given America's nuclear
superiority. The U.S. might conceivably rebuild after a nuclear
war, even with some of its major cities destroyed. Not so the
Soviet Union, for the destruction there would be that much
greater. And yet Khrushchev's public antics—taking off his shoe
and pounding it like a gavel at the U.N.—could make it seem
as though the Soviet leader was sufficiently unstable to risk his
nation's very survival for strategic advantage. Except Nixon knew
Khrushchev wasn't crazy; he was a showman, a gambler, like
himself. A gambler takes calculated risks. And he was betting
now that Khrushchev would instead put his chips down where
the U.S. was the weakest.

That place was Berlin, long a thorn in Khrushchev's side. And
this would be a good opportunity for the Soviet leader to try to
pull it out. By moving on Berlin, Khrushchev would be gambling
that the U.S. would let West Berlin go rather than start down the
path to war. Gates had said it plainly this morning: The only way
to defend that city was with tactical nuclear weapons. They'd
been incorporated into the Army's battlefield artillery in Europe
years ago. As president, he wouldn't even have to approve their
use; the commander in Europe had that authority.

The volumes in the bookcase by his chair had been arranged
in alphabetical order and he quickly found the one he was looking for: *Nuclear Weapons and Foreign Policy*. It was by a Jewish
fellow, Henry Kissinger, but a very bright guy, he thought.

He thumbed through the chapters looking for a passage that
had stayed with him since first reading the book when it came out
in '57. It said somewhere that the U.S. shouldn't rely on strategic
nuclear missiles and bombers, which would practically wipe out
civilization, but could freely use these small, short-range atomic
weapons that can be fired off from the battlefield like regular

artillery shells to efficiently stop the other side's troops. Kissinger believed the use of these tactical nuclear weapons didn't really carry any greater risk than conventional war—fighting in Europe with this type of battlefield nuclear weapon wouldn't escalate to the use of strategic nuclear weapons. He found the section he was looking for and read to himself. "Limited nuclear war represents our most effective strategy against nuclear powers..."

Kissinger wasn't the only one saying this. No one had much doubt that the U.S. would use these small nuclear weapons at some point, particularly to defend Berlin and other parts of Europe against the Soviet Union's superiority in tanks and guns and soldiers. He had said it himself as vice president. "Tactical atomic explosives are now conventional and will be used against the targets of any aggressive force," he told the invited guests who had come to hear him speak that day, the camera recording his words. These weapons, he said, "can and will be used on military targets."

Our battlefield nuclear weapons would eliminate division after advancing Warsaw Pact division. The Pentagon's war gamers concluded the Soviets would understand that the clash could escalate to general thermonuclear war if they retaliated with their own nuclear weapons. Our generals were certain their counterparts in Moscow would shrink from that prospect, knowing that even if they could destroy one or two of our cities with their strategic missiles or bombers, they'd come out on the short end of the stick in an all-out war. And so the fighting would be limited and the damage confined to military targets, without resort to the civilization-destroying, multi-megaton H-bombs atop huge rockets ready to fly across continents.

He had wanted to reread some of what Kissinger had written to help him think through this strategy, which he was beginning to fear might be overly optimistic. The Soviets now had tactical nuclear weapons in Europe, too. Wouldn't they think they had as much leeway to use them against us as we did against them? If so, the whole thing could escalate right on up to general nuclear war. The one way, the only way, to forestall that fate was to convince the Soviets he would not hesitate to fight just such an all-out war.

And yet, despite his many pledges to defend West Berlin, he could see how Khrushchev might think he was bluffing. If the Soviets knew better than to risk their survival for Cuba, why should they think the United States would risk New York or Washington in trade for half a city in a country that had so recently been an enemy?

His only hope of avoiding war was to persuade Khrushchev he was crazy enough to begin a nuclear war on the slightest provocation—convince the man who knew the most about playing the role of world leader most likely to go off half-cocked that Nixon, calm and measured in public, was the crazy one.

He called it his Madman Theory.

The theory really belonged first and foremost to John Foster Dulles and to Eisenhower, certainly, but it appealed to him no less, as powerful game-changing ideas often did. Eisenhower had ended the Korean War by getting word to the Chinese through a back channel that Ike would use nuclear weapons against North Korea unless a truce was signed immediately. A few weeks later, the war was over.

This was a game he knew something about. During his service in World War II, on a quiet island in the Pacific that the Japanese pretty much ignored, he made a study of the game of poker and the art of bluffing. As a result of his hard work, he'd come back from the war with a pretty good stake from the games he learned to consistently win over there, enough for a substantial payment on a new house.

The loud voice from the intercom startled him. "Admiral Radford and Robert Finch are here to see you."

He told Rose Mary to wait five minutes before showing them in. In that time he moved his work to his Oval Office desk. When he heard her escort Finch and Radford through the curved door of the Oval Office that led via the study corridor to her own office, he did not immediately raise his eyes from his desk. A leader could not appear eager or look tentative; he should look like he has something more important to do that he is stealing himself from to meet with those who come to see him. When entering a room, he frequently reminded his aides, a leader does not appear until his guests' anticipation is at its peak. And so he listened to the footsteps on the hardwood floor by the door and counted their paces across the carpet. When they were, by his practiced estimate, three quarters of the way to his desk he capped his fountain pen. To appear rushed he stood quickly and strode to the side of his desk just in time to shake Radford's outstretched hand.

"We will need your decision soon on my recommendation for relocation to the High Point Special Facility at Mount Weather, Mr. President," Radford said, as he opened a leather three-ring binder with a gold White House seal embossed on the cover. The sixty-six-year-old Radford sat ramrod straight in a claw-footed chair beside the president's double-pedestal mahogany desk with Finch in a matching chair on the opposite side.

If any other man had recommended evacuating the White House, the suggestion would have been easy to dismiss as the cry of a weak-spined fearmonger. He had pegged Radford as a man of steel back in '54, before the admiral's retirement, when he was still serving as chairman of the Joint Chiefs of Staff under Eisenhower. When it came time to bring on a military adviser for his 1960 presidential campaign, Radford was the man he wanted at his side. After defeating Kennedy, it was almost a given that Radford would come to work for him in the White House.

Despite his limitless respect for Radford, the idea of a government evacuation from the capital—carefully planned out in continuity of government reports and rehearsed with readiness drills to prepare for relocating vital government operations to an arc of sixteen facilities as far as 300 miles from Washington, including Mount Weather—seemed fantastical and at odds with a president's objective of doing everything possible to avoid war. The relocation sites were intended for circumstances all but impossible to imagine, making it hard to conceive of signing an order putting them into effect while the sun continued to shine in the sky as it always did. If war came, he knew it would be his responsibility to ensure—to the extent possible—that the government continue to operate sufficiently to keep order and tend to those in need. Allowing war, however horrendous, to render the federal government inoperable would be tantamount to defeat and taking preparations in advance of war would naturally increase the odds of government survival. Thinking of it that way, Radford's recommendations to take the first steps toward being prepared, just in case, might seem prudent—if they didn't so clearly conflict with his conviction that it was wrong for the president to leave the White House in the midst of a crisis and the feeling in his gut that national survival in the event of all-out war was a Pentagon pipe dream. The image of government officials fleeing the capital would send a message that war was imminent and few would take comfort knowing the evacuation was being done to ensure government operations could continue during a conflict.

"The Joint Chiefs are preparing to transfer their operations, also, to the underground Pentagon at Site R," Radford said.

"That's fine for them, but the president isn't going to put his tail between his legs and run away from a bunch of Communist thugs who think they can threaten us." He felt his chest puff out with these brave words. Hell, he sounded braver than the guys in uniform and he liked the sound of that, though it was not bravery he felt. It was an obligation to himself and the nation to appear strong in the face of danger. "Can you imagine the panic if I evacuated?" Now he looked brave and public-spirited, too.

As an admiral in the Pacific during World War II, Radford had earned a reputation for cold analysis, telling his men fighting the Japanese to "kill the bastards scientifically." Radford's analysis, now that evacuation was a better strategy than staying in the White House, might also be right in a calculated way. That wasn't enough, though. Radford and Finch—he knew instinctively Finch would want to get out of Dodge—would have to convince him that evacuation did not make him seem like a weak leader fleeing for his own safety.

"You're right, sir, that panic conditions could arise, even in cities outside the range of the MRBMs, if we implemented the White House Emergency Plan for evacuation and the JEEP, Defense's Joint Emergency Evacuation Plan," Radford said. "It would be impossible to conceal the large number of helicopters landing on the Mall and the other designated assembly sites. I stressed this to the Joint Chiefs and convinced them they could move some operations to Site R without fully activating their evacuation plan."

"I'll bet the military made sure its alternate Pentagon at Site R is rock solid."

"The risks there are actually greater than those at the Special Facility, since the SF was designed and completed earlier, before the advent of the more powerful devices in the Soviet inventory today. Even so, the risk at Mount Weather is a function of targeting accuracy and redundancy."

The president wasn't sure he understood. "Redundancy. Yep."

"Our intelligence indicates the Soviets may possibly possess the coordinates for Mount Weather, which was not constructed to survive a direct hit, the odds of which increase proportionately with the number of warheads dedicated to the objective."

"Then what's the point?" Here were the facts to back up his feeling that war was not survivable. "I'll use the bunker downstairs," he said. "If this thing heats up we'll camp out down there till the dust clears, you know—so to speak." He gave a grunt of a laugh to drive home his attempt to appear callous. "Hell."

"In the White House bunker, the probability of survival approaches zero in the event of a nuclear strike against Washington," Radford said.

"It isn't very comfortable, either," Finch added in his smooth, made-for-radio voice.

Raddy and Bob probably didn't know about the special group at an air base in Pennsylvania, far enough out where they can stay clear of the blast in Washington. Their job is to come and evacuate the president. If they don't make it in time, if there isn't enough warning, they've got heavy equipment, cranes and backhoes, to dig everyone out and put them in special protective suits and fly them to safety.

Finch snuffed out his cigarette in the standing ashtray by his chair. "The admiral's plan to quietly move just the minimal personnel out of Washington without activating all the continuity of government plans seems sensible to me," Finch said. "If we can keep this thing on the q.t., we should be able to avoid a backlash."

Radford nodded at Finch, adding, "At the present time I believe it sufficient for you and Mrs. Nixon, if she insists on returning from California, and a short list of key staff that I have designated for you at Tab B in your briefing material to travel to the Special Facility, which I recommend you do by automobile as a further measure to avoid arousing attention."

He felt an inexplicable connection with Finch, who looked at him now with an oh-please-say-it's-okay-to-get-out-of-here-to-someplace-safe expression. If his chief of staff wanted something, he sometimes felt himself—despite himself—wanting it too. Bob was the first person he talked to in the morning and the last person he spoke with at night and through it all just as bright and eager as when they'd first met, back in '47, when Finch was a twenty-two-year-old congressional aide with an office down the hall from his own official quarters as the new thirty-four-year-old representative from California's 12th Congressional District. Now, fifteen years later, Bob was still blond and movie-star handsome. He'd hired Finch without so much as a second thought when he needed an administrative assistant during his second term as vice president. Nor did he think twice in '60, before asking him to serve as chief of staff for the presidential campaign or, after that, as his right-hand man in the new administration. Over those years he'd come to regard Finch as something like the beloved younger brother he'd lost long ago to tuberculosis. He had half a mind to drop Vice President Lodge as his running mate in '64 and put Finch on the ticket instead.

Empathy for Bob and Raddy's risk calculus still weren't enough in his mind, though, to counterbalance the shame of abandoning the capital. "You might be able to move me out there and keep it quiet for a couple days, avoid any food riots and so on. But how long can we pretend the president is in the White House when he's really hiding out underground? The goddamn thing isn't going to fly, not for long," he said, unemphatically pounding the desk with his fist. "Anyway, I have to stay here to go on television tomorrow from the Oval Office." He could not leave the city solely to protect himself. The only sufficient justification would be strategic, something that strengthened his hand in the conflict with the Soviets and reduced the risk of war. In a moment of excitement, flush with the thrill he felt when putting together a grand concept, he cast his line: "What would be the strategic advantage of relocation?" As soon as he asked the question, he could see the same spark in Radford's eyes.

"In addition to concern about your personal safety and the continuity of government in the event of war, evacuation could serve as a precaution against a Soviet strike," Radford said, with the little enthusiasm he was capable of showing and without any sign that he had just swallowed the bait in front of him.

He knew exactly where Radford was going. "I don't understand."

"If you transfer to a secure location, the Soviets will judge that you are prepared for the worst."

"You mean it would show the president's resolve."

"And will serve as a deterrent to aggression," Radford added, tapping a finger on his briefing book.

"In other words, they won't know what I might do, which is what we want. Unpredictability is the greatest weapon a leader can have—I've always thought that." It was brilliant and he was angry for not arranging it so he got credit for an idea he'd thought of first. "Goddamn it," he said, punching the palm of his hand.

"Sir?" Finch looked at him, confused.

He flashed a smile. "Raddy's on to something, Bob."

"It's your Madman Theory," Finch said, returning the smile.

He was proud Bob made the connection. It showed it had been his idea all along. "If they don't know what I'm liable to do—"

"You might—"

"That's right, I might go off half mad," he said, throwing his arms up in the air to look the part.

"That will keep them in check." Finch was on the edge of his chair, eager and relieved.

"I might order an all-out retaliation. If they thought that, they'd really have to think twice."

"Before they—"

"They wouldn't even think of it," he said, rapping his desk to lead the chorus.

"Wouldn't dare," Finch said.

"We have to convince them I'm a madman." He leaned back in his tall leather chair, pushing with one foot up against his desk. "Let me explain something to you quietly," he began. He told

Radford and Finch about meeting with the aging and very wise president of South Korea during his vice-presidential trip to the region. This was a real mission from the start, an important job to do for the boss, not one of the sightseeing tours Eisenhower sent him on when he had to work like hell just to make it into a trip where he'd learn something about the world. Syngman Rhee believed—correctly—that Ike had made a fatal error settling for a divided Korea. Sooner or later the decision would come back to haunt the United States. But as vice president he had to be a good debater and argue Ike's case as best he could to bring home an assurance that Rhee would accept the division of his country. During these talks, the South Korean president spoke of his strategy for preventing war with the Communists in the North. "The key was Rhee's unpredictability," he told Radford and Finch. "The fear that he might start some action was a constant check on the Communists."

Finch gave a smile and Radford nodded, as though each had heard before about Rhee's advice.

Nixon threw a dog biscuit across the office at Checkers. The hard, bone-shaped snack slammed into the glass front of the antique Seymour Grandfather Clock, which marked the time of impact as 10:32 a.m. It made a sharp crack and everyone was quiet for a moment as Checkers chewed his treat.

He pushed a button on his desk and a steward entered almost immediately. "Get that shit-ass dog out of here." What the hell, he thought. Get to the point. "I have to do everything I can to make it look like I'd do anything."

"You might grab the football, Finch said."

"That satchel with the launch information—it's right outside that door," he said, pointing to the door to the Oval Office waiting room. "I might run with it, or try the long pass. That's what they have to think. I'm prepared to do that if the bastards dare try something."

"In Berlin," Finch said, limply lifting a finger toward the window.

Nixon wondered if Bob was trying to point in the direction of Germany. "That's the most likely place."

"I would agree with that," Radford said.

"You're preparing," Finch continued.

"Just in case. But they don't know that. I could be planning something. Because I'm taking all the necessary steps."

"Because you're moving operations to Mount Weather," Finch said. "Underground."

"Lodge can stay in Washington."

"The White House Evacuation Plan does call for you and the vice president to shelter in different locations," Radford said.

"If he starts crying, tell him he can go to Camp David."

"The new shelter there is very comfortable," Radford said, "but if I might add—"

"I hate the idea of leaving," Nixon said, putting his other foot against the desk. "They might use it to say I'm weak. But I don't give a damn what they say about me."

"If people only understood why you were going, they'd admire you greatly for it," Finch said.

"If I could just add, sir," Radford said. "If we are to send a message with the transfer of government to the SF we will need to employ non-scrambled communications."

"So they'll get the message. The Soviets, that is, not the public, will get the message," Finch said.

"That's the important thing, to get the message across every way we can. That's what I want done. And Bob, I want to you get with Klein and see what he thinks about how long we can keep this from the press. I think we'll only have a day or so—the jig will be up when I go on television. It won't be network fellows manning the camera and all that usual crap."

"I'll have Herb start working on a statement you can put out, frame it as just a precaution," Finch said.

"Good. Now I could try calling the editors at the major papers and say, Look here fellows, you've just got to hold this story that the president isn't in the White House because it's the right thing to do, you see, and I'll use national security. I might be able to get them to sit on it for twenty-four hours. That's my estimate and I'll say this, I know a little bit about the press." He smiled to appear humorous, then got back to business. "That'll give us some time to figure out what we can do to calm things down when word does get out."

"Or you could put out a statement denying the reports," Finch said. "The public will believe you before they believe what's in the papers."

"If the president says it, it's got to be true. Maybe you can sneak me back into the White House—I'll go through the Treasury Department tunnel and stroll into the pressroom. I'd like to see the expression on their faces then. See what Herb thinks, Bob."

"I would advise that Mrs. Nixon along with Tricia and Julie stay in California, sir," Radford said. "The shelter is no place for women and children."

"Pat would probably want to put up new curtains," Nixon said. He'd been out to West Virginia recently to see the government's newest shelter, code-named Casper, this one hidden under the Greenbrier Hotel, where members of Congress would be sent. That one was not as large and not as secure, but it was a little more modern, with country scenes painted on the glass panes of fake windows, already hung with curtains.

Chapter 3

Saturday, October 20, 1962

P AT NIXON GLANCED UP FROM HER WORK in the backseat of the Lincoln in time to see the group of seven or eight people in long, lightweight coats crowding together on the sidewalk in front of the appliance store window. Maybe the enterprising owner had set up one of those new-model washing machines and a salesgirl was offering a live demonstration, she thought, returning to the stack of letters in her lap. Los Angeles was never far behind with the latest improvements.

The next letter was in a child's hand, addressed, "Dear Mrs. President." The girl's name was Annie and she wanted to know if the president's wife still ironed her husband's pants, now that she was living in the White House. Annie's mother had probably saved the magazine photograph taken when Dick was vice president, the one of her posed in the living room of their Forest Lane house, pressing the family laundry.

By then, of course, she no longer needed to do the housework. It didn't matter.

When Dick was away on one of his frequent trips, or when she was worried about this or that, it always made her feel so much better to press his suits.

Anyway, that was what she told the society reporter the magazine had sent to the house. Maybe she should have told that girl how she so wanted to set the hot iron down on the backside of Dick's pants, just leave it there until it burned its indelible black mark. She'd have to find some other way, a way that would not be so embarrassing to her husband, a way that would allow her to keep her dignity.

"Dearest Annie," she began, as her secretary, beside her on the wide backseat, took the First Lady's dictation in neat shorthand on her steno pad, "a good wife, as you'll soon learn, will happily do whatever her husband needs to help him through his day."

When the car stopped at a traffic light, Pat looked through the window on the opposite side of the car and saw another crowd. She drew the last of the soothing warm air from her cigarette deep into her lungs. This time the group was larger, a dozen men and women staring at what she saw now was the flickering blue light of a television screen.

As the car began to move, she kept her eyes on the crowd. Jaw and bottom lip thrust forward, she blew a narrow white stream up at the car roof, snuffed the butt in the door-handle ashtray, and leaned toward the driver. "What's going on out there, Joe?"

The driver said he didn't know but would try to find out. He turned a knob and the small speaker on the dashboard came alive. "...In the lab late one night, when my eyes beheld a... Can you come out tonight, come come, come out tonight... Now do you love me, do you love... See the way he walks down the street, watch the way he shuffles his... This is Columbia's news head-quarters in New York once again and this is Bob Trout speaking."

"Here we go, Mrs. Nixon."

"...troop movements. But again, all we know for certain at this hour is that the White House has..."

"All right, turn it off, Joe," she said, speaking more loudly now to blot out the announcer's voice as she rubbed the base of her neck.

"Are you sure, Mrs. Nixon? It sounds important. The president is..."

"Turn it off, turn it off, turn it off," she repeated until Joe turned the dial. "You can listen while you're doing your errand—but I don't want to know anything about it when I get back. Do you understand?"

"Yes, ma'am."

Dick had given her clear instructions before she left for California. Under no condition was she to read any newspapers or watch any television news broadcasts. There was no need for her to get upset over things she couldn't control, he told her.

She had long ago accustomed herself to these protective news blackouts of his and hadn't paid particular attention to his most recent warning. All that registered anymore was a feeling that Dick still had some concern, some remaining instinct, for her welfare. Anyway, she had made sure she was too busy to focus on what she was sure would just be unpleasant news. She had learned years ago, learned the hard way, to let Dick manage his affairs without her advice or assistance—no matter what kind of hot water he got himself into without her organizing hand to guide him. She could find other ways to keep herself busy, staying on the move, maintaining her sense of purpose, making a life for herself apart from Dick, without ever showing a single crack in the happy face they presented in public.

She was finishing her dictation when Joe pulled up to the front steps of the red brick California Hospital on South Grand Avenue. He opened her door and she offered him her white-gloved hand. As she stepped from the car, her stiff, golden red hair glistening in the warm sunshine, a matronly woman came forward from the head of the receiving line. Pat greeted her with a thin smile that did little to soften the sharp lines of her cheeks and jaw. And still it accomplished so much. It was a smile she had mastered, one she could twist into something that was accepted as genuine.

She was a private person—yet she had allowed Dick to thrust her into the spotlight. And so she did what she had to do; she endured, as with so much before. She *would* endure. The pleasure for her, if there was any, came from endurance itself, from having the strength to bear it all without anyone suspecting she did not relish every minute of it. No. No one must suspect. She would as soon slit her wrists as expose herself. And she had learned to feel safe hiding behind her smile, learned to separate herself from the public woman the world knew as the First Lady, just as she had learned to do as an actress so many years before on the stage of the Whittier Community Players, standing apart from her character, a ventriloquist within her own body.

Only her eyes could give her away—pained, sad eyes looking for refuge.

Luckily, almost no one noticed.

And so it was that she drew now on every resource of her thin, angular body and extended her hand, once again the polite, cheerful, and smiling Mrs. Pat Nixon. The matronly woman introduced her to each of the well-dressed ladies standing at the edge of the long red carpet that had been rolled out from the main entrance to the curb. Some said how pleased they were to meet her. They welcomed her on behalf of the hospital and thanked her for honoring them with her visit. Others haltingly recited two or three carefully memorized sentences about how much they admired her husband for standing up to the Russians in Berlin, or how they appreciated the work she had done to publicize the achievements of women in the third world.

Making her way down the line, she found something individual to say to each woman, be it a compliment on a lovely hat or an interested question about the woman's work at the hospital, and with that she fell into her familiar role and began to relax.

The women could not see her, she knew now, though they would later say they had; they saw only what she wanted them to see. And with this realization, which always came to her but which she never allowed herself to expect and accept as a certainty, she could relax a bit more. And into that gap of relaxation the first stray thought came as she remembered the people she had seen peering in at the store-window televisions, and then the news on the car radio.

No, she was better off not knowing, she told herself, making her way down the line. It was a trap—a trap she had fallen into one too many times, she thought, already feeling the memory's sting.

It happened last year when she'd given in to her curiosity and her concern and, against Dick's wishes, followed the events in the *Washington Post* as Khrushchev tried to build a wall through Berlin to stem the tide of people leaving the Soviet-controlled section of the city for the Western sector. The United States and its allies responded by moving tanks along the autobahn toward Berlin, determined to block the construction. She knew, of course—we all knew it at some level—that any confrontation with Russia could easily escalate out of control. And so, when she saw the pictures in the paper of U.S. and Russian tanks facing off, muzzle to muzzle, she finally went to him.

Afterward, she could not forgive herself. Why had she believed this time would be different? Perhaps because the Berlin crisis, the first of his presidency, seemed so much more dangerous than anything that had come before. This time it was not just the press or his sworn opponents in the other party trying to destroy him politically, as bad as that had been. Or perhaps it had been Dick himself. He had gone for days without sleep, at one moment beside himself with anger, then, just as quickly, solemn and withdrawn. This time, she thought, she would be able to help. This time he would have no choice other than to accept her help.

As she moved now to the final woman in the receiving line, she could see the slow arc of his open hand moving toward her. The image repeated again and again before the woman in front of her came into focus, a short, pert woman in her mid-40s, hair in a bun behind her head, who was introduced as a long-serving financial administrator.

The woman was describing a letter she had written to the First Lady, saying something about how grateful she was for the note she had received in response. With a conspiratorial wink, the woman leaned closer and said she understood, *of course*, that the First Lady had not *actually* written the response herself.

Couldn't they understand she was a volunteer, just as some of them were, except that she probably worked twice as hard? She believed that everyone who wrote to her deserved a personal reply and when she was in Washington she spent four hours each morning reading and answering her mail. She knew—her staff had recently told her—that she had shaken the hands of more than 36,000 women from more than seventy organizations since becoming First Lady.

"I do remember your letter. If I'm not mistaken," she said, knowing she was not, "I may have offered some suggestions to help your fund-raising campaign for the new North Wing. Have you been able to reach your goal?"

The woman's mouth opened and, after a long moment, a stammered apology came forth.

Pat appeared to listen carefully. Then, with a musician's timing, moved away just a moment before the woman finished.

Walking side by side with the matronly woman who had greeted her at the car they tripped a beam of white light between two silver stanchions standing a few feet in front of the entrance, automatically opening the hospital's wide double doors. Surrounded in the lobby by a circle of talking women, she gave her attention to each for a moment, holding a woman's elbow briefly and then moving to the next, the swarm circling counterclockwise about her as she made her way forward.

She saw the television immediately. The matronly woman was taking her hand, steering her toward it for an introduction to the three white-uniformed women behind the front desk, one of whom was still stealing glances at the set. Pat pulled her hand back and the woman turned to her, quizzical. Oh, I'm just talking to one of these other ladies here for a moment, dear, she pretended, allowing herself to be led closer.

On the television she could see Walter Cronkite sitting behind a modest desk in the center of a crowded newsroom. A man hurried by, crouching down. Cronkite looked down, through thick black-frame glasses, at a teletype message on his desk. He slowly took his glasses off and raised his head to face the camera.

"You'll have a chance to powder your nose before lunch, Mrs. Nixon, but if you need to freshen up..." The woman was whispering in her ear as she guided her away from the desk, the circle of women forming about her again as they moved collectively to the elevator.

"What's your secret for remaining so calm at a time like this?"

"Will you cut your trip short to be with your husband?"

—⚭—

At first she had been happy to see Helene, waiting for her there in the backseat as she waved her last good-byes to the crowd of women in front of the hospital. Pat had invited her best friend to come with her to San Clemente to look at the house she and Dick were interested in and had sent Joe to pick her up while she toured the hospital.

Now she was beginning to have second thoughts.

Helene had been incredulous to hear that no one at the hospital had told her the news and she'd had to tell Helene that, no, she didn't know what all the fuss was about, and furthermore she didn't particularly care to know. "So, how's Jack?" she asked, hoping to persuade Helene to talk about her husband instead. "It's so wonderful he was able to take time out to work for a while in the White House. It's always such fun when I run into him there. I'm sure you can't wait till he's home again."

"Well, you know Jack, even if he's just hanging around waiting for Dick to find something for him to do, it's a thrill for him to be in the White House and to be honest, it's a relief to have him out of my hair for a while."

She and Helene Drown went back to the first days of her marriage to Dick, when her friend's name was still Colesie. They were both teachers at Whittier High then and they'd become quick friends.

Helene, who'd started at the school during what would turn out to be Pat's final year there, wasn't like the other women on the Whittier faculty. Most of them were older, and though they had been outwardly polite toward her since she had arrived four years earlier, she could sense their resentment toward the young newcomer in their midst. Was it just her youth and inexperience? Or might it have something to do with her appearance, she wondered.

When she looked in the mirror, after properly making herself up, she did see a rather pretty young lady, with smooth curls of red and gold hair; clear skin; high, rosy cheeks; and a nice, sharp jawline. She wanted so much for the other teachers to like her and just couldn't bear the thought she might stand out.

So she made herself as helpful as she could, always offering to do some extra typing or taking charge of the cookies and coffee at meetings, while the others took care of business.

Helene was young, too, and such a free soul. There was something about being around her that Pat liked from the start. With Helene she felt her own carefree spirit grow stronger and it seemed possible to live life any way she wanted, without caring a fig for what people might be saying behind her back.

And then there was this other side to Helene, she remembered now, sitting next to her in the car. She didn't easily give in.

"Come on, Buddy. How can you just bury your head in the sand?"

"There's nothing I can do, so why should I worry about it?"

If only Helene understood that Dick didn't want to hear her opinions, that he no longer took comfort from her presence. She'd have to go through the whole litany with her, starting with Dick's very first campaign, in '46. She'd have to tell Helene about the time when Dick was in the radio studio preparing to give a speech—the same speech she'd heard him give a hundred times—when she walked in. He turned to face her and she saw it first in his blazing black eyes. "Get the hell out of here," he shouted. "You know I don't want to be interrupted when I'm working!"

In the silence that followed she could hear the pitying thoughts going through the minds of the other men in the studio and wanted to turn and run as fast as she could. Instead, she turned and walked away slowly. For most of all, she wanted to appear strong and unhurt and to fend off their concern.

"You know I don't talk to Dick about his work," she said to Helene now, without turning to face her.

Not anymore.

It was a hard-won lesson. After that first time with Dick, she should have known better; instead, she soon repeated her mistake, and again got the back of his hand. After that, she had gone on with her responsibilities, greeting as many voters as she possibly could, doing everything to look her very best, never, ever letting anyone see her when she wasn't smiling.

It did not take much more of this treatment before she stopped talking to him about anything he didn't think was her business.

And as time went on, they talked less and less.

"It's such a pleasure to meet you, Mrs. Nixon," the real estate woman said.

Pat touched the woman's outstretched hand and stepped from the car, returning the smile.

From the outside the house resembled all the other houses in San Clemente, with the same red-tile roof and white stucco walls.

"Isn't it wonderful," the real estate woman said, stretching an arm wide to take in everything, from the lush vegetation all around the property to the inlaid stones of the path where they stood, to the house itself.

"It's charming," she said. Yes, charming. That was the word she and Dick both used when they started coming to San Clemente on their Sunday drives together down the coast, before they married.

Helene introduced herself to the real estate agent and the three of them went inside, where they were greeted by the stale odor of windows and drapes closed too long against the sun.

As they began their tour of the house, she easily imagined the rooms fresh and clean again. She would choose light, billowy material for the curtains to replace the dark, heavy fabric that hung there now. And those canvas awnings would have to go.

As they went through the house she had new decorating ideas for each room. She and Dick had moved so many times since they had married and each time she had worked her magic, transforming a dreary apartment or house into a cheerful home.

Silently she practiced the lines she would use tonight on the phone, when they would talk only of the house, and the girls.

She would start by telling him how all but one of the fourteen rooms opened onto a square courtyard at the center of the house, and about the fountain right there in the middle with its four green frogs spraying water and the cupid on top. Or maybe she would start with the setting. Five acres of palm and eucalyptus trees. And somehow she would have to tell her husband how the house was set on a cliff overlooking the beach. San Clemente beach.

She assured Helene and the agent it was all right, to please go on ahead. When they finally left, after Helene gave her a long look, she opened the latch on the wide window shutters and swung them out of the way.

The bright light took her by surprise and she put an arm up to shield her eyes. When she looked down at her purse, it was hard for her to see. But its contents were orderly and she found her sunglasses quickly.

The light reflecting from the blue water and white sand was tamer now behind the small dark lenses. They even seemed to absorb the tension in her neck. She always seemed to feel it first in her neck.

After lighting a cigarette, she crossed her arms on the wide slate sill and leaned out, watching a surfer's wave come riderless to shore. She and Dick must have walked for miles along this beach, bare feet splashing in the shallow surf, Dick's Irish setter, King, off running even before one of them released the stick, spinning up in an arc and landing in the shallow water.

Turning now, she saw the high cliffs and tried to find Dana Point. Somewhere up there was the dirt road they drove down at sunset. Dick had parked the car—her car—right at the edge of the cliff, so close the Oldsmobile seemed about to take wing over the Pacific. She wasn't surprised when he turned to her and asked the question. He had asked it so often she had made him promise to wait three months before bringing up the subject again.

This day they both knew the waiting period was over.

As the sun disappeared behind the water that March day in 1940, its pink glow illuminating the clouds at the horizon's edge, she wasn't sure how to answer. She was earning a good salary as a typing teacher, maybe more than Dick was making as a new lawyer in town, and was enjoying her independence. She hadn't fallen for him the way he had for her.

Maybe it was love all the same.

That first night, when they met, she had hardly noticed him. She was too upset at having let herself get roped into joining the local theater group.

"This is all your fault," she had said to her friend, Elizabeth Coles, as they'd left St. Matthias's Church when the evening's tryouts were through.

"What do you mean?" Elizabeth asked, looking hurt. Then, smiling, "You got the part."

"Yeah, *that's* what I mean." She drew on her cigarette and it burned red in the dark field. "I don't like performing in front of big audiences."

"Hey, would you girls like a lift?"

He stood about five or six inches taller than she did, about an inch shy of six feet. His hair was thick and wavy, almost curly, and jet-black. There was not enough light to judge his eyes in the dim moonlight; inside the church, though, she had seen a dark intensity. When he smiled, small crinkles formed at the edges of his eyes and his white teeth sparkled. She noticed his clothes, too, and the evident care he took with his appearance.

Elizabeth showed her a conspiratorial smile, then turned to Nixon. "That's very kind of you."

"Are you sure it won't be any trouble?" she asked him.

"Are you kidding? Come on, my car is right over here."

Elizabeth seemed eager to climb in first. Then he helped Pat up and closed the door of the black Model A behind her.

They talked for a few minutes about the play and their respective roles before the car slowed to a stop at the four corners. With his left hand still on the wheel, he leaned across the seat, ignoring Elizabeth, and looked straight at her. "I'd like to have a date with you," he said.

She tried to move against the door. There was no room there, anywhere, nothing she could do but wrap her arms tight against her chest, nowhere to hide from this horrible spotlight. No one had ever been so forward with her, except those movie producers she had met in Hollywood when she was working her way through college as an extra. Now, as then, she was flattered; more than that, she felt cornered. So she laughed, right in his face. "Oh, I'm much too busy," she said.

He leaned back across the seat and drove on, the only sound the grinding of gears.

A week later the Whittier Community Players met again to begin their rehearsals. She made sure to sit by the door again when Dick drove them home.

"Are you still too busy to go on a date with me?" he asked, leaning across Elizabeth.

This time she rattled off every chore and project and social obligation a girl could possibly have. At least he's good humored about it, she thought. If he hadn't been so aggressive, if he hadn't embarrassed her in front of Elizabeth, if he hadn't asked her out before they'd had a chance to become acquainted, she might have said yes. He *was* kind of handsome.

"This time *you* sit next to him, Pat," Elizabeth whispered in her ear as they walked to his car after the next rehearsal.

"No!" she practically yelled under her voice.

When Dick leaned over this time, Elizabeth squeezed back in the seat, as if to give them another inch of privacy. "When are you going to give me that date?"

It was his stubborn foolishness she laughed at this time. Not even trying to make excuses, she shook her head no. Maybe he could tell she was laughing at him because he turned serious, instead of laughing along with her. He pointed his finger and said, "Don't laugh. Someday I'm going to marry you."

She looked at him, unable to speak. At first she thought he was joking, until she saw there were no crinkles around his eyes this time, no smile. Finally, she burst out laughing, right in his face, at this absurd man.

When opening night finally came she wanted to have some fun and so she finally gave in. He wanted her to meet his parents right then and there.

The next time he saw her after that he asked, "When are you going to go out with me again?"

"I can't go with you."

"How come?"

"I have another date."

"Oh."

"With a boy in Los Angeles."

"I'll drive you!"

"What?"

"I'll drive you to Los Angeles. You shouldn't go alone."

"You're crazy, you know that? How would I get home, anyway?"

"I'll wait for you in the car."

"All evening?"

"Sure. That way I'll get to be with you."

In Los Angeles, she smiled and nodded at her date, trying to look as though she were listening. All the time she couldn't get her mind off Dick, waiting for her in the car. Was she being cruel? After all, it was his idea. She wondered if he would get along with her roommate, Margaret.

"I think you should ask Margaret on a date."

"Only if you'll be there when I come to pick her up."

Margaret said it was Pat, Pat, Pat, all night long—that was the only thing Dick wanted to talk about.

When she answered the phone it was him. He wanted to know if she would go for a walk.

"I have loads of homework to grade."

"I'll come over and help you."

She had already had one marriage proposal, she told him when they met for sodas at the drugstore. "I'm not ready to settle down. I want to travel all over the world. I'm really a Gypsy, you know."

"I've never heard of an Irish Gypsy before," he said.

She laughed, not wanting him to know. She would never tell him what it had been like when she was a girl, never tell him how her father told her stories about leaving home as a young man and traveling to every one of the forty-eight states, working along the way at whatever job he found—prospector, whaler, and everything else. She wouldn't tell him how those bedtime stories had wormed their way into her dreams, dreams of strange rituals from the other side of the world. Telling Dick would only bring it back—her father lying ill in his bed that final year of his life, she, at eighteen, doing all the things he couldn't do for himself anymore. Nor could she talk of how the end had come in much the same way for her mother four years before her father was taken.

Two years after her father's death, her childhood dreams hardened into adolescent desires, she left home. Someone had mentioned an old man and his wife who needed a driver to take them back east from California. So she loaded the couple's luggage in their Packard, slid in behind the big wheel, and headed toward the Atlantic, driving for weeks down the two-lane roads that wove across 3,000 miles of nothing she had ever seen before.

She was sure her two brothers in California understood when she wrote to say she wouldn't be coming back right away, that she was staying in New York City, working with their aunt at a Catholic hospital. She loved being cheerful for those unfortunate patients, no matter that she had to watch them slowly succumb to tuberculosis. She put on a smile and for a while they forgot about their illness, especially the men. She never feared their contagion, as she had not feared contracting that very disease from her father.

Almost two years later, riding the bus home, she began planning all her future trips. She had always envied her teachers, free each summer to travel wherever they pleased. That, she decided, would be her life. A wage earner for the school year, a Gypsy for the summer.

She worked forty hours a week sweeping floors and bookkeeping and typing and then taking care of the apartment she shared with her brothers, until all the work finally paid off. She got her degree and a job at Whittier High. That first summer of freedom was just months away when she auditioned with the Whittier Community Players, and met Dick Nixon.

She wasn't going to give all that up, not when it was almost within reach. And so she went off that summer without him, and didn't call when she got back.

She knew he would call anyway, or write. He seemed almost to prefer writing, at least when it came to expressing his feelings. As long as he didn't keep talking about marriage, it could be nice to have someone to go on double dates with. Then there was Dick's little brother, eight-year-old Eddie, who was such fun to roughhouse with and take places. And Hannah, their mother, sure could use some help baking those fifty pies every morning before the sun came up to sell at the Nixon grocery store and filling station in Whittier, even if it did mean listening to her Quaker prayers. She loved to read—it was almost as good as travel itself—so why not go to the beach with Dick on Sundays with their books, even if he did look a little silly in his long-sleeved shirts?

The nice thing about him was he didn't pry. Why open those old wounds? It was bad enough he told her how he had lost two brothers. No sense telling him the same disease had struck her father down, no sense bringing it back. She didn't think she could stand that. Otherwise, he wasn't much good at talking about himself, either.

And so, when Dick drove the Oldsmobile to the cliff's edge that afternoon and asked again if she would marry him, maybe that was why she said yes. Or maybe it was because she sensed Dick was going places. She wanted to go places, too.

She took a last look at the beach now as she crushed her cigarette butt against the outside wall. She pulled the shutters tight, careful to flip the latch back into the locked position. Slowly, she folded her sunglasses and returned them to their place in her purse.

On the phone tonight with Dick there was something else she'd say. "I think we should buy the house."

Chapter 4

Sunday, October 21, 1962

T HE BIG BALD HEAD LEANED WAY BACK, a mouth full of crooked teeth opened wide in great gasps of sadistic, mocking laughter. The guffawing skull came closer and the demonic cries echoed louder until the president was awakened by his own screams.

Sitting on the edge of the empty bed he wiped the sweat from his forehead with the monogrammed sleeve of his blue cotton Brooks Brothers pajamas. The chintz drapes Pat had chosen for his bedroom were not yet backlit by the sun. On the bedside table the self-illuminating hands of the Baby Ben confirmed the predawn hour.

His clothes for the day were set out when he returned from the bathroom in his silk robe and leather slippers. His dark blue suit and white shirt hung on the outside of the closet door, above his freshly shined black wingtip shoes; underwear, socks, White House cufflinks, and blue-and-red-striped silk tie were neatly arranged on a side table. By now he had no conscious memory of a dream that had seemed on awakening to be an ugly portent for his confrontation with Khrushchev, which entered a new and more dangerous phase today. And yet as he buttoned his shirt and knotted his tie his thoughts remained with the possibilities and perils of war. He thought of the Air Force planes that would soon destroy the Soviet Union's antiaircraft batteries, MiG fighters, and IL-28 bombers in Cuba, before targeting the missiles being readied, and those already able, to unleash their nuclear payloads on their own designated set of targets in the United States.

The uniformed elevator attendant, showing no surprise at seeing the president on his way to work at five in the morning, bowed slightly and followed him inside the small car for the slow two-story descent from the family quarters. The president looked to the floor; he said nothing. Each day the U.S. planes would go after more targets until, on the fifth day, all would be destroyed, allowing the Marines to begin the invasion that would liberate Havana. If Khrushchev intended to strike the U.S. from Cuba, the premier would have to act soon, before his missiles were destroyed.

The elevator door stood open and the attendant waited. "Ground floor, Mr. President."

The elevator lobby opened onto the long, wide ground-floor corridor that ran the length of the original section of the White House, an elegant cross-vaulted ceiling overhead with worn, hospital-green carpeting underfoot. The United States had not experienced war at home since Lincoln had lived in this house, haunted as it was by every effort made within its walls, both revered and reviled, to preserve, protect, and defend the Constitution. Nearing the corridor's end he wondered if Lincoln would be remembered with the same reverence had he ordered the North to fire the Civil War's first shot, or if he had fled Washington for safer ground.

The frosty air of this last morning in the White House stung his face as he opened the Garden Room door. Later this afternoon, a car would be waiting nearby to take him to Mount Weather.

Walking the length of the West Wing colonnade to his office he imagined a classroom of young children at their desks with pictures of all the presidents taped in a neat row along the length of one wall and halfway down another. The teacher moved from Lincoln to Theodore Roosevelt to Woodrow Wilson to Calvin Coolidge to Franklin Roosevelt and now was telling the students how General Dwight Eisenhower had kept the nation at peace through two administrations. His own picture was next on the wall and he wondered if the glint would be gone from the teacher's eye when her pointer landed on him.

He hoped she would say that President Nixon's decision to bomb the Communist missiles in Cuba saved the world from war. And he hoped she would tell the children that President Nixon did not leave Washington in fear. "Now raise your hands if your parents are planning a trip to sunny Cuba this winter? That's something else we remember President Nixon for."

He was entering the Oval Office when he realized the paradox: There might be no alternative but for his presidency to be immortalized for keeping the world safe. Otherwise—if he did everything possible to prevent war, and still it came—a nation struggling to rebuild would have little time for history lessons.

He stirred what remained of the ice in the etched crystal Scotch glass, leaving the silver spoon on the side table by his easy chair. It was quiet inside the small first-floor suite in the massive Old Executive Office Building opposite the White House, where he often came to escape the steady flow of administration staff in the West Wing. This morning had been especially busy as he maintained his regular schedule of appointments—having his picture taken with a Harvard professor—Watson—who'd won a Nobel prize for something in biology and most of the New York Yankees, who'd won the World Series against the San Francisco Giants—to pretend to the press all was normal. After the cameramen had the film they came for he closeted himself here to work on tonight's television address; review reports from Gates, Radford, and Lemnitzer on the start of military action against Cuba; and prepare to leave later this afternoon for Mount Weather. First there was a personal matter that needed his attention.

In a manila folder labeled MRS. NIXON in his briefcase he found the agenda for this afternoon's call. One of the items was the house she'd gone to inspect in San Clemente. He struggled at first with the prospect of discussing their plans for the future when no one could say where the present would lead. Pat still knew nothing of what he would say tonight on television and there was no need to tell her just so she could ask her incessant questions. It was as necessary to keep up appearances with her as with the press. Preparing again to pretend all was normal, he was able to look forward and imagine periodic escapes to California. There the demands of those who constantly bothered him with their memos about this or that domestic problem that needed his immediate attention—the stack growing ever higher while he devoted nearly all of his working time to Cuba—would be a continent away, freeing him to focus as he was now on creating a more peaceful world for generations to come. In California he would see only the people he wanted to see. There were very few of them anymore—Finch and Radford, primarily, who would fly West with him. If he wanted to talk with anyone else he would need only to pick up the phone for them to soon be at his side.

He emptied the glass and put it down next to the phone, waiting for the fourth ring to answer the call back from the White House operator who he'd asked moments earlier to please get his wife on the line.

They hadn't been talking long when Pat asked of the San Clemente house, "Do you think we can afford it?" In California, the First Lady smoothed out her blue and gray starburst-patterned skirt and said, "It'll need some work, you know." Her husband's salary was almost triple what it had been when he'd been vice president and they really had no need for their Washington house now, even though it wasn't that long ago she'd finished decorating so it would be just right for Dick to invite over all the important people he dealt with as vice president for informal entertaining. They'd only been on Forest Lane four years when it was time to pack the things they wanted to take with them to the White House. The modern décor in the guest room at Helene's wasn't quite her style, but sitting here in her friend's leather Eames lounge chair and talking on the pink Princess phone this morning, she vicariously felt the contentment of settling in one place.

"I'll arrange for some military and White House staff to help with some of that. J.B. can fly out there to oversee the workers, for one thing." Between that and hiding the improvements Pat wanted as security enhancements, he figured that most of the costs should be covered.

"Oh, Mr. West has to be the best chief usher the White House has ever had," Pat said, thinking of how essential he'd been as she restored one dowdy, run-down White House room after another with period antiques and authentic colors, an Oval Office makeover being only her most recent achievement. The way the Eisenhowers left the place, filled with furniture from Sears, was a shame for such an historic house. "I'm sure J.B. would love to do it—if it doesn't keep him away from his family for too long."

"We'll fly him out so he can work there two or three days a week."

"I'll call him right away," she said, lighting a cigarette from the burning butt hanging from the corner of her mouth. It seemed as though her life had been one house redecoration after another, Tilden Street in '51, Forest Lane in '57, the White House in '61, and now San Clemente. It was her responsibility to make a comfortable home for her family and she would smile and do a job she could be proud of.

"Tell J.B. the president said it was okay." If West objected, he'd find a way to have him fired. If the Secret Service could corroborate his suspicion that West was a homosexual, it would be out of his hands; they would insist he be let go as a security risk.

"I'd like to come out here with J.B., when I can get away." Oh, to get away from the spotlight that followed her everywhere in Washington. In San Clemente she would go where she wanted without the press harpies demanding to know what she was up to now. For a few days at a time she could even pretend to be divorced, without Dick to kick her around.

His wife's desire to spend time in California was like a bolt cutter snapping the heavy chain that tied him to Pat. Every day she spent in California would be another day she couldn't butt into his business, ask to share a drink with his group during a plane ride, or embarrass him with her attempts to kiss him when they were in public. The next time she tried something like that he'd get her alone and give her a good slap. If only she could live at San Clemente until he called on her to fly back to Washington to appear in her supporting role as First Lady at a State dinner or another occasion when her presence was required to keep up the appearance of a happy First Couple. "I don't know if you'll have the time, Buddy. You have an awfully busy schedule. No, I don't think so."

The bastard hated giving her what she wanted. Whether it was out of spite or from some other motive, she didn't know. Beyond never telling her, or anyone, what he was feeling, he oftentimes seemed not to want to reveal what he was thinking, either. It was as though he had to lie to avoid giving himself away, or to become the person he thought people would like and respect. Part of it she could understand. It was necessary for her to lie a little when a reporter asked a question that could not be given an honest response that wouldn't air dirty laundry. In private, too, with any of her friends or with Dick, especially, there was no use scratching away at old sores; as Dick knew as well, that only made them worse. She only wanted to steer free of bitterness. With Dick it went further. Maybe he was trying to seem concerned she would overextend herself. Was he concerned? She still wanted to think so. "I'm sure I can find some time to spare."

"Now that you're there, why don't you stay a few more days and get everything settled for buying the place." Even with a lawyer he'd arrange to look over her shoulder and report everything back to him for his approval, it went against the fiber of his being to give her any kind of responsibility. If he couldn't persuade Pat to stay in California, though, he would have to tell her about the shelter and insist she go. If she were there in the room with him now he would turn his back to her, acting as though he wasn't listening as she listed her reasons for not wanting to go to Mount Weather. He would tell her she didn't have any choice and immediately leave the room. Or he would tell her how much the girls would love it there, how they would run giggling, chasing one of the shelter's electric carts that regularly shuttled workers, staff, and officials as they went about their duties. The tunnel-like hallways were what he remembered most from his trip to High Point for an exercise to test whether the government could be run from the bunker deep inside the mountain. Tricia and Julie could swim in one of the ponds they'd showed him on his tour. There wasn't a shallow end—ten feet deep the entire 200 feet across, they said. One of the Secret Service agents, maybe Jack Sherwood, would play lifeguard. As long as the girls didn't piss in the drinking water. An underground bunker is no place for young ladies, Pat would say, never having set eyes on the place.

There were no major White House social events scheduled for the next few days and she could keep up on some of her responsibilities with long-distance telephone calls from Helene's that could be charged to the White House. It was just that Dick seemed to be in an awful hurry all of a sudden for her to close on the house. He must be desperate to take the opportunity of a lull in his schedule, without any out-of-town appearances where he needed her as a prop, for a holiday from her. She fixed up his houses, raised his children, campaigned with him, and made him look like a happily married man. Otherwise she was excess baggage to be put on a shelf until he needed her again. She had gone over it again and again, each time coming to the same conclusion. There was nothing she could do to put things back to the way they were when they were courting and first married and yet nothing would be worth the humiliation for her and the children of not having a husband and a father. For now, all she could do was play his game. If he was anticipating being rid of her a while longer, he'd have to beg for it. "I don't know if I can extend my stay. I still have so much work to get ready for the social season."

"Can't that wait?" He held his head in his hand as he waited for her answer.

She paused to savor the moment. "Oh, I suppose I can stay a *bit* longer."

"The sooner we get the sale completed, the sooner we'll be able to start using the place." When he got off the phone he would give Finch strict orders that no one was to tell Pat about the shelter. By the time the press got wise to his relocation, he was thinking, Pat would have watched his television address and would know along with the rest of the world of the fighting in Cuba; then he could tell her it's no longer safe to travel and she'd be glad to know he's somewhere protected. Whatever happens, she'd be able to ride it out in California, where none of the MRBMs in Cuba could reach her. If his fears about Berlin were realized and the threat of general war escalated, plenty of L.A. shelters would gladly receive her and the rest of the family—the girls, their grandmother, and their four uncles—as honored guests.

"Once it's fixed up, I'm coming here with the kids once a month." Even without adding, "with you or without you," he would understand. If she could move into the San Clemente house full time she would, and not miss her White House obligations one bit. It was certainly a thrill to meet all the fascinating people from around the world who called on the White House and it had always been her dream to travel to the exotic lands she'd visited on her trips with Dick. And she had been very happy to fill their house with all the wonderful and exotic pieces their hosts had presented to them—rugs from the shah of Iran, a marble inlaid chest from Chiang Kai-shek of Nationalist China and so many more. What hadn't been in her fantasy was traveling as part of an official delegation that required her to wear her well-worn smile for the popping flash bulbs, give her same happy answers to the reporters, and make small talk with the wives of the heads of state. She worked so hard to say nothing that might betray her thoughts. She could do it endlessly if she had to, and oftentimes it seemed as if she had to. If Dick had been satisfied to be a successful lawyer in private practice they could have traveled to the same lands as ordinary tourists, taking trips when the children were not in school so they could learn, too, rather than leaving them home, crying. With that she would have been happy.

"I'll tell you when you can go and when you can't. Is that clear?" He could feel the anger beginning to rise, a satisfying and familiar feeling he embraced.

"Don't get upset—I was just joking." She didn't know why she tried to soothe him, especially on the phone; it was an instinct at odds with her judgment.

The hell you were, he thought. She used every chance she could to make him angry then made him angrier still by denying she'd done any such thing. Last week when they were about to leave for the airport to fly to New York where he was to appear at a rally in support of Governor Nelson Rockefeller's reelection, Pat had intentionally, he thought, made him wait. Being on time was like keeping a promise, and he took the promises he made seriously; it went with being well prepared, and he owed much of his success in life, from his early days in school to winning the presidency, to thorough preparation. People who were habitually late always had some excuse. "Time got away from me," someone had once told him on arriving late for a meeting and he had never forgotten that phrase. It conjured up some slippery, elusive force forever changing shape to fool us into misjudgment when in fact time was one of the few constants in life. Pat was as meticulous and conscientious as any woman in other ways and he had to believe her failure to be on time was intentional. Sometimes she made herself late simply to needle him for his punctuality. On other occasions it was in protest over whatever grievance she harbored at the moment. Or it could just be a stab in the back for the resentment she harbored, for him and their life in the public eye.

"Can you at least promise that we'll come to California as often as we can when the girls are on school break?" As much as she wanted to get out of Washington she wanted even more for Julie and Tricia to not be spoiled by their pampered life in the White House.

"Yeah, sure." Why even bother answering, he thought. Whatever he said, she probably wouldn't believe it. Ever since breaking the promise he'd made her not to run for a second term as vice president she didn't believe half of what he said. The promised vacations he had never found the time to take, the promised dinners together he couldn't make, those were different. Work came first. No wife liked to hear that her husband wouldn't be home for dinner and he was sure they all complained.

Underneath, they understood a man had important obligations. Tearing up his promise not to run again for vice president in '56 was different—it was a gamble he had to make. He knew Pat would have to go along with his decision to stay in politics. She didn't have the guts to walk out—she'd never make it on her own. The gamble was with their relationship. He didn't know what the cost to him would be, only that he had no choice but to find out. What use was peace at home if it meant withdrawing from the great arena of world affairs, where man is tested against man? He also owed it to his mother and her Quaker idealism to stay in the game, dedicated to ensuring peace.

"When we're all together here it'll be like we're an ordinary family again," she said.

He took her remark like a right jab. She took every opportunity to remind him how much happier she would have been if he had just set his sights on being a rich corporate lawyer. Of course she knew he had no interest in working just to make money, joining exclusive golf clubs or attending swank Fifth Avenue parties with the in social set. That may have been what he'd been aiming for when he graduated from Duke Law School in '37, ranked third in his class, and came to New York looking for work, only to be sent away. He should have known they'd turn their noses up at his type, poor and from the wrong schools. They forced him to go crawling back to little Whittier for a job mother brokered at a two-bit firm where he listened, red-faced, to women tell their sordid stories of adultery so he could file their divorce papers. Returning to Wall Street to look for work instead of running for reelection as vice president in '56 or president in '60 would have been the ultimate humiliation. He'd be leaving politics a defeated man—defeated by his wife, no less. Even so, even if he had let Pat break him, he wouldn't have given those New York rich boys a second chance, eager though they'd be to have the name of a former vice president of the United States on their letterhead. He wouldn't give them the satisfaction.

And now he wasn't about to give Pat the satisfaction of acknowledging her resentment at being forced to live a public life. In all things it was best to ignore her and every petty thing she said. "Someone will contact you when it's time for you to return." With that he put down the phone and picked up his drink.

She held the pink receiver to her ear, knowing the line had gone dead. What use was it getting him mad again over the choices they had made—or the choices he made and she had settled for? She didn't know on this morning any more than she knew any other day. He was gone from her and he was there. They were divorced in spirit and together in fact. She wanted nothing to do with him and was obligated to do right by him. A wife took care of her husband. That was one thing of which she was sure. As long as they were married, and she knew they always would be, her responsibility was to take good care of her husband. If only he didn't make her job so difficult.

———⚬⚬⚬———

"President Eisenhower will be with you in just a moment, Mr. President."

"Tell him I can wait." He ran a finger along the green desk phone's rows of clear plastic buttons, each small rectangle ready at the push to immediately connect him with the major departments of government. He drew a line through "1:05 p.m.—The President will speak by telephone with Mrs. Patricia Nixon" on his typed list of daily appointments. The call with Eisenhower was the last item of White House business before "The president will motor to the High Point Special Facility at Mount Weather."

Can't do anything to rush the old man, frail as he is. Not now, when he needed him more than ever, maybe as much as he had during the '60 election. You had to be especially careful with a man who had already had a stroke and a heart attack while president. He would never receive the credit he was due for accommodating the old man, putting at risk his own election—his life's goal—out of concern for Ike's health. His enemies, who thought of him as an evil man, would never believe him capable of such charity.

As he waited for Eisenhower to come to the phone, he tried to prepare himself to appear thoughtful and analytical. That had been his approach since his first conversation with Eisenhower about Cuba, soon after the missiles were discovered, as it had been throughout his vice presidency. He had listened carefully to what the former president had to say, never interrupting, thoughtfully deliberating and responding in a tone he tried to make sound respectful. If he ever raised questions Eisenhower could perceive as challenging, he couched them in deferential terms and tried to sound something like an Oxford don providing an objective consideration of all sides of the problem. In the end, most of it was for show; they had agreed it was necessary to bomb the missile sites and send in the Marines to root out the Communists from Cuba.

"Sorry to keep you waiting, President Nixon. President Eisenhower is able to take your call now, if you still have the time."

"Put him through," he said, pushing a small button on his desk.

"President Nixon?"

"I wanted to let you know I'm going to take your advice and announce both the bombing and invasion when I go on television tonight."

"That's at eight o'clock, is it?"

There was a gravity in Eisenhower's voice that he'd seldom heard. "That's right, sir. This way there will be no question about our firmness on this thing."

"Yes."

"My feeling, and I wanted to ask if you agree with me on this," he said, knowing Eisenhower would, "is that this should help do away with any thinking that the United States can be deterred from its course or that we'll tolerate a move against Berlin, for example." He pointed at the fireplace and mouthed the words "more wood" for the steward standing in the Oval Office doorway.

"My idea is this," Eisenhower said. "The damn Soviets will do whatever they want, what they figure is good for them."

"That's right." Wasn't he always right? The general probably thought it went without saying.

"And I don't believe they relate one situation with another."

"Berlin and Cuba."

"Just what they find out they can do here and there and the other place. If they go into Berlin, that means they've got to look out that they don't get a terrific blow to themselves."

Eisenhower had told him from the beginning of the Cuban crisis that bombing the missile sites and invading the island would not lead to war and in the days since he had sometimes used the excuse of updating the former president about plans for installing a new government in Havana, or seeking advice about using a congressional resolution passed before the crisis as the basis for initiating hostilities against Cuba, to hear once more from the nation's most experienced military authority that responding with force to the Soviet aggression in Cuba would not trigger World War III. "You've told me this in the past, and I believe it very strongly, that the best thing we can do at a time like this is to lead with our resolve, so there'll be no doubt on that score."

"That's my position."

As vice president he'd known how to handle his disagreements with Eisenhower: Salute and then go off and chew on it in private. Sitting in the president's chair now, looking at the fire raging across the room, he was grateful that he'd not had any major differences with the former president on the great foreign policy issues facing the country these last two years, be they in Berlin, Laos, or Vietnam. "I also wanted to get your opinion on an initiative that Radford put forward to move some essential White House operations to Mount Weather."

"Radford put this idea out?"

"He believes it helps build our case that we're prepared to see this thing through to the end."

"Only if the Soviets know you've evacuated."

"We would have our communications in the clear so they could pick that up."

"I always thought Mount Weather would be a last resort, if war were imminent. We're at a very dangerous pass now, of course—Mamie and I are praying every day for God to grant you the wisdom you need—but unless I'm mistaken, I don't think this will cause them to shoot off their missiles."

He swept his arm across his desk, sending memos and reports fluttering and falling to the floor, at the suggestion that without divine intervention he didn't have the smarts to outfox Khrushchev. Struggling to hide his anger, he took comfort in Eisenhower's judgment about the risk of a wider war. Maybe Radford was too pessimistic, or was being overly cautious. No matter what his advisers said—each had his own interests to advance—he had to rely on his gut, which told him to bank on his Madman Theory and leave Washington, even as its anxious churning kept him in a perpetual state of stage fright.

"Radford says that once we start our action in Cuba—that will be very soon now—well, that begins the period of danger, for a Soviet response."

"The invasion—if anything is going to cause a response, that'll be it."

"I would just add this, the important thing is the signal we send by activating Mount Weather."

"Well, you know I agree with that. I suppose this will hammer home the idea that you're capable of doing what it takes."

"Yes."

"Of doing anything."

"That's what we need them to believe, yes, sir."

—— ⌘ ——

Khrushchev was having dinner at home with his twenty-seven-year-old son, Sergei, when the call came. He listened, asking few questions. The moment he ended the call, his trembling hand reached for the other phone on his desk, which linked directly to the Kremlin. "Call all Presidium members and tell them to gather at Kremlin in one hour. I'll tell them what it's about when they arrive. Call Malinovsky and Gromyko and have them come as well."

"I probably won't be back tonight," he told Sergei as he put on his overcoat. "Tell your mother."

He watched his Lenin Hills villa recede in the distance as his ZIL limousine sped east and wondered if he would ever see it or his family again.

"We have received word this evening that American airplanes have commenced bombing island of Cuba," Khrushchev told the Presidium members in as steady a voice as his agitation allowed. "We must conclude from this aggression that United States knows of missiles we provided our brother revolutionaries for their protection."

Anastas Mikoyan, in his usual seat in the Presidium meeting room, stared at his folded hands on the large rectangular conference table's green woolen surface. As the missile project was being planned, Mikoyan had not feared to describe all that could go wrong. It would be hard to conceal so many missiles and so many ships, he'd warned. Now that it had turned out just as the sixty-six-year-old Mikoyan had predicted, Khrushchev saw that his friend, who did not look up, would not cause any embarrassment and was grateful to be spared his just reproach.

"This may end in big war," Khrushchev said from the head of the table, pointing at Malinovsky. "You blew it."

When the defense minister tried to speak, Khrushchev dismissed him with a wave of his hand. "Sit down. We don't want to hear from you." Malinovsky should have warned him this would happen. He wiped the sweat from his brow, sensing his face was glowing red; it did not concern him. Only one thing did. Peace was all. Everything he would do from here on, every thought, every action, must be directed toward understanding what had happened and preventing it from escalating into a catastrophic war with the United States.

He had been wrong to believe in Pliyev as well, the general he'd sent to Cuba to command Soviet forces. His old World War II comrade, who had recently led troops in forcefully putting down demonstrators in Novocherkassk, must have failed to properly conceal the missiles from American spy planes. Because of Pliyev's stupid errors, Cuba might be lost and there could be a war more horrible than the one they fought against the Germans, when it was not yet possible to imagine anything more horrible.

Lightheaded and dizzy, he looked down the long table, grasping the legs underneath as though they were two anchors, and felt everything he'd counted on and thought he knew coming unmoored. If he did not perish in his Kremlin office suddenly sometime in the next few days, his rivals would wait until the crisis was over and then put the blame on him for having lost the country's foothold in the Caribbean and bringing the world to the brink of war. They would get together in secret and plot to take power. If he couldn't stop them any other way he would have them killed before they could strip him of everything he'd worked for, or worse.

"We were not going to unleash war," he said to remind his colleagues that his intentions had been peaceful. "We just wanted to intimidate them."

Andrei Gromyko, the foreign minister, rose to speak. "It is regrettable that those responsible have allowed our missiles to be seen from sky, but it is Americans who are to blame. They are using their lucky discovery to justify long-standing imperialist plans to capture Cuba."

Silently he thanked Andrei; here was something else to hold on to. Andrei, who had given his support to the missile deployment, was rightly shifting the blame to the Americans. Nixon, in particular. Unlike the Democratic Party candidate in the 1960 election, an unknown whose name Khrushchev was unable at this moment to recall, no guessing was needed about Nixon.

During eight years as vice president, including a Nixon trip to Moscow, there had been plenty of opportunity to size up this brash young man—still a boy for a man of Khrushchev's sixty-eight years—as a true reactionary. As vice president, Nixon had waged a campaign in the White House with Secretary of State Dulles to undermine Eisenhower's efforts to seek a peaceful accommodation with the Soviet Union. As president, Nixon had shown in Berlin he was bent on continuing Dulles's dangerous policy of bringing the world to the edge of war to get his way.

To the extent Khrushchev had allowed himself to question what might happen if the Americans discovered the missiles prematurely, he assumed the president would be able to control the warmongers in the Pentagon eager to seize on any excuse to launch their rockets. He should have thought more about what might go wrong; he had been so sure.

"We do not want war. But they have attacked us and we must decide how we will respond," he told the Presidium. The first order of business was to raise the alert level of all Soviet armed forces and the forces of the Warsaw Pact countries. He must prepare for war as he tried to stop it.

Grabbing at the first idea that came to mind, he suggested telling the Americans, "All of our equipment belongs to Cubans and Cubans will announce how they will respond. We will not let Castro threaten U.S. with our missiles, but we could let them threaten to use tactical ones."

He let the twelve members discuss his suggestion even as he decided against it. It would be too dangerous to give control of the missiles to Castro. He loved Fidel like a brother but knew he had a hot head sometimes. The opposite was needed—more control from Moscow.

Already, Soviet and Cuban soldiers were firing on American planes. General Pliyev had no choice, the Presidium agreed, but to fire back when fired upon and was carrying out his orders to defend from air attack. They decided they could not tell him to cease fire.

"But we must prevent anything else from happening that we have not thought through," he told the Presidium. "This requires that we give clear instructions to our commanders in Cuba regarding use of all nuclear weapons."

It did not take long before the Presidium agreed to issue instructions ordering Pliyev not to use any of the missiles without authorization from Moscow. There would have to be some response to the American aggression, but no one at the table was ready to launch the operational R-12s against U.S. cities.

When the discussion turned to how the 45,000 Soviet soldiers in Cuba would defend themselves against an American invasion, if it should come to that, Khrushchev and the Presidium members agreed they had no choice but to give them the means for self-defense. The only way to prevail against a much larger American force would be to use the short-range tactical nuclear weapons sent to the island for that very purpose. Khrushchev had sent these arms in accord with Soviet military doctrine, which anticipated that in any clash with the West, battlefield nuclear weapons would be used against N.A.T.O. or American troops. In any event, the Americans would not invade, Khrushchev thought. Even Nixon wasn't that idiotic. In fact, the very presence of these small atom bombs would prevent an invasion. "We have weapons to sink their mighty ships before their soldiers even get their boots wet trying to come ashore."

Still, preparations had to be made.

And so language was added to the cable: "In the event of a landing of the opponent's forces on the island of Cuba, if there is a concentration of enemy ships with landing forces near the coast of Cuba in its territorial waters, and there is no possibility to receive directives from the U.S.S.R. Ministry of Defense, you are personally allowed to take the decision to apply the tactical nuclear Luna and FKR missiles as a means of local war for the destruction of the opponent on land and on the coast with the aim of a full crushing defeat of troops on the territory of Cuba and the defense of the Cuban Revolution."

"It is tragic," Khrushchev lamented aloud. "We had come so close to ensuring peaceful relations."

Chapter 5

Sunday, October 21, to Monday, October 22, 1962

O F THE FIFTEEN COWS IN THE PASTURE on Blue Ridge Mountain Road, five were standing; the rest sat on their folded legs. He'd been told cows could sense a change in the weather and would seat themselves, perhaps as protection from an approaching storm.

He did the math in his head. A 65-percent chance of rain, give or take.

"We'll be at High Point in about ten minutes, Mr. President" came a voice from the limousine's radio telephone. With one finger nudging his white shirt cuff, he checked the time. Very close to two hours, start to finish, as Rose Mary had said.

His previous visit to the High Point shelter at Mount Weather had been coordinated with Operation Alert 1961. As civil defense sirens sounded in cities and people were ordered off the streets and into shelters, as television and AM radio stations went off the air to allow CONELRAD emergency radio-system broadcasts, he rode in a secret convoy with thousands of officials along these same lonely Virginia roads to practice procedures for continued government operations in the event of nuclear war. After a short meeting with his Cabinet, he was given a tour of the 434-acre site and introduced to a few of the 240 or more people who worked at the facility.

Now, on a yellow legal pad he listed the eleven names he remembered from that visit.

The 34-ton blast door to High Point had been swinging open for more than ten minutes when his limousine approached. The metal door was 10 feet tall, 20 feet across, and 5 feet thick, a giant bank vault entrance that easily swallowed the president's 1961 Lincoln as it entered the tunnel under a guillotine gate.

Inside he transferred to an electric tram and was driven through a maze of tunnels and roads connecting twenty underground office buildings until stopping at the entrance to the one everyone here called the White House.

He stepped out onto a sidewalk, illuminated under the harsh glow of florescent lights in the arched ceiling five stories above. The wide front door to the plain concrete structure, another vault-like, four-inch-thick block of steel, had what looked to him like a metal car steering wheel in place of a door handle. One of the Navy ensigns in dress uniform standing guard saluted and spun the wheel, pushing it open with his shoulder.

Inside was a long corridor strung with clear incandescent bulbs. An electric cart was waiting.

A young Navy officer saluted. "Good evening, Mr. President. If you'll climb aboard I'll drive you to your office. I understand Mr. Finch will be there to greet you upon your arrival."

The corridor, wide enough for two carts to comfortably pass in opposite directions, stretched to a point of light far off in the distance. As the cart hummed its way there he pulled the draft of his television address from his briefcase, not yet satisfied that it struck the right tone after working on it most of the day, first at the White House in Washington and then in the limousine. He didn't see Bob until the cart came to a stop.

"We've got the studio mocked-up—it's all ready for you, if you'd like to take a look. You go on the air in two hours."

"Give me about twenty minutes," he said, holding up the typescript. "Is Rose Mary here?"

"She's standing by to type the final copy, when you're ready."

⌾

"My fellow Americans, I have asked the networks to set aside this time tonight so that I may speak to you from the Oval Office about a very serious matter that concerns all of us. Over the past year many of you have probably read in your newspapers, or heard me speak on television about my concern with the large quantities of military weapons the Soviet Union has been shipping to the island of Cuba. The Soviet ambassador to the United States, Mr. Dobrynin, assured me these were purely defensive weapons. Of course, we know better than to trust the Russians, don't we?"

He looked up at the camera from the script on his desk and, despite himself, his mouth formed a wry smile. Across the country and down the years, at campaign stop after campaign stop, on television and radio and in print, at airports and in auditoriums, from the back of trains and atop flatbed trucks, from the well of the House and the Senate Floor, in the White House as vice president and for the last year and a half on the largest stage of all, as president, he had made the same warning to whomever would listen. They're backstabbers.

"So I issued a secret order to our military. I told them to keep a close eye on those Russian ships."

When he looked up at the camera again, it was with a frown, eyes narrowed. Speaking more slowly, voice lowered, he said, "On October 15, I received information that confirmed, beyond all doubt"—he emphasized these last words with a slow shake of his head—"that the Soviet Union had begun sending offensive missiles to that imprisoned island. Clearly, the purpose of these missiles is to provide a nuclear strike capability against the United States. The Communists' secret plan is to threaten us with unthinkable devastation if we don't play along with their plans for world domination." He felt the beads of sweat on his upper lip and patted them dry with his handkerchief as they were about to break free to roll as tears across his mouth.

"Let me be clear. Some of these missiles are already operational and pose a direct threat to cities in the southeastern United States, including our nation's capital." He reached for his water glass, pausing as much to let his words resonate as to wet his throat.

"The Soviet Union is also working full steam ahead in Cuba to ready missiles with a much longer range. These missiles would threaten almost all of the continental United States and parts of Canada as well."

Holding his script with one hand he balled the other into a fist. "Make no mistake," he said, bringing down his fist, "the basic objective of the Soviet Union is to impose Communism on the Western world.

"And so, after careful consideration of all the alternatives, and with the unanimous encouragement of our most senior military leaders, the Joint Chiefs of Staff, I gave the go-ahead for our Air Force to eliminate the nuclear threat from Cuba. This action is under way as I speak to you tonight. Of course, we would be doing only half our job if we simply destroyed the Soviet missiles and then withdrew." When you bite the bullet, bite it hard—go for the big play. Surprise the hell out of your enemies, put 'em off balance. Change the game to your advantage. He was going for all the marbles—getting rid of the missiles, unmistakably, and Castro, too. "What would prevent Premier Khrushchev from sending additional missiles to Cuba at sometime in the future? No, we must go to the root of the problem, and that is the presence of a Communist regime just ninety miles from our shores.

"Nuclear weapons are not the solution to the difficulties that divide the world in this modern era. Their use would unleash unconscionable suffering upon mankind. This we must avoid at all costs. But let there be no mistake." He looked squarely at the big camera lens in front of him, wanting to deliver his message directly to Khrushchev. "We will defend ourselves, and our allies, against any and all Communist aggression with every means at our disposal. And we will prevail, *whatever the cost.*"

⚬∞⚬

Her husband's words made her brain shiver, like goose bumps across her mind. On the Magnavox in Helene's living room, outside Los Angeles, he looked pale and tired. She was sure he hadn't slept much.

Helene, sitting beside her on the sleek two-shades-of-blue Finn Juhl sofa, looked increasingly concerned as Dick told the nation how the U.S. had caught the Soviet Union attempting to build a secret nuclear missile base in Cuba and began to describe the actions he was taking in response.

Her friend wasn't seeing what she saw. Dick knew how to perform. On stage, with the Whittier Community Players, she had seen how he had taught himself to bring tears to his eyes. He knew how to appear gay when he was sad and strong when he felt weak, to sound optimistic when he feared the worst and, most important, how to sound convincing saying one thing when he believed another, whether addressing the entire nation, or just her. Now, watching him bring his fist down on his desk for emphasis, she wondered how much thought he had put into that simple gesture as he'd prepared for his speech. These, she supposed, were the skills a politician had to learn, and Dick, despite his youth, was one of the best—had been from the beginning.

The only thing he hadn't mastered with all his study, she thought to herself with a smile, was how to look spontaneous, though he practiced that too.

"Let me be clear. These missiles threaten our nation with the prospect of unthinkable devastation."

She sensed Helene looking at her, trying to gauge her reaction. She couldn't face Helene. Right now she couldn't look at her husband, either; she stared instead at one of the speakers that flanked the television screen at the center of the American Modern console.

It couldn't be as bad as he was saying; if it were, he would have told her about it on the telephone instead of letting her learn the news from the television along with everyone else. Or was he afraid she would ask him questions? Is that why he didn't tell her? Surely he knew better by now; she'd been good about that. It had to be that Dick was overstating his case because he very much wanted the nation to take this threat from the Russians seriously. That's why he said those things—to focus the nation's attention on the problem and get everyone behind his plan for getting rid of that awful Castro. And there, he just said using nuclear weapons was unconscionable. She was sure Dick knew best.

What Dick may not have realized is just how terribly frightened people were going to be; they wouldn't be seeing the stagecraft and the acting the way she could and would take his words at face value. She would explain all this later to Helene so she wouldn't worry. For the other housewives, she could see them rushing to their neighborhood stores as soon as they opened tomorrow morning, fighting one another as they struggled to load their shopping carts with bread and eggs and canned goods. And mothers everywhere around the country were going to be so worried tomorrow about sending their children off to school. Will that kiss good-bye they gave their husbands as they headed off to work be their last? And of course everyone will want to know all about the fallout shelters their local communities had established and stocked with supplies, just to be safe. She needed to do something to help. Something reassuring.

Right away, when she was able to look at the screen again, she saw it. At first, hearing Dick describe the horrible Communist treachery in Cuba, she'd put it to the back of her mind. Now she stared and didn't notice the salted peanuts fall from between her fingers.

"What is it, Buddy?"

Pat pointed at the TV. "Those aren't my curtains."

"What are you talking about?"

"Look, quick. King should be right there."

"King?"

Pat grabbed one of Helene's leather and stainless-steel chairs. Sitting inches from the convex screen she was sure now, even without being able to see the colors. "It's a goddamn *set!*"

"What in the world are you talking about?"

"Did Jack say anything?"

"I haven't been able to reach him. The White House operator keeps saying he's busy."

———— ✦ ————

Oleg Troyanovsky, Khrushchev's foreign policy aide, listened on the phone as an official at the Foreign Ministry in Moscow read from the statement the U.S. Embassy had delivered minutes earlier—it was now just a little after two in the morning in Moscow—and that President Nixon would deliver on American television in one hour.

"'We would be doing only half our job if we simply destroyed Soviet missiles and then withdrew,'" Troyanovsky said in Russian to the Presidium members. Again he listened then translated, "'Nyet, we must go to root of problem, and that is presence of Communist regime just ninety miles from our shores.'"

"Read this final sentence again." Khrushchev knew what he'd heard, but what he'd heard couldn't be. Yes, those were the president's words. That did not mean he had to believe them, that he had to believe Nixon. He had learned not to trust what this man said. Even so, he clenched his muscles to prevent an embarrassing accident.

He had ordered missiles sent to the Caribbean to prevent an American invasion. In so doing, had he handed Nixon a justification—something the president could twist into a justification—for snuffing out a beacon for all the unfortunate, exploited peoples of Latin America? Had he opened the door for the capitalists to deliver a terrible blow to Marxist-Leninist teaching that would cast the Soviet Union away from Latin America?

"'We will defend ourselves, and our allies, against any and all Communist aggression with every means at our disposal. And we will prevail, whatever may be cost.'" Troyanovsky looked at Khrushchev. "This last part is emphasized in text."

"Nixon is threatening us," Malinovsky said. "If we try to stop Americans, lunatics might start World War III."

He had never been able to convince Malinovsky that the next big conflict would be a missile war; the general was only sixty-three, but old in his thinking and insisted that big armies and their conventional weapons would always play an important role. Now Malinovsky looked scared and Khrushchev wondered if his defense minister finally understood. "It's one thing to threaten with nuclear weapons, it's another to use them, Rodion Yakovlevich." It went unsaid, Khrushchev knew, that he had threatened the United States many times with war to intimidate the Americans, without any intention of initiating hostilities. Now he tried to convince Malinovsky, and himself, that the American president's statement was itself an opening gambit meant to intimidate, that Nixon would not follow through on his threat to invade Cuba, knowing it could lead to a wider war.

Soon the president would make clear the meaning of this ploy. Perhaps tomorrow a cable would arrive offering a deal. "Nixon wishes to frighten us to get something in return. Keep this in mind and it will strengthen your resolve," he said for his own benefit as much as for the glum faces around the table staring into their tea glasses. They would all soon know if Nixon's sword was made of steel, or if it was just wood, his threats hollow. For now, the best they could do, he told the Presidium, was to frighten the Americans into believing an invasion would lead to general war and the death of 70 million of their citizens. This would deter invasion.

Khrushchev said he would try to find the right words to send to the Americans. He would also compose a letter to Castro, praising him for bravely fighting back against America's air assault and reassuring him that the Soviet Union would continue to defend the revolution. In the meantime he told the Presidium members to go to their offices to get some sleep. He would call them in the morning to resume their meeting.

In his own office he began dictating a message to the American president that would take him until dawn to complete. The bombing of Cuba, he said, is "an act of war that is pushing mankind toward abyss of world missile-nuclear war." Khrushchev proposed a summit meeting, offering to go anywhere to meet Nixon. To show he was serious about seeking peace, he told the American president he was ordering all ships en route to Cuba with additional armaments and troops to return to port. He also ordered the submarines armed with nuclear torpedoes he'd sent to protect the fleet to reverse course.

The Soviet Union was showing unprecedented restraint with these actions and in not responding militarily to America's illegal bombing of Cuba, he told Nixon; this would only encourage those who wished to see their nations go to war. And then he warned Nixon about what would happen if the president carried out his threat to invade. He would no longer be able to restrain his military "and we will all meet in hell."

⁓⊗⊗⊗⁓

President Nixon wore his blue velvet smoking jacket over his suit, as he would if he were in the comfort of his hideaway office across from the White House, where he would have ordered more logs to make the flames jump higher in the fireplace. During his tour of Mount Weather as vice president, he was not shown the cold, concrete-walled fortress of a room that was to serve as the president's office, should the site be activated. He had feared it would be undersized, as were many of the offices he'd seen at the facility. Instead, his decidedly rectangular office here was large, if not airy, with enough room for him to comfortably meet with a dozen men around the conference table at one end of the room. Nearby were two doors with access to the main corridor. One opened first onto a small office where Rose Mary took up her position; the other exit led through a small room with green filing cabinets and a table. At the opposite end of the room from the two doors was his desk. It was plain in comparison with the intricately carved wooden structure he was accustomed to sitting at in the Oval Office, large and utilitarian, topped with wood veneer. There was a pen set, a blotter, and a dial phone with rows of clear plastic buttons, similar to the one he used in the Oval Office. Behind the desk, on a small table, was another phone; it was red, without a dial. Next to it the U.S. flag hung limply from atop a tall pole in a brass stand; a matching stand seven feet away held the state flag of Virginia. Between the conference table and the desk was the sitting area where he was trying to get comfortable. Nearby were two brown leather couches, a glass and aluminum coffee table, and two more easy chairs—pieces not that different from those the Eisenhowers had used in the White House.

After shaking hands with the military crew in charge of the Mount Weather television studio, he had walked slowly down the long passageway, eschewing the offer of a ride in one of the carts that were always nearby and glad to be away from the heat of the lights. Walking with his hands in his pants pockets and his head down, he still saw the lumbering camera aimed at him, as the words he'd spoken minutes before paraded again through his mind.

He'd gone with very little sleep for most of the last three days and now, with Scotch and Seconal beginning to work their way through his system, he looked again at the list of calls he'd received—patched through from the White House switchboard as though he were across the street in his Old Executive Office Building hideaway—since going off the air, calls he'd begun taking and making hours earlier with an almost giddy excitement washing away the fear and dread of these last few days. Foreign heads of state, Cabinet members, members of Congress, old political friends, and some who hadn't always been so friendly, had called to praise his steely determination, offering to help in any way they could, assuring him the whole country was praying for him as he struggled to bring a quick and successful end to Khrushchev's perilous provocation.

What he saw were the names that were missing from the roster.

I don't need them, he said to himself. Fuck 'em. Silently he went through the roll call of his Cabinet. Every one of them should have called, he told himself. He ran through the names of possible replacements he could make at various positions around the Cabinet table after the mid-term elections—this time he'd be sure they were men who knew how to be loyal to their president.

"Bob, where the hell are you?" he said in his second call of the evening to his chief of staff.

"I'm in my office. Our offices aren't as close together here, but I could be over there in ten minutes."

"No, stay there. I want you to make up a list of all the people who should be calling after a big speech like tonight's. Then the next time I can just go down the list, circle the ones who don't call, and we'll know who's not with us."

"Yes, sir."

"Dulles still hasn't called me, you know," he said of CIA director Allen Dulles. "His brother would have been on the phone to me even before I'd gotten off the air."

If only he could talk to Foster, the man most of the world knew as John Foster Dulles, Eisenhower's secretary of state until late in the president's second term, when Foster's rapidly spreading cancer forced his resignation.

His skull sessions at Foster's house in those years had been like a political finishing school for a young vice president still developing the maturity he would need to confidently guide the nation through dangerous waters, should he someday become president. Night after night in Foster's study, thinking through all that was so disturbing in the world, a drink in one hand, the other free to point, point, point into the soft leather arm of the club chair if it would help make their case, they shared their frustration with their president, who talked—just talked—of standing up to the Communists, afraid of committing American troops to a protracted conflict in Vietnam or Laos and refusing to tap the growing arsenal of small nuclear weapons designed to ensure quick and decisive victory.

He was sure Foster would approve of the decision he had announced to the nation this evening. Foster would have understood the risk and would not have shied from it, as had Hall and some of the other gutless men who had cautioned him not to send in the Marines to finish the job, or not to bomb the Cuban missile sites for fear of how Khrushchev might respond. Men afraid of taking large risks never made large advances.

The direct message he inserted at the end for Khrushchev would be clear inside the Kremlin: The U.S. was ready to use nuclear weapons if the Soviets caused any trouble in Berlin or elsewhere as their missiles were destroyed in Cuba and Castro was eliminated. By threatening a war no one could win, the Soviets—and his enemies at home—would see the tough bastard he so wanted to be. By threatening Khrushchev with Armageddon he was able to look brutally tough when in fact he was doing everything possible to prevent a war.

"The secretary would have been proud of you, sir—it's just what Foster Dulles would have done," said Finch, who had watched the speech from the studio.

"Do you know the first one to call me was Jack McCloy? Of all people."

He had expected Jack to join Jacob Beam, ambassador to the Soviet Union, Hall, and the others who initially favored a soft line on the missiles in Cuba, expected him to say these weapons really didn't change the nuclear equation, that it didn't much matter if we got hit by a missile launched from the other side of the world, or one from Cuba, who believed he would argue that we should negotiate or put up a blockade and insist Khrushchev remove the missiles. Just insist. So it was a shocker when Jack made the case for air strikes to destroy the missiles and even agreed, perhaps a bit reluctantly, to sending in ground troops.

"What did McCloy have to say about the speech?" Finch's voice was perkier now.

"Said it was absolutely top notch."

"Which of course it was."

"It was a goddamn effective speech. And I know a little something about speechmaking."

"The best you've ever made, Mr. President."

"It was tough, that's the thing."

"It couldn't have been tougher."

"But see, even if they didn't like it—Beam and Hall and the rest—they should have called. I mean, I told Rose Mary, god-damn it, anyone who calls is to get through. So I just wonder what the hell's happened."

"Everyone I've talked to has nothing but praise for the speech, sir." Finch's voice betrayed only the barest hint of dismay.

"Is that right? What did they like about it, Bob?"

"Absolutely everything. Everyone agrees the tone was just right. They all respect your decision and they understand what a difficult time this is for you."

"Well that's right," he said, reaching for his glass. "It all comes down to the president. He's got to make the big decision. It's all on his shoulders. But I don't lose any sleep over it." The realization returned with the first moment of consciousness each morning, before he was able to open his eyes after a few hours' sleep, a dread that covered him like a lead blanket, a weight he carried through each day of the crisis, from that grim waking to fitful sleep, each morning looking darker, each day growing longer, each night becoming shorter.

"But you have that decision behind you now that the next phase has begun—the military phase—so maybe you can get some rest. It's almost two o'clock now."

"I wrote most of that speech, you know. Writing's damn hard—that's why I have a lot of respect for writers, they have to be smart—but I think I pulled it off pretty well, don't you?"

"Yes, sir."

"I'm kind of an egghead myself, you know. No one believes it." Maybe they'd believe it if he'd been able to afford to go to Harvard with that scholarship the school offered. The Nixons had been poor, maybe not as poor as Pat's family, but poor enough that he had to work hard—very hard—for everything and there would still be the cross-country trips from California and the living expenses he would be required to fund, and so he had been forced to go to Whittier College instead, forced to smile politely whenever someone claimed never to have heard of the place, or lied that they had.

Without that Harvard education, without those connections, he was forever the outsider, forced to prove himself by working harder than anyone else, overcoming the laughs and the slights and the snubs through excellence and personal gut performance, while the Harvard boys sat on their fat butts. The same hard work that had propelled him from the starting gates to become one of the brightest stars in the political firmament for single-handedly ferreting out a dangerous Red who gave our government's secrets to the Communists, front-page newspaper headlines chronicling every twist and turn of his investigation of Alger Hiss—one of the New Deal era's best and brightest, admired by Republicans and Democrats alike—and the trial that led to Hiss's conviction for lying about espionage.

"Hiss was one of those Harvard men, Bob."

"Yes, sir."

The best PR minds in the country couldn't have dreamed up a better publicity photo than the one newspapers across the nation featured on their front pages when he finally got the goods on Hiss—the intrepid young congressman Nixon staring intently into a magnifying glass at a microfilm strip of stolen State Department secrets he'd discovered hidden in a hollowed-out pumpkin on Whittaker Chambers's Maryland farm.

"Don't be an informer, Bob. Look how it ruined Chambers. And one of *Time*'s best writers."

The liberals never would accept that Richard Nixon had gotten the goods to prove Hiss's treachery, couldn't believe their favorite son had passed America's secrets to its sworn enemy, or just refused to care. Hiss was one of them, an Ivy Leaguer, and who was Dick Nixon? Some hick from—what was the name of his school?

They hit him with every smear in the book—forgery, drunkenness, insanity, thievery, perjury, bigamy, adultery. Adultery? Sure he could if he'd wanted to—anytime. He'd seen those young girls jumping and jumping and jumping to see him as he campaigned in '60, their skirts flying. He just didn't go in for that stuff.

"Too many liberals," he said into the phone now, as it all flashed brightly in his mind.

"Sir?"

"We have too many liberals in the Cabinet, Bob. That's why they haven't called. They've hated my guts ever since I went after their darling boy, Hiss. They'll do anything to see me fail—anything. But they're not going to stop me this time. They'll see just how tough Richard Nixon is."

"They'll have to give you the credit you deserve."

Would it be enough for them if he destroyed the missiles threatening the nation from Cuba, liberated the island from Communism, and averted nuclear war? It would be enough to make another president a national hero, he thought, drifting off for a moment before waking again. Exposing Hiss had made him a hero to some, propelling him in just a couple years to the Senate, surpassing every member of his freshman class in Congress, Kennedy included. He was just beginning to learn the ways of the upper chamber—in nineteen months there had hardly been enough time even to think about reelection—when Eisenhower anointed him, a thirteen-year-old junior senator from California, as his vice presidential running mate in '52. Oh, how Kennedy must have envied him.

"Kennedy was one of the first to call tonight, Bob. Said he supported me 100 percent. Of course he might have to take a different line publicly."

If bringing down Hiss had made him a hero to some it also gained him a permanent corps of hard-core opponents in the press and among Democrats, of course, and within his own party, too. The enemies he'd made—also for exposing the Socialist voting record of that woman, Helen Gahagan Douglas, who opposed him in his 1950 Senate race—were ready to do anything to stop him from becoming vice president, knowing he'd have a straight shot at the presidency in '60.

"Remember how they tried to get me off the ticket in '52?" he asked Finch.

Someone on the campaign train was handing him the newspaper and all he could see was the headline. NIXON SCANDAL FUND.

Some of his aides tried to restrain him. Others could not face the spectacle of his rage and turned away. He saw them look to the door and to one another, scared and uncertain.

"At first I just dismissed the story, Bob—I didn't have any secret fund. The usual pack of lies—that kind of thing."

Finch said nothing; he'd heard it before.

"I'll tell you, though, the temptation was always there." When he turned to pour another Scotch, the telephone receiver squeezed between his shoulder and ear fell to the floor. "Shit. Did you say something, Bob?"

"You were saying the temptation's the worst."

"Maybe I should have accepted some of those fat legal fees some of the other senators were taking on the side." A $15,000 salary, even with another $6,600 from lecture fees, didn't make a man wealthy, even in '52, not when you had a wife and two growing kids to support. "There wouldn't have been anything illegal about it. But it didn't seem right, Bob. Maybe I should have put Pat on the government payroll for all the long hours she worked at the office. Those fucking reporters. They were just waiting for their chance to destroy Dick Nixon."

In Tulare and Fresno, Merced and Stockton, reporters bolted from the lounge car of the Nixon Special as the train made its way north through California on the first leg of a whistle-stop tour of fifty cities in eleven Western states to spread the word about the danger to the nation from the fifth column that had infiltrated the government and the growing cancer of dishonesty in Washington. They ran to the nearest telephones, knocking on the doors of nearby homes if the phones at the station were unavailable, climbing back aboard the train with other reporters sent to ride the story of his secret fund, all of them brimming with questions and innuendo.

They shouted at him as he walked through their car on his way to the platform at the rear of the train to address the crowds that gathered at each stop. He pretended he didn't hear the reporters, looked straight ahead, marched on.

"Senator Nixon, have you talked to General Eisenhower yet?"

"Senator Nixon, will you resign from the ticket?"

Eisenhower wasn't going to come to his rescue. No one was. No one ever had or ever would. Instead, Ike gave him thirty minutes of prime time on a national television hookup; rope to hang himself or save himself.

Yes, he'd expose everything, expose Pat, too, count up all they owed and the little they had while the whole country watched, open the bedroom curtains at night and let them all watch, do anything, be Eisenhower's errand boy, if Ike would only keep him as his running mate, stay up nights on adrenaline preparing for those thirty minutes, try like hell to think through all the angles, too hepped up to sleep without a pill, too tired to get through the day without another Benzedrine.

He was just about to leave for the television studio when Dewey called. Thomas Dewey his friend, his supporter, his booster in Ike's camp calling to tell him he should end his address by resigning from the ticket. Hell, Dewey was saying he should resign from the Senate, too. It was what the people around Eisenhower wanted, so it had to be what Ike wanted, too.

"If Dewey calls," he mumbled to Finch now, "tell him to go to hell."

"Yes, sir."

"They all hate me, Bob. But this time, with Cuba, if I go down, they all go down with me."

"Sir, it's very late and you've been working very—"

"Those fancy New York Republicans didn't care if I was innocent of the charges." They didn't like his kind—unsophisticated, self-made, nothing handed to him on a silver platter. "Going on television was the only thing left to do for me to clear my name. But you know who was against that? I'll bet you do."

"Was it—?"

"That's right. Pat. 'There's only one way to deal with these lies,' I told her. 'I'm going to go on television and give a complete accounting of our personal finances.'" He didn't need to tell his wife he would be speaking in front of the largest audience in history ever to watch a man desperately try to rescue his career.

"You know what she asked me? Pat's the one who really suffered through all of this. She asked, 'Why do you have to tell people how little we have and how much we owe?' She thought we should be entitled to our privacy."

He couldn't bear to tell her the truth, that they would never have their privacy back. He was afraid of what she might do if she really understood. The unfairness, the betrayal, the meanness—all of it was eating away at him, too. Maybe he'd endured enough, put the family through enough, the girls coming home in tears from the mean things the other kids said about him at school.

It was three minutes before the rope would be his to do with it what he could, when he felt the tears welling up behind his eyes. "I just don't think I can go through with this, Buddy," he whispered in his wife's ear. He would resign his place on the ticket and go back to Whittier, where she could lead the quiet life she craved. It would be a relief to call it all off, to let the pressure beating down on him finally break through. Then he could tell them all to go to hell. They wouldn't have Dick Nixon to kick around anymore.

"It took a lot of guts for me to go on TV like that, Bob. I was putting it all on the line."

Pat wouldn't let him give in, couldn't bear seeing him broken, no matter how much his public accounting would shame her. Without her encouragement, he knew, he wouldn't have had the strength to stand up to Eisenhower and wouldn't be president now.

"Of course you can do it, Dick," she said. "If you don't, your life will be marred forever and the same will be true of your family, and particularly your daughters." She took his hand, knowing the encouragement he always took from that simple gesture, and led him into the auditorium, empty but for the camera crew.

When he told millions of people Pat owned no fancy coat, the camera turned in her direction, catching the taught, embarrassed face of the pained yet adoring wife, which must have embarrassed her more.

My wife's sitting over here. She is a wonderful stenographer. She used to teach stenography and she used to teach shorthand in high school. That was when I met her and I can tell you folks that she's worked many hours at night and many hours on Saturdays and Sundays in my office, and she's done a fine job, and I am proud to say tonight that in the six years I have been in the House and the Senate of the United States, Pat Nixon has never been on the government payroll.

"I wouldn't be here without Pat—you know that, Bob, don't you?"

"She called when you were on the phone with de Gaulle. She's on your call-back list."

"You see, if people were going to believe I wasn't a crook," he said, speech slurred, "I had to lay it all on the line," the 1950 Oldsmobile, the $20,000 equity in their Washington house, the $3,000 equity in a California house where his parents lived, even the $4,000 in life insurance. It wasn't very much.

It was the only way to prove they had not lived in a style beyond his salary. People wanted more than the Price-Waterhouse audit that cleared him of all wrongdoing.

But Pat and I have the satisfaction that every dime that we have got is honestly ours.

He was one of them, he wanted to say, one of the majority who came by everything they had through hard work. He wasn't one of those Harvard elitists.

One other thing I probably should tell you, because if I don't they'll probably be saying this about me, too, we did get something—a gift—after the election. A man down in Texas heard Pat on the radio mention the fact that our two youngsters would like to have a dog. And believe it or not, the day before we left on this campaign trip we got a message from Union Station in Baltimore saying that they had a package for us. We went down to get it. You know what it was? It was a little cocker spaniel dog in a crate that he had sent all the way from Texas, black and white, spotted, and our little girl Tricia, the six year old, named it Checkers. And you know, the kids, like all kids, love the dog, and I just want to say this, right now, that regardless of what they say about it, we're gonna keep it.

He walked off the stage in a daze as a friend, one of the few who had not betrayed him, approached. He heard the congratulations, felt himself shaking hands, as he tried to hold back the tears. There are photographers here. It didn't matter. There was nothing he could do to stop himself.

He put his head down on his friend's shoulder and cried. He had saved his career, and he would never be the same.

The letters that poured in forced Eisenhower to keep him on the ticket, begrudgingly, resentfully, and always holding the power to end his career with a few words.

"You're my boy," Ike would tell him the next day in West Virginia.

"Have we heard anything from Eisenhower about the speech, Bob?"

"I'll have to—"

"Eisenhower hates my guts as much as the rest of them... those establishment bastards...if they don't...I'll..."

"You have a full schedule of meetings tomorrow—I've put virtually all your other business on hold and..." Finch's voice cracked and he paused to regain his composure. "The next week will be, well, sir, the most difficult of your presidency—of any presidency, I should say. But you should know that you will have the full...the full support of...sir, are you still there?"

On Finch's end of the line there was silence and finally a click as the line went dead.

Castro shot one fist into the humid air and then the other as he pictured Soviet missiles blasting off from Cuba toward the United States and said again what he had been saying for hours, since taking refuge in the control room of his unfinished underground command post with General Pliyev. "The imperialists must suffer the consequences of the war they have begun, which is extermination!"

It was the first time since the bombing had begun that the Cuban leader had not been madly riding a Jeep from one end of the island to the other, checking that his troops were properly digging in against invasion, assisting their Soviet comrades to shoot down American planes, and directing sufficient artillery at Guantanamo. He was high on the danger and excitement of once more defending the revolution he'd forged less than four years earlier against his giant nemesis from the north; enraged at the lives lost and the damaged factories, homes, schools, and clinics; crazy with fear that everything he had worked for and built, the progress to come in Cuba and the shining example he was setting for all of Latin America, was at risk; and through it all as alive and vibrant as he'd ever been in his thirty-six years and ever would be.

Nixon's war on Cuba had been building to this moment since his meeting with the then vice president in Washington. Starting with bombings of sugar-production plants, burning crops, sinking ships loaded with goods for export, and countless other acts of sabotage and terrorism aimed at crippling the Cuban economy, it escalated to open warfare with the CIA-led invasion at Trinidad last year. The CIA invaders who survived and made their way to the Escambray Mountains continued the fight with their raids on Cuban forces, factories, and farms.

When Khrushchev offered to defend the revolution with Soviet missiles, Castro grasped at it as the only way his tiny nation could fend off another assault from the Americans, convinced as he'd been since the Trinidad invasion that Nixon would attack again, this time with warships and Marines instead of poorly trained Cuban exiles.

Now that Nixon had publicly announced an invasion was imminent it was time to use Khrushchev's rockets.

Pliyev closed the door that led to the bunker's central tunnel, which was sealed at the far end with a giant steel plate that could be opened to let in men and materiel. Seated again across the small conference table from Castro, the fifty-eight-year-old general spoke quietly. "I have ordered missiles fueled and warheads readied so launching will be immediate on my instructions to fire. In meantime, Major Gerchenov is doing excellent job shooting down many American airplanes." He paused and waited for the translator. "I cannot do more without orders from Moscow. Then we will know how to act," Pliyev concluded, wiping his brow.

Castro stood again and leaned over his chair toward Pliyev. "I will send a letter to comrade Nikita myself to tell him what I have told you, that he must not repeat the mistakes of World War II when Stalin was warned the Germans would invade but did nothing. You are a military man so you understand that a force that remains in its barracks is lost, but I must educate the premier about this. What use are your mighty rockets, general, if we allow the Americans to obliterate them?" Castro asked, waving at the American planes flying somewhere overhead.

"Will you advise my country to make nuclear first strike against United States?"

The general was twisting his words to make him sound as though he'd lost his reason. "I do not wish to make such a direct statement," he said, returning to the table and his third sausage of the evening. "What I wish to say is that we must not wait to experience the perfidy of the imperialists, letting them decide that Cuba should be wiped off the face of the earth." Castro squashed the bottle cap with his army boot as it hit the concrete floor; the beer, which still tasted cold, was the only relief for the heat, worse now. "Once the Americans have bombed all of your antiaircraft defenses, and then your missiles, they will begin their invasion. How will we defend ourselves? Every man, woman, and even grown children will fight to the end to defend the revolution. I have seen that the morale of the people is very high and they will meet the aggressor heroically, but we cannot fight forever against the imperialists without your rockets. That's why the rockets are here! We must give Khrushchev the moral strength to use them before they are all destroyed."

"And what then? We do not have sufficient rockets in Soviet Union to eliminate enemy's ability to retaliate against us with their nuclear weapons."

Castro stretched out his long legs and put his hands up to stop Pliyev. "Tell me this again. I cannot believe my ears. The Soviet Union is not inferior in nuclear weapons to the United States. Nikita speaks as a man who is confident he possesses the weapons to make good on what he says. But you are telling me otherwise—or that is how I heard you. Perhaps because our engineers have not finished the ventilation work"—Castro held out his arms—"you're words are influenced by a lack of proper oxygen."

"It is truth only few are privileged to know and I trust you will not speak of it to anyone. Premier's threats are tactic—and very effective—to scare enemy. Should there be war between United States and Soviet Union, enemy will have plenty of nuclear bombs left over when they get done with us to drop few on you also."

Castro examined his hands, which were uncharacteristically still, and decided this confounding information only reinforced his point. "However harsh and terrible the solution, there is no other, general, but the one I have put forward."

"My men and I are here to defend Cuban revolution. Let us hope that my orders from Moscow arrive soon so I know what I am permitted to do. Now I think it is time for us to inspect damage that has been done today."

Chapter 6

Monday, October 22, 1962

WHEN PAT FOLDED DOWN the green and yellow polka dot cover on the guest-room bed closest to the phone, instead of the matching single bed she'd slept in till now, the clock radio's radium hands glowed at two o'clock. In another ninety minutes the sun would be coming up on the east coast, where Dick might be getting an early start or might still be working. She wanted to tell him what a wonderful speech he had made on television. That was always so important to him and it satisfied her to help him feel confident in his performance. Then she would want to lay into him with questions about why in the world he hadn't been able to make his speech from the Oval Office and where in the White House they'd constructed that look-alike set and why in God's name he hadn't told her when they talked yesterday about the construction going on in the Oval Office that required fooling people with that sham set. Turning the clear plastic knob near the 3 on the clock's black face until the tab pointed to *RADIO ALARM* and keeping the red needle set to six, she knew he wouldn't tell her anything she hadn't heard for herself on television or could read in the morning paper. He might even try to deny that he'd made his address from a stage set. That would really get her angry and she could already hear the argument they'd have. Not that she put much hope in getting a call back. He often froze her out when he had something to hide, as he did now—and not just from her this time. Under the covers in her peach satin pajamas, eyes closed, she waited for sleep to come, determined to assume her responsibility as First Lady in the morning. He would expect no less of her.

———∽∾∾————

Joseph Quinn, the Los Angeles civil defense director, gestured proudly at the narrow door beside the doughnut shop. "This is the entrance here, Mrs. Nixon."

It was a pity all those harried office workers, air-raid sirens wailing in their ears and thoughts of their children hiding under desks at school going through their minds, would be entering this grand structure through such a forlorn little entrance, she thought, looking up at the twelve-story, granite Subway Terminal Building, constructed in 1925 to resemble a fifteenth-century Florentine palazzo.

While Quinn struggled to open the padlocked door, she looked for the familiar orange-and-black civil defense sign that would tell one and all that they could take refuge here, should our military detect missiles coming this way from Cuba.

Charles Fisher, chief of the Army Engineers' civil defense section for Los Angeles, anticipated her question. "We'll be getting signs up as soon as we can. One problem we've been having is that building owners don't want us drilling holes in their buildings."

"Everyone around here already knows this is a shelter anyway," said Charles Alexander, the third of the First Lady's escorts and the Terminal Building's general manager.

"There are five schools, including Belmont High, within a fifteen-minute walk of here, Mrs. Nixon," Fisher said. "And another... What is it, Chuck, three thousand people?" Alexander nodded. "Another three thousand people work in the Subway Building who'll be wanting to come down here."

"And I've been getting calls from people who work in some of the other buildings here around Pershing Square who know about the shelter," said Quinn, who now had the door open. "Some of them have asked if they can make reservations."

She thought that sounded like quite a proper approach. They could even set up a little makeshift reservations desk right out here on the sidewalk so people could line up to check in.

Quinn looked at her, shaking his head. "Can you believe that?"

"The ideas some people have." She made a tight smile and entered the narrow corridor, careful to keep her white-gloved hands clear of the grime-covered walls.

"Oh, how interesting," she said now and again as Alexander told her the history of the building and the Pacific Electric subway line that had run underneath. She was having to work harder now at looking chipper after what seemed like an eternity in this dark and twisting hall. They must have walked the length of a football field, she thought; the worst part was that they could be near the end or still have just as far to go—there was no way to tell and the last thing she was going to do was ask.

She walked down the seventeen steps carefully in her high heels, declining to hold the banister.

"You're quite the trooper, Mrs. Nixon. Chuck tells me that hall is 112 yards."

"Just sixty yards from here to the platform," Alexander said.

Her feet were beginning to swell, which only made her more determined. "Please continue, Mr. Alexander. You were saying how the trolley cars were red. That's such a lovely color." She smiled and picked up the pace.

It was funny how turning a corner and seeing a place you hadn't visited in years could immediately bring back old memories. She'd stood on this old subway platform as a young woman; she remembered the excitement of being in a crowd, the grand concourse upstairs, and how proud she had felt riding the red trolley cars. Yes, they were red—the Red Car Subway, they called the trains that had once brought commuters from the San Fernando Valley and the Westside into the heart of downtown, until the line was shut down in '56.

Now the trains and their passengers were gone and brown boxes, stacked four high, stood waiting instead.

"These boxes contain enough biscuits so that everyone can have sixty-four a day for two weeks," Quinn said.

"That's wonderful," she said, wondering how anyone could survive two weeks on old biscuits.

"There are also plenty of medical supplies and sanitation kits in there," Fisher said with evident pride.

"And each of these can hold seventeen-and-a-half gallons of water," Quinn said, pointing to a row of containers, also stacked four high. "That's enough for everyone to have a quart a day."

"Hey, Joe," yelled one of the photographers who had kept to themselves till now. "How about we get a shot of you pouring Mrs. Nixon here a drink."

"That would be lovely," she said. Her throat felt like parchment after that horrible walk.

Quinn whispered something in Alexander's ear, and the building manager scurried off. Almost as quietly, he said to her, "We'll have you a drink in no time, Mrs. Nixon."

Turning to the reporters, he said, "Actually, boys, we haven't filled these containers yet."

"You mean we been duped?" one of them yelled.

"Aw, come on guys. We can fill all these jugs from the building's water supply in ninety minutes flat. Why jump the gun?"

"Yeah, as long as one of them atom bombs from Cuba don't make a mess of the plumbing," a reporter yelled, getting a good laugh from his buddies.

The photographers settled for a picture of her and Quinn examining a carton of biscuits. Alexander, panting and holding a half-spilled glass of water, stood off to the side. "Joe, move your fat mitt, you're blocking your own damn civil defense seal on that pretty box."

"All right, watch your language, boys."

The popping bulbs lit up the dark platform and she smiled her good-for-all-occasions smile.

⁂

"I'll walk you back to your hotel, Mrs. Nixon," Quinn said when they were back out on South Hill Street.

"That's awfully kind of you, Mr. Quinn."

"That way these press boys won't bother you." Only two had stayed with the tour and they were now following at a discrete distance.

Ahead of them on South Olive Street, across from the Biltmore, was a desolate, grass-covered block. It was lunchtime and the streets all around were filled with office workers on their lunchtime breaks. Almost no one was in the park, and she could see why. Even if anyone had a notion to enter the barren square they would have to dodge the automobiles streaming up and down the ramps on either side to the underground garage that had been built in the early 1950s.

"Oh, it's such a shame what they did to Pershing Square," she said. She remembered it as it was before, a lush oasis of tropical plants with a lovely fountain at its center.

"You can't stop progress," said Quinn, himself the image of the modern man in his dark suit, white shirt, and narrow tie. "Besides, we can use the garage as another fallout shelter. It would be the biggest of all—there's room down there for fifty-four thousand. Without the cars, of course."

"Oh, the rations alone must take up an awful lot of room." She wondered if the garage had plumbing to fill the water containers.

"They will, they certainly will," Quinn said as the doorman at the Biltmore bowed slightly and they entered the grand Italian-Spanish Renaissance lobby. Quinn whispered something to the reporters and they stayed outside.

She looked at him, smiling. Was he trying to say the biggest shelter in the city wasn't stocked yet? What if the sirens sounded today? What would happen to all the poor people who took refuge there, people who were counting on their government to shelter them until it was safe to emerge and return home? She motioned for him to sit down on an ornate sofa, in a quiet corner of the lobby under the high Moorish beamed ceiling. Maybe there was something she could do to help.

"To tell you the truth, Mrs. Nixon, there have been a few difficulties, but isn't that the way it always is? I'm sure everything will be just fine," he said with a smile.

"This whole mess with Cuba will blow over soon enough, I'm sure. But if there's anything I, or my husband, can do to help, please don't hesitate to ask."

She'd seen this many times before, a local official who realizes that meeting with the First Lady is as close as he'll ever get to the president, that if there's an appeal to be made it will have to go through her. Yet, nine times out of ten, these men were reluctant to level with her. Maybe they didn't think she really wanted to help, or didn't think she was interested in anything more than showing up for goodwill tours. They'd seen the pictures of her in the magazines, smiling up at Dick, the way any good wife would. That's what he expected, and she demanded no less of herself. They didn't seem to believe she could be a good wife and a hard worker.

She decided to try one more time. "Do you have everything you need?"

After a moment, Quinn looked up from the floor and she saw a different expression on his face. The pleasant tour guide was gone; now he was the determined public servant she imagined his colleagues would recognize.

He leaned forward across the coffee table and looked at her directly. "I'll be honest with you, Mrs. Nixon. We had both better pray none of those missiles come this way."

"Well, of course, but once you get that garage stocked, and..."

"I have two hundred tons of supplies in a Long Beach warehouse. That's enough to take care of forty thousand people for two weeks."

"Plus the Subway Terminal shelter?"

"Yes, and we have one other stocked shelter in the city, the Army Engineers headquarters building, which can handle three hundred people. So even if I can get those supplies out of the warehouse—and let me tell you, the city council won't even give me the money to do that—we can shelter 50,300."

"Where will the rest of the people go?"

"There are 2.6 million people in the city of Los Angeles, Mrs. Nixon, 2.6 million."

He leaned back and she saw the intensity in his eyes recede. She didn't know what he was seeing, only that it wasn't her, or anyone else in the lobby. Maybe it was all those other people.

She thought of the aerial pictures of that demonstration in Washington against the war in Laos, with tens of thousands of people on the Mall, a sea of humanity, and imagined it bigger and bigger and bigger, the crowd stretching to the horizon in every direction. Was that 2.6 million?

Finally, she asked: "What about the Valley, the people outside the city?" When she was growing up many of those towns were sleepy hamlets; she knew that was not the modern California reality of 1962.

"If they're lucky, they've built their own shelter, though the men will be off at work—this is if it comes during the workday." He was talking now as though divorced from his own words.

Maybe, she thought, that was the only way the poor man could live with what he knew.

"Dad won't have time to make it home. The kids, they'll be at school. A few of them might be able to make it home in time, or they can take shelter at their schools. But none of the schools are stocked with supplies. That leaves mom. But it hardly matters," he said, his voice trailing off. "So few of them took our advice to build shelters."

She leaned forward in her chair. It was really all so simple: "What if they evacuate, wouldn't that be the answer?"

"It would be chaos, all those people on the roads, running for their lives. Besides, there just wouldn't be time."

"How much warning will we have?"

"We estimate about fifteen minutes."

"Then they have to leave now, just stay away until this nasty business is over, that's the only way." Tears were beginning to well in her eyes. She refused to let them emerge.

"It sounds good at first, Mrs. Nixon, but if we evacuate our cities—and I'll tell you, Los Angeles is hardly the only city without adequate shelters—the Russians will think we're preparing for war, you know, getting ready to attack them and we think in that case they'd strike first."

She leaned back, deflated. They've obviously thought all this through. She should have known that. Those smart men in Washington aren't going to let all those families suffer. There could only be one answer, one reason there weren't shelters for everyone. It was because Dick and the other men in charge didn't think they'd ever really need the silly things. There were a few, to make it look like we were doing something, she thought, laughing to herself about the tour she'd just taken. She'd been part of the charade, helping to reassure the public that everything was under control. That was okay with her, and maybe it made sense for those who really believed all that talk—that's what it was, just talk—about atomic war. It's just that crazy Khrushchev testing us. He can't be so stupid as to do something that would kill so many innocent people, and not just our people—lots of innocent Russians, too. This thought made her feel better. Oh, what a scare.

"Mr. Quinn?"

He was still looking at her without really seeing, and didn't answer.

"There's really no need to be concerned," she said, returning to the chipper tone she used in public. "I'm sure my husband has this whole thing with Cuba under control."

———∞∞∞———

"Why are there Russians in Cuba, mommy?" Julie, the fourteen-year-old, wanted to know.

Chet Huntley was tapping a map of Cuba with a rubber-tipped wooden pointer. The late afternoon sun, beaming into the living room from the two-story foyer, made the newscast hard to see, but the message was clear.

"Helene, would you mind turning off the TV?"

Coming in from the kitchen Helene gave a What-could-I-do? roll of her eyes. Tricia and Julie had run to meet their mother at the front door, both of them in tears, upon her return to Rolling Hills from touring the Subway Building shelter. She had pulled them in close, her hands resting lightly on the backs of their heads. She sat her girls on the orange sectional sofa by the free-standing fireplace and tried to explain.

"Fidel Castro is the president of Cuba, honey, and he's a Communist, just like the people in the Soviet Union."

Tricia nodded at Julie. She seemed to think this was a good enough answer for her sister, who was two years younger. "But why did they bring missiles with them?"

"Buddy?" Helene was in the open kitchen, pouring milk into multicolored plastic tumblers to go with the sandwiches on the kidney-shaped tray. "Can I talk to you for a minute?"

"Okay, girls. I want you both to get out the books you brought with you and read quietly. And no more television." She looked at each in turn until she was satisfied they understood. "Now go on. We can talk more about this later." With an arm on each of their shoulders, she pulled them in close for a last hug, and whispered for them not to worry.

She followed Helene upstairs to the master bedroom, where they stood by the door.

"I didn't want the kids to hear," Helene said, glancing down the stairs, "but Jack finally called from Washington while you were out this afternoon."

"Did he say what was going on that they couldn't broadcast last night from the Oval Office?"

"No, Jack said he wasn't free to say much, but we talked about bringing Maureen home from Purdue until, you know."

She didn't want to know.

"I mean, until this is all over. Jack said it would be the shortest war in history—maybe just a couple weeks."

Turning from the window to look at Helene, she felt disoriented.

Helene hesitated a moment. "Maybe he didn't use that word, war, but what else would you call it when we're bombing Soviet missiles and sending our troops to invade another country?"

Seeing everyone going about their usual business downtown today, it certainly didn't seem like the country was at war. "Helene," she said, putting her hand on her friend's arm and smiling again, "we're not at war."

Helene sighed and said, "Call it whatever you want—are you going back to Washington or not?"

Chapter 7

Monday, October 22, 1962

*T*HIS MORNING THE WORLD HOLDS ITS BREATH. *By stationing offensive nuclear missiles on the island of Cuba, at America's doorstep, Soviet Premier Nikita Khrushchev has left mankind teetering on the brink of World War III. No U.S. president could permit these missiles to remain on the island and this newspaper fully supports President Nixon's decision to bomb these missiles out of existence. Yet we deeply regret that the president has also ordered our armed forces to invade the island, with the apparent objective of toppling the Castro regime. While this page has often condemned the reckless policies of the Communist government in Havana, the inevitable confrontation between our soldiers and the Soviet troops stationed in Cuba to protect Khrushchev's missiles appears destined to destabilize an already precariously delicate situation.*

An angry hand scribbled in the margin of the Daily News Summary, by the *St. Louis Post-Dispatch* editorial: "Appeasers!" He'd have the editors crawling on their knees; Finch would see to it: "F: *Post-Dispatch* gets no WH access for 1 mo. Cut them off," he wrote.

The *Dispatch* editors, like the others he'd spoken with on the phone, had gone along with his request to hold their stories on his relocation. To avoid running anything that wasn't accurate—as though they ever care about that when they go after him—they omitted references to the White House and the Oval Office from their copy. Though the calls were strictly off the record, he took the opportunity to explain how important it was to send in troops to make sure all the missiles had been destroyed, so the editors knew he had no choice but to invade. And yet they couldn't pass up an excuse to bash Richard Nixon, even now. His chance to get rid of that fucking bastard in Havana had arrived, had finally, finally arrived, and he wasn't going to screw it up this time, no matter what the damn press said, no matter what anyone said.

The *Dispatch* reporters and all the other press boys won't believe their damn eyes. Every Cuban in Florida will want to be at the Miami airport to catch a glimpse of him when he emerges from his big Boeing 707, MILITARY AIR TRANSPORT SERVICE proudly spelled out above the passenger windows of its aluminum-silver fuselage glinting in the bright Florida sun, arms up over his head, giving the V sign this time for the return of a free Cuba, for the sweetest victory of his presidency.

Hell, why not fly that presidential jet right into Havana? He could see them lining the motorcade route to the capital, an endless sea of Cubans, even more than the quarter million who came out in Poland in '59—largest ever for a Western leader in a captive nation—to throw roses and shout "Long Live Nixon."

On his yellow pad he made some notes for the speech he would give, starting by remembering some of his best-received lines, all of them new to his Havana audience.

Doomed to defeat in the world struggle unless... must risk as much to defend freedom as the Communists are willing to risk to destroy it... may the time never come when any president feels it necessary to apologize for trying to protect the U.S. from surprise attack... America will not tolerate being pushed around.

The pen was on the floor, the phone on the side table was ringing, and for a moment he didn't know where he was. "Yeah?"

"William Pawley asks to speak with you," Rose Mary Woods said from her desk in an adjoining office. "The White House switchboard patched him through."

"Do I have time before the NSC briefing at nine? Anything other than the Cuba thing can wait."

"I understand Admiral Radford is on his way now to High Point. And Mr. Pawley says he wishes to speak to you about the Cuba matter."

"All right, Rose Mary, I'll talk to him. But when the admiral gets here, send him in immediately," he said, looking for the Benzedrine bottle in the side-table drawer.

"I will. Here's Mr. Pawley."

"Congratulations, Mr. President."

"We're finally going to get the bastard, ambassador, gonna feed Castro his own balls for lunch," he said, slapping the arm of the same chair where he had slept, until being awakened by an early morning phone call. After a shower and a shave he returned to his office where he had a quick breakfast of orange juice, wheat germ, and a glass of milk while reading his morning briefing book.

"It's a wonderful day for Cuba and for the United Sates, thanks to your leadership. Your speech last night was just superb. I want you to know that Bebe and Senator Smathers and I watched it together here in Florida."

He flipped through the yellow legal pad on his lap until he came to the page with the list of names he had begun making last night and had reviewed again this morning. He added Pawley's name to the list. "I talked with Rebozo last night—invited him to the White House for a ring-side seat. I thought he'd enjoy that. Anyway, it was a hard-hitting address, you have to say that. It came across, did it?"

"The part where you said we weren't going to settle for a halfway solution and pointed to the Communists in Cuba as the root of the problem was especially strong. I have to tell you that the three of us were on our feet, applauding."

He smiled as he imagined Pawley in his white suit and maybe his broad-brimmed straw hat and Glorious George—Is there a woman on his arm Bill didn't mention?—with Bebe leading the cheers, and maybe sharing the young lady's affections. The competition among the three men to choose the one who could be said to hate Castro the most would have been intense and difficult to judge.

George had been representing Florida in the Senate since defeating "Red" Pepper in '50—an ugly campaign that was worth it to get rid of that left-winger—the same year George introduced Bebe, whose Latin blood certainly made him the most vociferous Castro hater of the three, even if Pawley was the only one who'd been raised on the island. Smathers had proved himself a true lover of the free-wheeling Cuban way of life, where a man could put aside his responsibilities for a few carefree days in the sun, free to try his luck at the roulette wheel or the blackjack table, if that was his pleasure, or satisfy his other desires. So strong were Smathers's ties to the island, so hard had he fought to clear the way for a return to that way of life, that he didn't object to being called the senator from Cuba.

Of the three it had been Bill who he'd found the most useful in his attempts, beginning even before he became president, to get rid of Castro. All of them had agreed from the beginning, of course, that Castro had to be eliminated. Only Pawley, however, could back up his tough words; he had influence and his considerable fortune behind him.

"It's almost too good to be true," Pawley said now. "To think that we can look forward within a week's time to finally getting rid of that bastard, after working so hard for this for so long."

You said it, Bill. And you could have said it's about time, too. It had been more than three years ago and he was still vice president when Eisenhower gave the green light and he took it upon himself to become the advocate in the White House for Castro's elimination. His plan was to have it done with by November of '60. It was that, he had been sure, or have Kennedy beat him up for not getting rid of the Communists at our doorstep, with the implication that if Nixon couldn't handle a tin-pot dictator ninety miles from Florida, then voters shouldn't buy the Republican's talk about freeing the enslaved people behind the other Iron Curtain. That's exactly what Jack did, of course, and it did very nearly cost him the presidency.

"Some of the little shits in the press say I should take the easy political path. This morning's editorials are already kicking me." He swung his leg at the *Post-Dispatch* on the floor. The paper was too far for him to reach. "We support the president on the bombing and the missiles have to go, some of them give me that—plenty you know are too damned scared even to go that far—then they say the president is taking too great a risk with this invasion."

"People who say we shouldn't finish the job are just fuzzy thinkers. Any jackass can see it was Castro that turned Cuba into a welcome mat for the Kremlin. This is just the kind of thing we were trying to prevent."

Tried and failed, he thought, kicking one of the coffee table's aluminum legs with his wingtip and rattling the glass, tried and failed. Bill didn't say it; he didn't have to. There it was, his failure, as vice president and then for almost three years as president, a failure he was sure wouldn't escape his critics' notice when this was all over. If Nixon had gotten rid of Castro, the Soviets would have never built a missile base practically under our nose and the whole confrontation could have been avoided, they'll say. It was all Nixon's fault. Yeah, they'd blame him for this, too. Anything to get their licks in, he knew that. For now, though, they were rallying around the flag. At least he had that.

"I had the leaders from the Hill over on Sunday, Bill. And I have to say, they were very supportive. Johnson, Fulbright, Kennedy, Vinson, and all the rest. They're all as eager as we are to finally get a solution to the Castro situation."

"It's been a slow game till now. With the boys we put in at Trinidad bottled up by Castro's—"

"All the supplies we've dropped them and they're still—I know you handpicked some of them, Bill, but it's like they're sitting on their goddamn dead asses up there in the mountains. Your boys'll finally see some real action again—they'll join up with the Marines when they come ashore on Friday and with the Guantanamo troops. So this is our opportunity."

"To do it right."

Yeah, to do it right this time. Meaning what? Nixon's to blame? For God's sake, Bill, don't you remember you were one of those who came up with the idea to send in that CIA-trained army of exiles after you and Dulles couldn't hire anyone to take a shot at Castro? After you two sold Eisenhower on your cockamamy scheme it didn't matter how many times I said, do it right and send in the Marines, but at least do something before the damn election. How many times did I say that? Do it right. Dulles kept insisting the exiles weren't ready and Ike wouldn't pull the trigger and fucking Election Day comes and Castro's still suckin' on his fat cigar.

What the hell would have happened if Kennedy had been elected, he wondered, staring across the room at a large map of Cuba? Who knows how Jack might have screwed up the invasion. Would Kennedy have had the balls to call in American air strikes and order in Navy ships? No. *I* did. *I* saw to it that those exiles came ashore all right at Trinidad and made it up into the mountains, everything according to the plan, just as

Eisenhower had approved it. He's the great general, after all. So what went wrong with your boys, Bill, all those CIA-trained exiles so eager to go in there and take over? Where were the thousands of disaffected Cubans who were supposed to join in to take on Castro? Trinidad was supposed to be a hotbed for opposition to Castro—that's why I wouldn't approve a change to that other landing site, the Bay of Pigs, no way to get into the mountains from there anyway. That plan was sure to fail. So our boys are still sitting in the Escambray Mountains and only a couple hundred Cubans have joined their little shit-ass army. Well, I wasn't going to sit on my ass, too.

He put his feet up on the coffee table he'd knocked askew and said, "I couldn't tell you this until now, Bill, but late last year—of course this is long before anyone suspected Khrushchev would try to sneak those missiles in there—I ordered the Pentagon to start planning a full-scale invasion. No more half-assed stunts. I'd decided to do it right, go for the big play. Create a pretext, go in, get it over with."

"I know that was your thinking from the beginning, to mount a full-scale invasion. If Ike had taken your counsel we wouldn't be facing down these Russian A-bombs there."

It was a little late now to be sucking up. "Yes, but I'll tell you this, it's a good thing we did that planning. Because now Defense has done all its training exercises for an invasion and is staged and ready to go in. We're as prepared for a full-scale invasion as we can possibly be."

"That's very good news, Mr. President."

"Politically, we're in good shape, too, because you see, now we have a legitimate provocation, though the one I had been working on would have seemed legitimate, I mean, if Glenn, uh—"

"John Glenn?"

"Uh, well anyway, it was a pretty damn good plan. I can say that honestly. But now we can say we're invading because we have to make sure all those missiles are destroyed. That's my public line."

"It almost makes those missiles a blessing in disguise—if we can just get through this thing without it escalating into something just horrendous. To be honest, Mr. President, I know a number of families who have left Miami and others are, well, let's say they're putting their affairs in order."

"So you'd say the mood down there is pretty grim, is it? You're right there in the thick of it, of course."

"The antiaircraft missiles on the beach here—I know they're necessary, we all do, but seeing them pointing up at the sky, and with all the soldiers here, we can't help but imagine the worst."

He doubted whether Pawley or any other civilian could imagine the emptiness and the silence the generals had described to him. Maybe it would be different on the edge of the blast zone, where the greatest danger would be firestorms and fallout. Would there be screams? Over the last week he woke up more than once screaming himself, waking from a dream he only half remembered. The part he could recall was similar each time. He was running through ruins to escape a pack of survivors, one carrying a thick rope tied into a noose. "I'm sure you understand that those antiaircraft missiles are there as a precaution. Just the fact that they're there means it's less likely we'll need them. I want you to get the word out down there about that, Bill."

"We're all going to be holding our breath till this is over."

"I sent Khrushchev a clear message at the end of my address: 'Hands off Europe, or we go nuclear.' And I'll tell you why I said that, it's to keep the peace. As long as Khrushchev is scared of what I might do—we want him to think that SOB Nixon might lose his marbles and push the button, you see—of course, there's really no big red button, the way they show in the movies—but this way we won't have any trouble from him. That's my theory."

"What about the missiles, what if he decides to fire one off from Cuba before they're all destroyed?"

"Here's what matters when it comes to these nuclear weapons—Khrushchev's not suicidal. If he launched one of those missiles, yes, the devastation, the loss of life, it would be unspeakable, almost beyond our ability to comprehend. But if he used even one nuclear weapon against us, I wouldn't have any choice, and he knows this. My response would be practically automatic—boom, no more Soviet Union." He snapped his fingers. There was no sound and he was angry he tried.

"Well, the nation is grateful you've thought this through and to have such an experienced man as yourself in the Oval Office at this critical hour, not some greenhorn playboy senator."

That was tempting bait. He thought about it then thought he had a lot to do today and there was one other thing he wanted to talk with Pawley about. "Now I've done a lot of thinking on this, Bill, about who to put in there when Castro's gone."

"And the others, we have to be sure to get rid of..."

"Yep, all those bastards, Che, brother Raúl. Did you see what he said, the brother, this is a couple years back, that he wished he could drop three atom bombs on New York? Well, they all get it at dawn, as we've said. But see, after that..."

"Yes, I've talked to Finch about this, the provisional government, but—"

"Let's get down to nut cutting. You know how I feel on this, Bill."

"Kohly."

"We can trust him. I've talked to him on a number of occasions, not in person, of course, can't risk the president being seen with him."

"No."

"Rebozo agrees with me on this, Bill. He's been sounding Kohly out on this and says he's ready to take it on."

"And the CIA, do they—"

"Absolutely. Dulles assures me Kohly can handle things for us down there. State is a different matter, but I'll handle them."

"Hell, they betrayed Cuba, I'm not concerned about them."

"Good."

"There's no doubt but that Kohly considers himself Cuba's president-in-waiting, sir. I'm just afraid the exiles, all these different organizations, well, I just don't know if we can get them to line up behind Kohly."

He shuffled through some of the papers on the end table; he couldn't find what he was looking for. "Two of these Miami groups, the Christian Democratic Movement and the Movement of Revolutionary Recuperation, whatever the hell they call themselves, they sent me a telegram."

"I don't know if they represent—"

"They held their own election this summer."

"They're behind—"

"Kohly, that's right. I just think he's a very impressive fellow, former investment banker in Havana—hell, you know all that. But let me tell you, he's got the balls of a brass monkey."

"But there are some other groups that think Kohly—"

"You know these damn Cubans as well as anyone, Bill. They're good, hardworking people, but—and Rebozo says this himself—they can't agree on whether the damn sun's coming up in the morning. See, Kohly will play ball with us. That's the important thing here."

"Right."

"You understand, I'm sure."

"He'll cooperate."

"We don't want any trouble. There'll be a lot of these people coming back to Cuba when this is over, and some of them just as bad as that little shit Castro."

"Lots of them will be Communists."

"We don't want any more trouble from their kind. I know you agree with me on that, Bill, but this is the thing about Kohly, he can, well, he can take care of all that."

"He knows who's who, I'll give you that."

"They're sneaky SOBs. I don't have to tell you."

"I'll get together with Bebe, Mr. President."

"Good deal," he said, fastening his suit jacket's center button.

"I'll talk to Bebe, and then we'll speak again in a few days."

He motioned to Finch, waiting at the door, to take a seat by his desk, where there were four sturdy leather armchairs with oak legs. "Now another thing, Bill. I was thinking I might go down to Havana when this is all over. What would you think of that?"

Finch smiled and gave a thumbs-up.

"That's an excellent idea, Mr. President. I can guarantee you an extremely warm reception."

He knew Pawley would like his idea and wanted to hear more; he wanted to hear just how good an idea it was. "A big crowd, you think?" He smiled and nodded at Finch.

"You'll be very happy you went, I'm sure of that," Pawley said.

"Well, I'd like you there on the stage with me, Bill. Would you do that for me?"

"That would be an honor, sir."

He turned to face Finch. "All right."

"Good talking to you, Mr. President."

"All right, Bill." He threw the receiver into the cradle and shouted at Finch, who stood abruptly. "Where the hell is Radford? Goddamn his ass, he's supposed to be keeping me up to date."

"He's en route from Site R. He'll join us as soon as he arrives."

The president walked from the sitting area to his desk, hands clasped behind his back, head down. "Anyway, that was Ambassador Pawley. He's not so sure about our putting Kohly in, but I think he'll come around."

"Pawley's main concern, as I understand it from talking with him about this a couple of times," Finch said, one hand on the chair back, the other in his pants pocket, "is that the new government compensate him for what he lost when Castro took over."

Standing behind another of the other chairs flanking his desk, Nixon grasped the brass-riveted edge of the tall backrest with both hands. "Why don't you talk to Kohly. Have him assure Rebozo that he'll return the gas company and the bus system and whatever the hell else Bill owned down there. That ought to do it."

"All right, I'll call Kohly. I'm sure he'll agree to that."

"Pawley has a few people he wants us to put in. We both think Rebozo would make a heck of a finance minister," he said, looking at Finch with a quick smile to counteract his feeling that he couldn't let Bebe move to Cuba if it would take much longer to bring him up from Havana than it did now from Miami.

"Bebe wasn't born in Cuba, was he?" Finch asked.

He shook his head and added, "He'll be back as soon as the shooting stops anyway." Quick smile again. No, he needed to keep Bebe in easy reach. "I don't need him. Hell, a president can't have any friends. Anyway, he's got Cuba in his blood just like all the rest of them. They fuckin' love it down there. And you can have a hell of a good time in Havana. Half of Miami'll be on boats headed down there."

"We've got some difficult days ahead before we break out that champagne," Radford said, striding forward with his hand outstretched.

Seeing Radford for the first time at Mount Weather, Nixon felt that extra sense of assurance a president looks for in trying times, when he cannot help rethink his decisions and finds himself anticipating all that might run afoul in the days to come. He had gotten his first taste of Radford's toughness as vice president when the admiral was chairman of the Joint Chiefs and came to talk to him about Vietnam. "This is where the French are pinned down," he could remember Radford telling him while rolling out a map on the conference table. The name on the map, by Radford's finger, was Dien Bien Phu.

Radford may have come to see him that day looking for any assistance a vice president could lend in making a case to the president. Or maybe it was because Radford knew he had been in Vietnam the year before, with Pat, as part of a two-month trip through the Far East, making him one of the few other men in the Eisenhower administration who was familiar with a map of Vietnam. While Pat had been visiting a hospital, his French army escort had handed him a helmet and they'd ridden in an American Jeep to the front lines where he'd watched French soldiers fire American-made shells at the Communists, even then sensing France's coming failure.

Radford's plan—Operation Vulture—was to save the French, who had, indeed, gotten themselves pinned down by the North Vietnamese. "There is a possibility that massive conventional bombing may fail to rout the enemy," Radford had told him. "In that eventuality we will employ from one to three low-yield nuclear devices."

"We can't afford to let the French lose." They had both said it. And those were the words they agreed to use when they went to see Eisenhower.

"We can't engage in active war over there. It would be completely unconstitutional and indefensible," the president told them, fully prepared to let the French lose rather than approve Radford's plan.

Neither of them reminded the president of how, at other times, he'd told them a Communist takeover of Vietnam would be intolerable.

"What have you got for me?" Nixon said, moving to his leather desk chair. Radford sat to his right, Finch to his left.

"First, we have a disturbing report that the Soviet military, including the Strategic Rocket Forces, have been put on high alert."

His desk chair rolled backward when he jumped to his feet and he hardly noticed when it knocked the map of Cuba to the floor. He faced Radford with his fists on his waist, suit jacket pulling at the center button. Get very angry when you're losing. It was a lesson he'd learned early, on the Whittier College football field. "The bastard thinks he can bully me!" he shouted at Radford and Finch, anger smothering fear.

"It could be a bluff, but—"

"That's exactly what it is!" he shouted. A bluff, yes, and yet it showed Khrushchev wasn't completely cowed. So what else might that bald bastard do? That was what concerned him. Meanwhile, Radford and Finch needed a president who was strong. "He wants to scare me into canceling the invasion. Well I'm not going to fold," he said, pounding his fist against his palm. Finch cowered; Radford looked back with a calm and steady gaze.

"The alert is also a credible threat," Radford said. "There are as many as 110 nuclear-armed ICBMs that could reach the United States from Soviet territory, in addition to their strategic bomber force. We'd be able to stop most of the bombers, maybe all, but as you know, we would not be able to prevent the missiles from getting through, unless we destroy them first."

He turned his back on the two men, busying himself with the papers on the table behind his desk, trying to ignore what he was hearing. As much as he feared the consequences of a Soviet move against West Berlin, unable to sleep each night as his mind relentlessly imagined the consequences, now he felt the ever greater danger of being pushed into a corner where he could be pressured to respond with force to forestall a Soviet attack. Radford was a military man at heart and the admiral, no less than his former colleagues among the Joint Chiefs, did not shrink from the thought of preemptive war to forestall an attack.

When he heard his national security adviser say that, in the final analysis, it still was unlikely the Soviets were ready to launch a nuclear strike against the U.S., he knew Radford would not be pushing for a first strike, and was able to turn around. Leaning his forearms against the tall seat back of his chair, which Finch had replaced, along with the map, he said it would be as suicidal for the Soviets to attack the U.S. as it would be for us to strike at them. His job was to keep anything from upsetting this balance and he emphasized this with Radford, concluding by saying, "So that's the thing, keep to our plan and make damn sure no one goes off half-cocked."

"I think you make exactly the right point, that miscalculation is the greatest danger," Radford said, tapping the base of his pen against his left palm.

"Raddy, I want you to get the word out around the Pentagon that the president feels the Soviets are blowing a lot of hot air raising their alert level. This is the point to get across—we're monitoring the situation very closely, of course, but for now we're keeping our powder dry."

Radford finished writing a note to himself, then continued. "The Soviet transport ships we've been tracking—"

"These are the ships bringing more missiles?"

"Yes, sir. Missiles and troops, we believe." In the margin of his notepad Radford drew a small circle, with successively lager circles around it. "They continue on course for Cuba."

"Hell, sink 'em. We're already bombing their damn missiles in Cuba, for Christ's sake. How are the ones headed there by ship any different?"

"No difference in kind, sir. I'm just surprised they think they can pull into port in Cuba while our iron is raining down. My money says they'll turn back to the Baltic before they reach our blockade line."

"All right. Keep an eye on them," Nixon said, leaning over his desk and studying his notes. "Those are transport ships. Now, what about their navy?"

"Yes, this was the next item I had for you, sir. We've identified four Foxtrot submarines in the Atlantic that appear to be headed to Cuba. This is the first time Soviet subs have been this close to the continental U.S."

"That cocksucker!" This time his anger was genuine. Khrushchev had given his word to Ambassador Beam that the Soviets were not planning to build a submarine base in Cuba. Here was another Communist betrayal to add to the list—yet more justification for bombing and invading the island to drive the Communists out of the Western Hemisphere. "Khrushchev's word isn't worth shit," he said, shaking his head in disgust.

"A submarine base at Mariel would be the most likely explanation—I would agree," Radford said. "Short of that, the simple presence of Soviet subs in the Atlantic is a disturbing precedent."

"Sink them, goddamn it," he yelled, feeling the blood in his face rush to the surface. "That's an order," he yelled again, trying to sound sincere.

"Maybe we should track them for a while first," Finch suggested, his voice cracking.

"I agree with Bob," Radford added. "They don't pose an immediate threat to our fleet. These are Foxtrot-class diesel subs, quite noisy—easy to detect—and they aren't carrying nuclear torpedoes."

It felt good to be able to show his anger and prove he wasn't going to let himself be humiliated, knowing Radford and Finch would temper his impulses, providing a way to back down without looking like he was giving in. "Hell, all right. But I want a close eye kept on those subs."

Radford nodded compliance and Finch said, "I'd think we'd get a cable from Moscow soon. That should give us a better idea of what they're thinking."

"State says this afternoon at the earliest," Radford responded, looking at Finch and then at the president.

Nixon drew a line through the question on his legal pad and moved his fountain pen to the next item. "What's the latest on our alert status?"

"U.S. nuclear forces worldwide have fully achieved DEFCON 2 status, per your order. SAC reports it currently has 172 missiles and 1,200 bombers on alert capable of delivering 7,000 megatons. At least 60 B-52s—each carrying two thermonuclear devices—are on twenty-four-hour missions flying to their positive control turnaround points where they orbit until heading home."

"Positive control point, I see. That's what LeMay calls the fail-safe point. Is that it?"

"Yes, sir. If the communication system fails, the pilots return to base. They only proceed to their targets if they receive their go codes over the radio."

Unscrewing the cap of his pen and studying the nib, he listened as his national security adviser went on to describe how the Strategic Air Command had doubled its nuclear bomber capability as the number of ICBMs and Polaris submarines on alert also increased, how quick-reaction-alert aircraft in the Pacific and Europe had been readied for immediate launch with nuclear weapons as bombers were sent to forward bases in Great Britain and Spain where, together with other forward-based aircraft, they were prepared, if called upon, to destroy a preset list of targets throughout the Eastern Bloc.

Without quite smiling, Radford conveyed a sense of satisfaction. "That, Mr. President, is what can be described as a credible deterrent."

He pictured Khrushchev, hands raised, back-stepping away from the atomic gun barrel pointed at his shiny skull. Scare him shitless, keep the peace. At the same time he was thinking of something Radford had said earlier. "Those go codes you mentioned—the president is the only one who can issue those."

"No, sir. President Eisenhower gave the SAC commander that authority—but only if the Soviets use nuclear weapons and he can't get in touch with you."

"Because the president has been killed, I presume."

"Yes, sir. Or because the phone lines are down and he can't reach you."

Swiveling around in his chair to pour a glass of water from the metal pitcher on the table behind his desk, he remembered having been briefed about these protocols as vice president. At the time they had seemed like preparations for a fairy-tale world. Now, when it was too late to go through the bureaucratic machinations that would be necessary to change them, he could only trust that Eisenhower had thoroughly considered the consequences. "The next level of readiness," he said, turning back, "Defense Condition 1—I mean, that's it, short of war. Is that it?"

"Exercise term, Cocked Pistol, yes, sir, that would be the maximum readiness posture, to be used if war is imminent. I believe we've put in place a very carefully calibrated response," Radford added. "Moving to DEFCON 2 proved very effective during the Berlin Fence crisis and I believe the Soviets will once again get the message that the United States stands ready to defend its interests, come what may."

Last year, when the Soviet Union began building a barbwire and brick barrier along the line separating East and West Berlin, he had ordered tanks modified to serve as deadly armored bulldozers into position along the barricade in Berlin where they sat, engines idling, as the fence started to become a wall. McCloy gave him the predictable State Department line. The Soviets had no choice except to stem the exodus from East to West and it was all quite legal as the construction was entirely within the Soviet-controlled sector. What McCloy didn't give him was a way to explain going back on the vow he had made so often to never let the Soviet Union bring its Iron Curtain down around yet more freedom-loving people. He could not turn his back, turn freedom's back, on the people of East Berlin.

He also knew that if he listened to those who told him to smash the barrier—"Tear it down, Mr. President," his Republican friends said, "you must tear down that fence"—there would be a terrible price to pay.

His solution was to move the military to DEFCON 2 and in so doing he became the first U.S. president to issue that order.

He decided to call what had happened in Berlin a victory. After all, construction had stopped. Yes, the fence remained and some brave souls seeking their freedom in the West did not make it across. The larger truth was that the most determined found the escape routes a wall would have forever sealed, judging by the blueprints later smuggled out showing plans for a brick fortress with guard towers and a no-man's-land where German snipers could cut down anyone crazy enough to attempt an escape.

It was also the first vindication of his theory that while nuclear weapons may have no practical use, because of their horrible destructive power, they did have a diplomatic purpose. By acting as though he was prepared to use them to defend U.S. interests, he was able to scare Khrushchev into backing down.

He took another drink of water and moved to his next question. "What do you have for me on the bombing, Raddy?"

"We have completed 249 sorties targeting the air defense system, airfields, and the operational MRBM sites," Radford said, standing now by the map of Cuba and pointing out some of the sites that had been hit. "Aircraft from Air Force bases Homestead and McCoy in Florida, from our carrier fleet in theatre, and from Guantanamo are all participating in Operation Scabbards."

"How many planes have we lost?" He knew there would be American casualties in the fighting—there would have to be. He could only hope the fighting would be over quickly, keeping losses to a minimum, and remind himself that he'd been left with no choice but to order these men into combat.

"We believe the Soviet MiGs, SAM SA-2s, and antiaircraft artillery are being jointly controlled by ground radar, which is proving very effective against our aircraft, so our losses are heavier than we'd anticipated. I'll have updated figures for you later today."

"I want those numbers on my desk as soon as they come in."

"Yes, sir. SAC has readied some of its B-47 Stratojets to go in with nuclear weapons to finish the job, but I still think iron bombs will prove sufficient."

If using conventional weapons against Cuba and getting rid of Castro wasn't enough to provoke Khrushchev in to retaliating, surely detonating nuclear warheads on the island would. He could only imagine that this was another of LeMay's ideas. "Whatever we need to get the job done, Raddy."

Nixon looked down at his shirt cuffs and adjusted just how far they extended from his suit jacket before continuing. "Now there's something else I've been going over. It's this question of when the Soviets are most likely to respond—if they do. I received a message from Ambassador Beam in Moscow. He's pretty sure there'll be a military response. And by the way, in his opinion this'll be limited to conventional weapons. He doesn't see them needing to go the nuclear route to make their point. Now to get back to it, Beam thinks this shit will hit the fan after we invade. Beam knows the Soviet mind pretty well and in his view the military will gain the upper hand in the Politburo once we invade. Well, I know something about the

commie mind too and let me say this. If Khrushchev decides
to cause us trouble somewhere, he'd do it now, rather than
waiting."

"Rather than wait for the invasion?" Radford asked, returning to his chair.

"Khrushchev is thinking that if he moves on Berlin or Korea
now, maybe he'll be able to prevent the invasion. Communist
control of Cuba, that's as important to Khrushchev as the missiles. I did a lot of thinking last night and I think they snuck
the missiles in there in the first place to keep us from invading.
But once we've gone in and we have our man, this fellow Kohly,
in Havana and Fidel's facing a firing squad with Raúl on the
50-yard line of his stadium, well, the game is over."

Radford slowly closed his binder. "I agree with your analysis,
to a point. Yet we should not discount anger and retaliation as
motivators of Soviet aggression, whether in Berlin or elsewhere.
You and I have seen that play out before. In that light, I anticipate
a heightened threat into the new year."

"Can't let our guard down, absolutely." He made a note on
his yellow legal pad. *Continued vigilance necessary.* There should
be a way to use that in next month's congressional elections.

"Out," Castro shouted at the Cubans manning the radio and
marking the wall map. "What does it say, general?"

Pliyev finished reading the orders from Moscow, brought
to him at Castro's bunker, where he had relocated with his staff
from his aboveground command center at a villa southwest of
Havana. He set the papers on the table, holding them, re-reading
the Russian. "We will not be able to use our strategic missiles
without authorization from Moscow."

"Impossible!" Castro threw his cigar stub to the floor, where it
hissed in a small puddle. "Nikita's letter to me pledged to defend

Cuba against American aggression, yet he will not let you use the means you have at your disposal?"

"These orders were sent before your letter arrived in Moscow, so perhaps you will be able to change premier's mind. Americans have not yet destroyed all our operational missiles."

"What else do you read?"

"Yes, there is good news. Tactical nuclear weapons are under my control."

Castro flung his arms around the general's shoulders. After a long hug he stepped back and spoke in triumph. "We will vanquish the Yankee invaders!" Taking a fresh cigar from the box on the table, he paused to run it under his nose, before handing it to Pliyev; the general put it in his shirt pocket, the uncut end poking through a turned corner of the buttoned flap. "You will return to Moscow, my friend, as the hero who saved the Cuban revolution."

Pliyev read the cable again, nodding his agreement with its terms. "Presidium has decided wisely." He held up the cable and continued, "I am good soldier and would have followed orders to destroy American cities, if that was what this told me to do. I know that is what you and your brother wish for but I believe it would have been mistake. Result would be war of annihilation."

Castro was offended. "This is something no man in his right mind would wish for, general. What I tried to convey in my letter to Moscow was that Nixon is loco and will use his missiles against the Soviet Union and Nikita should be prepared to strike first."

"You have met with Nixon and I have not, but I hope he is not loco, as you say. Let us just hope that Lunas and FKRs will be enough to save us."

Castro tried to make sense of this as he added the cigar smoke in his lungs to the room's stagnant air. "The Americans will never set foot on Cuban soil. We will destroy them while they are still on their ships. And their illegal occupation of

Guantanamo will soon come to a swift and bloody end, so they will get no help there."

"And what if Americans have their own tactical nuclear weapons? Nothing will be left of us either."

Triumphant again, Castro stood as tall as he could. "I have always been ready to give my life in defense of my country, general. As long as we kill the American aggressors I will die a happy man and I know you will too."

⸺⸺

McCloy didn't break stride as he handed Rose Mary his wool overcoat and hat. "Chocolate drop, Mr. President?" McCloy asked, reaching out with a palm full of bell-shaped candies pulled from a pocket of his gray flannel suit—"They're awfully good"—before taking his place in an armchair beside the president's desk.

"No thanks. Now, about that cable." He was eager for Jack's reaction to the rambling message from Khrushchev that he'd been waiting for since publicly unmasking the Soviet Union's secret Cuban adventure. He was finally able to read it, page by page, as each was torn from the Teletype in the Mount Weather communications room and brought to him by military courier, while McCloy flew by helicopter from Washington. From one sheet to the next he swung from feeling morose over the cable's threats of war to euphoria at Khrushchev's promised concessions.

"It was so long, it took quite a while coming in," McCloy said.

"When was it sent? Do we know?" He wanted every detail.

"Ambassador Beam says it was dropped off at the embassy at three a.m. our time in Moscow," McCloy said, looking at his watch. "About twelve hours ago. The cable's an odd brew—threats of nuclear war, an offer to negotiate, and—thank God—a major concession on—"

"That was my first reaction," the president said, suddenly aware McCloy might be referring to Khrushchev's offer to negotiate. "I'm talking about the submarines and the ships, the ones transporting more missiles, returning to port."

"Right."

"Well, I talked to Radford again, just before you got here, and he says there's no sign they've turned around. It could be a trap."

"I believe we need to take Khrushchev at his word."

You would, Jack, Nixon said to himself. "Well, you may be right, but if we analyze this thing, we have to ask, what's he going to do with more missiles, anyway? We'd just bomb those too."

"So you think it isn't—"

"Maybe it isn't a damn concession at all."

McCloy said he agreed Khrushchev might have more to gain by sending the ships back to port, but not so with the submarines. "Khrushchev's concession on the subs shows the Soviets don't want to confront us militarily."

"Maybe," Nixon said. "Or the subs are just to protect the transport ships, so they're not needed any more."

McCloy looked skeptical. "Possibly," he said.

"The rest of the cable is full of Communist propaganda— you expect that sort of crap. But I'll tell you what surprised me about it. It's the way it rambles on." He put his forearms on the unfamiliar desktop and leaned right, toward McCloy. "It makes you wonder what the hell's going on over there." More than that, it had undermined his firmly held idea of Khrushchev as an ultimately rational opponent.

"It does almost seem like the man's a marble short," the stocky, five-foot-ten secretary of state said with a quick tilt of the head for emphasis.

"I'll tell you how I see it," Nixon said, eager to dismiss his own doubts by explaining how Khrushchev's ramblings could mask a foxily crafty poker player. "There's some pretty tough language in there, too," he added, "but it doesn't scare me—he's just blowing hot air with this shit about meeting in hell if we invade. Don't you agree?" McCloy started to answer but Nixon cut him off. "I'll tell you why I'm not backing down. Because he can't back up his threats—he's holding a losing hand."

"That would explain his offer to negotiate," McCloy answered. "The question is whether the offer is made in good faith."

Before McCloy arrived he'd quickly written down a list of arguments against accepting Khrushchev's offer to meet. Now he decided he didn't need them. "It's a moot point, Jack. There's nothing to negotiate." He leaned back in his chair and shot a yellow wad of paper toward the aluminum trash can.

"A note from Pat," Nixon said, as McCloy grabbed the rebound and made a successful underhand toss.

"I *am* troubled," McCloy said, "that the cable explicitly refers to 'thermonuclear war' and how we're pushing toward the abyss."

"Khrushchev's got a lot of fucking nerve saying that when he's the one who put those damn missiles there and tried to cover it up," Nixon answered, seeing McCloy's small eyes narrow. "After you cut out all the crap"—he waved the Soviet cable above his head—"he's threatening us with..." He slapped the sheaf of papers down on his desk. "Hell—he says it'll escalate into general war, but I say it's another damn bluff is all, like putting their rocket forces on alert. That's all he can do with those shitty cards he's holding." A bluff would be a sign of calculation and consideration, a reassuring sign.

"His words were—"

"Yes." The president had read them over and over; now he wanted to hear the proof that Khrushchev wasn't crazy.

McCloy pulled the cable from his satchel and flipped the pages until finding the section he was looking for. "It says, 'You will get in response whatever you throw at us.' I interpret this language, Mr. President, as a possible threat against our nuclear missiles in Turkey, for starters."

Suddenly, he was shot through with a new worry. In focusing so intensely on the danger in Berlin, had he failed to give due consideration to Turkey? "Those are Jupiters, aren't they?"

"They were approved by Eisenhower in '59, but they were just recently deployed—fifteen in all. They carry 1.4 megaton warheads, if memory serves," McCloy said, resting the cable from Moscow on the edge of the president's almost empty desk.

"I'll be talking to Gates soon," Nixon said, looking at his watch, "and I'll make sure they're taking whatever precautions they can over there. I want you to talk to the Turkish ambassador, Jack. Don't say anything about the cable, but you can bring up whatever parallels there might be between the Jupiters and the missiles in Cuba. If they get hit I don't want General Gürsel yelling that we kept their government in the cold." If the cost of getting rid of Castro were to be the loss of obsolete N.A.T.O. missiles in Turkey, he'd consider it a bargain.

"We'll put together some options for you that you'll want to consider, should the Turkey scenario play out. God help us if it comes to that," McCloy said, crossing himself.

He had known there was more to McCloy, gray-haired and eighteen years his senior, than the Mr. Establishment label some commentators used to describe his surprise pick for secretary of state. As a graduate of Harvard Law School, partner in a Wall Street firm, president of the World Bank, chairman of the Chase Manhattan Bank, and confidant of past presidents, McCloy certainly moved easily in the social circles that had always excluded Richard Nixon. It was harder to overlook the role some said Jack played in trying to convince Eisenhower to drop his vice president in favor of a new running mate in '56. He'd chosen to believe those who denied these rumors because, like himself, Jack had been born poor and had worked his way through college. Looking across his desk at the secretary now, with thin lips and large ears, it was easy enough to imagine him in a dirty miner's suit instead of an impeccable dress suit. Most importantly, Jack had never condescended to him, as so many others of his ilk had. Until now, though, he hadn't thought of McCloy as a God-fearing man. "You know, Jack, I talked to my friend, Reverend Graham, early this morning. He's a good man. Did you know I appeared with him at Yankee Stadium during his crusade in '57? I can give you his number, if you'd like."

"Yes, thank you, I would like that," McCloy said, smiling his appreciation.

"I'll have Rose Mary give it to you on your way out."

McCloy looked away, seeming for a moment to be lost in thought, as he said, "I think we can all use some spiritual guidance in these times."

"Let me tell you, I say a quiet Quaker prayer every night." He would, beginning tonight.

McCloy came back to attention. "I know you've been working practically around the clock, Mr. President, and of course you carry the awful burden"—he closed his eyes now—"of having made such a momentous decision."

If McCloy was trying to talk him into letting his hair down, it wasn't going to work. "We chose the only course that was open to us, Jack."

"Absolutely. Khrushchev boxed us in by putting those missiles there secretly. But what I wanted to say, if I might"—McCloy scratched the back of his neck with one finger—"is that, as trying as these days have been, it's only now, with that decision behind us, that it's possible to hear the clock ticking, if you know what I mean."

"Not the doomsday clock, I hope," he answered with a forced laugh.

"Not exactly, sir, but—well, I know you've thought about this quite a bit. We've maneuvered ourselves into a very dangerous spot over the past eight years." McCloy leaned forward, his forearms on his thighs, hands clasped together. "I don't like to speak ill of the dead, but our policy of massive retaliation—you've heard me say this before—begun by my predecessor has become so inflexible that any miscalculation by Khrushchev might force you into a response that could be, well..." The secretary's voice trailed off; when he tried to finish he was barely audible. "Ungodly."

As McCloy struggled, Nixon focused on a long crack in the ceiling, recalling some of Jack's other attempts over the last eighteen months to soften the policy Foster and Eisenhower had put in place. McCloy's idea all along had been to allow the president to choose from a range of options, rather than an all-out retaliatory response.

Nixon waited for McCloy to conclude, then began, "Let me just say this, Jack, that the danger you refer to—just the idea of it is *unthinkable*"—he shook his head in disgust, emphasizing each syllable of the popular Mount Weather shorthand he often heard the professionals there use to mask what they had spent their careers thinking about quite explicitly, but now, with the world on the brink of atom bombs bursting in air, didn't have the stomach, or the manners, to describe. "But precisely because it is so unthinkable, we're able to keep things in check." Just as long as Khrushchev keeps his wits, he thought.

"It's always been a paradox to me, Mr. President," McCloy said, hands palm up in befuddlement.

Jack's Harvard education was getting in the way of his common sense, Nixon thought. "Here's the thing to remember," he said, pointing his finger, "the Soviets don't want war with us any more than we do with them."

"I accept the premise, yet I'm afraid we may be heading into the abyss and be unable to turn back," McCloy said, looking at the edge of the beige carpeting where it stopped a few inches from the wall, before closing his eyes.

Jack, the president thought, simply wouldn't accept the logic of deterrence and there was nothing, it seemed, he could say to change that. "Now, to get back to it," Nixon said, tapping his desk with a pen to get McCloy's attention, "would you say our Jupiters in Turkey are really comparable to the Soviet missiles in Cuba?"

McCloy drew his eyebrows together. "The distance is almost exactly the same—they're one hundred miles from Soviet soil, ten miles further from Key West than Cuba. And I dare say the Jupiters may have contributed to provoking Khrushchev to try for an equivalency in Cuba. We have reports they made him quite livid. He seems almost to believe they're pointed directly at his dacha, which is on the Black Sea across from Turkey. I'm concerned that Khrushchev thinks he's going to give us a taste of our own medicine. That could be a very nasty business."

Nixon nodded at McCloy and thought: No, it would be a very clean way of bringing the crisis to a peaceful conclusion. The Soviets would destroy the Jupiters—probably located where there'd be few casualties—and the U.S. would loudly protest that the Soviet attack was in no way comparable to the U.S. attack on the missiles in Cuba. "This whole parallel thing—Turkey, Cuba—it's total bullshit. We didn't pledge to never put offensive weapons in Turkey then turn around and install them *secretly*," he said, leaning toward McCloy and drawing out the last word, while slowly shaking his head in disgust. "And what about Dobrynin telling me to my face there were no nuclear weapons going to Cuba, when I had the photographs to prove otherwise?"

"Soviet duplicity at work once again. We know it well."

"There's another thing. Our missiles in Turkey are defensive. The Soviet's missiles in Cuba aren't there to defend the island, they're there to attack us." He'd send Lodge to the United Nations to prove there was no parallel between Soviet missiles in Cuba and N.A.T.O. missiles in Turkey, playing up a Soviet attack on the Jupiters as an act of wanton aggression. Then he'd demonstrate his bona fides as a peacemaker, calming the clamor for retaliation and calling for an end to hostilities.

"You make an excellent case for why we'd have to respond to Soviet aggression against Turkey, Mr. President."

Before McCloy became too convinced by this straw man argument, he needed to start laying the groundwork with Jack for ultimately accepting a hit on the Jupiters. "There's one fly in this ointment. Gates tells me our missiles in Turkey were obsolete by the time they became operational."

McCloy pulled a long, fat cigar from his jacket. He clipped off the tip and struck a wooden match against the sole of his shoe. The secretary brought the flame to the end of his cigar and, before lighting it, said, "Perhaps we can use that to our advantage."

Watching McCloy suck the flame toward the cigar, he felt himself falling into a trap. "How's that?"

"As I read the cable, Khrushchev may be open to a deal. If the Jupiters are obsolete in our eyes, but perceived as a threat by the Soviets, perhaps we're in a position to use them in a trade and receive more in return than they're worth."

Now he could see where McCloy was heading. "So you think if we agree to remove the Jupiters, Khrushchev will agree not to retaliate in Berlin—is that it?"

"In Berlin or elsewhere. But I don't think that alone will be enough."

The cries of foul that would be hurled at him for sacrificing Turkey's security to appease the Soviets were already ringing in his ears, making it hard to think what else McCloy was prepared to concede.

"As you know, Mr. President, my position has always been that the premise justifying invasion is the need to inspect the missile sites to assure they're beyond repair."

"That's right." McCloy had never been part of the group in his administration that believed Castro's ouster was imperative for keeping Communist influence from spreading through the Caribbean. So far, the two lines of thinking on Castro had co-existed without creating major policy conflicts in the administration.

"But I thought about it last night—I have to say I haven't been getting much sleep either—and then with the Soviet rocket force going on heightened alert and with the cable today I think we might well give more consideration to whether the CIA could accomplish the same ends—do the inspection, that is—through photographic surveillance."

This was just the type of woolly-headed vacillation he had feared from Jack all along, ready at the drop of a hat to negotiate when we're holding all the cards. "I agree with you, Jack, that the point here is to deal with the missile threat."

"Castro is a..."

"A bonus. Right." No, Castro was always the point, but to get McCloy to support the invasion he had always stressed with him the necessity of verifying that all the missiles are destroyed and that no more reach the island. "I've always said, Jack, that if there's a way we can ratchet this thing down, I'm going to be the first one in line standing behind it. I just don't know if what you suggest is possible."

"I think it's worth exploring in more depth."

"So you think suspending our invasion plan and dismantling the Jupiters will lessen the risk of this thing escalating into a wider war?"

"If I may paraphrase, the devil taketh Khrushchev up into an exceeding high mountain and sheweth him all the kingdoms of the world and the glory of them and saith unto him, All these things will I give thee if thou wilt fall down and worship me."

"That's from Matthew?"

"Very good. 4:8-9."

"You're saying we need a way to get Khrushchev down off the mountaintop?"

"This may be the only way."

It wasn't going to be his way—there was no going back on getting rid of Castro. And agreeing to trade the Jupiters for a Soviet non-aggression pledge would make him look cowardly. The rub was, he didn't want to risk splintering the support within the administration that he'd lined up for his plan and had to play along with McCloy. "Why don't you get together with Dulles and have him look into this verification-by-air thing. In the meantime, I want you to start drafting a response to this cable. Maybe someday we'll have a direct Teletype connection with the Kremlin," he said with a grin that he hoped would grease the wheels.

"We'll put that on the agenda to discuss when this is all over. But I would say we'd have to settle whether it's technically feasible to thoroughly inspect the island from the air before drafting our response."

He caught himself scowling and immediately flashed a cover-up smile, angry at McCloy and disappointed with himself. He was in Jack's trap with both feet now. To appear open to considering McCloy's negotiation proposal he'd have to wait for an answer from Dulles before responding to Moscow. He had played along with McCloy and he was stuck.

⸺ɣ∞◦ ⸺

"Jack's soft," Nixon said in summation over the secure phone line to Langley. "You know that, Allie." As obvious as it was, Dulles was probably too friendly with McCloy—and the two of them too much alike—to notice. Jack went to Harvard and Allie to Princeton—that was their biggest divide. "He's just like all those impossible fags over there at State. I knew I shouldn't have put him in the Cabinet." The president calculated that there was no need, for the moment, to spell out how he'd nominated McCloy for secretary of state only after Allie had provided assurances Jack wouldn't be an obstacle.

"Jack is awfully upset over—"

"It's what I get for bringing an internationalist into the Cabinet." Maybe the rumor was true after all about McCloy being one of those establishment bastards who tried to talk Ike into kicking him off the ticket in '56. Those stuck-up assholes thought they were better than Nixon, with their money, their fancy schools and upper-crust families. When he made the mistake of going to one of their parties once, some of the guests—he could see them now and seethed again at the memory—refused to speak with him. "I only nominated him because you swore he wasn't part of the dump-Nixon crowd. But maybe we don't know the whole story on that." In other words, Allie, you're responsible for getting McCloy to drop his proposal.

"I've known Jack even longer than you, Mr. President, and you and I have been friends, for what is it now, thirteen years? Jack means well."

The president didn't remember exactly when he and Dulles had met, but he would never lose track of how their friendship had almost come to an abrupt end during the '60 campaign when the director told Kennedy about Eisenhower's secret plan to send CIA-trained Cuban exiles to overthrow Castro. With that, Kennedy was able to back him into a corner in their fourth radio-television debate, forcing him to oppose the very policy he was privately pushing harder than anyone else in the Eisenhower administration. Any effort to overthrow Castro, he had to say in answer to Frank Singiser's question, would break five U.S. treaties, lose us all our friends in Latin America, be condemned at the U.N., and, "would be an open invitation for Mr. Khrushchev to come into Latin America and to engage us in what would be a civil war, and possibly even worse than that." At least he'd been right about that last part.

"I'll say this, Allie," Nixon said now. "Jack plays a useful role—helps us with that whole U.N. establishment crowd. But we need to keep him in line on this Cuba thing. I want Castro out of there, damn it!"

"I'll check with my photo interpretation staff, Mr. President, and see if Jack's idea for verification by air holds any water and I'll get back to you on that before I give Jack the verdict."

"I don't give a rat's ass what your fucking interpreters think." Do I have to spell out everything for you?

For a moment, static was the only sound on the phone line. "I understand," Dulles finally answered. "I'm afraid my old friend Jack doesn't sufficiently appreciate the opportunity we have to—"

"A *marvelous* opportunity."

"Most definitely, yes, to bring freedom to Cuba."

"I'm gonna have Castro's balls bronzed and put the damn things in a frame on my office wall." The Oval Office, he almost said. Of course it would be the Oval Office.

"I'd be honored to be the one to present them to you, Mr. President."

"Sure."

"If you'll permit me, when Jack calls I'll engage in a bit of subterfuge. I will appear to take under advisement his question as to whether air surveillance alone is sufficient to determine if the missile threat has been vanquished. After a short interval I will report back that it is not within our technical means."

"Tell him it was a damn good idea. You can say the president thought so too."

"Yes, and it's just terribly unfortunate it isn't feasible."

That was what he wanted to hear. "Let me say this too, I want you to drag your feet on this thing, you see?" Of course Dulles wouldn't understand—he'd only just grasped it himself. McCloy hadn't trapped him. It was Jack who was cornered. The delay in the diplomatic process might be just enough to avert any further State Department meddling.

"Are you certain? That will slow our response back to Moscow and—"

"The invasion's the thing now, Allie. If we can stall for a day on this it'll be too late for Jack to try any more tricks to stop us."

⁂

"We have intercepted radio communications indicating Americans have activated underground presidential command facility outside Washington and have increased readiness of nuclear forces."

The men of the Presidium tried to make what sense they could of Khrushchev's words—of those present, only the defense minister knew in advance what the premier would say. The silence in the meeting room broke quietly as one and then others murmured ideas among themselves.

For the second time in twenty-four hours Khrushchev reassessed his conclusions about the man in the White House, or wherever Nixon had fled to. Until he heard the president's words translated early this morning, he hadn't considered Nixon reckless enough to invade Cuba with Soviet forces present to defend the island. And until tonight he never thought Nixon would come this close, with these preparations, to nuclear war.

Advisers had warned him a moment like this might come. Yes, of course, it was possible. Any idiot could see that. No, they did not think the premier was stupid, they'd said, and good for them. They said they had an obligation to present him with the facts. And so he sat and listened as they explained how America would win a nuclear war against the Soviet Union. You are the stupid ones, he told them. How could America be victorious with so many of its citizens killed and its most important cities destroyed? You know nothing, he told them. It was so preposterous, any fool could see the United States could never initiate a nuclear strike, just as he never would. The Soviet Union itself had barely survived as a nation after suffering only a third as many deaths in World War II. American casualties alone in a new war would be more in one day than the total lost by all nations in the last war. No man would ever begin such a war of annihilation.

Even as he had counted on American sanity and self-interest in his dealings with Eisenhower and Nixon, he had encouraged them to believe their foe might not be as rational. And looking around the table now at men in clothes rumpled from sleeping on their office couches and working another day without returning home, he knew some of them were thinking their premier had played his role too convincingly. Threatening the United States with an inflated image of Soviet missiles being turned out "like sausages," then putting them under America's nose, might have scared Nixon into believing the Soviet Union was ready to go to war. If that is what they thought, they should have said so when they had their chance.

Mikoyan was standing, requesting permission to speak. Khrushchev was unsure how long he'd been there, unseen.

"If war is coming, comrades, everything is lost." While Mikoyan paused to regain his composure another member heaved into a handkerchief and left the room. "We should all take our families to countryside."

Chapter 8

Tuesday, October 23, 1962

"HONEST TO GOD, BUDDY, I thought you'd gone off the deep end Sunday night, but it looks like you were onto something," Helene said. She pointed to the newspaper on the breakfast table. "Get a look at this."

NIXON WORKING FROM UNDISCLOSED LOCATION;
MANY OFFICIALS STAY IN WASHINGTON

Pat unfolded the paper to find three stories on the front page about the president's relocation to what the *Los Angeles Times* variously described as a shelter, a secret relocation center, and a continuity of government facility. Each noted that the location was unknown, undisclosed, or top secret. The articles did not say where the president had been when he spoke on television Sunday evening.

Helene filled Pat's cup with coffee and said, "I take it Dick didn't mention any of this to you."

The newspaper's reflection in the silver percolator was all Pat could see. "I can't believe it."

"You said it yourself, Buddy, when we were watching him on TV."

"I've never heard of these shelters they're talking about in the paper, Helene. I never thought, well—"

"That he evacuated?"

"Why would he do that?" And why didn't he say anything?

"Are you serious, Buddy? He left because it's too dangerous to stay. Now do you believe me?"

"It says here"—Pat tapped the paper with her polished, natural-color fingernail—"that all these other men are staying in Washington."

"Yeah, I don't understand that either. If it were me, I'd get the hell out of there—pronto, as our Mexicans say."

Pat continued reading while Helene returned to making breakfast. "It says, 'The White House would not disclose when the president relocated.' I'll bet he left on Sunday."

"Do you think he'd already left when you talked to him on the phone? Wouldn't he have told you?"

"I don't know." What would Helene think of her and her marriage if she said he lied to her often enough that she had no reason to trust anything he told her? In her mind, one lie was enough to stop trusting someone. At that point you knew the person was capable of not telling you the truth and if they were capable of lying they could do it anytime. She could see that problem coming up in a normal marriage, or a marriage to a normal person. With Dick, the problem was on a different level. "I don't see why he would have kept that from me."

"Maybe he couldn't tell you because, you know, maybe Russian spies can tap our phones," Helene said, filling the Mary Proctor Foursome toaster with sliced bread.

"It wasn't a secure line—that's true." Maybe he wanted to say, but wasn't allowed. That could explain why he hadn't returned her call Sunday night. "Certainly he can tell me about it now, since it's in all the papers."

"But not where he is. I'll bet he won't be able to tell you that," Helene said, sounding excited at being in the middle of a mystery.

"He must be in a hotel somewhere," Pat said.

Helene leaned back against the sink. "That's it! And the government booked all the rooms so no one will know he's there."

Pat felt her friend's enthusiasm and turned in her chair to face Helene. "Probably someplace far away."

"I'll bet it's in the mountains, somewhere. Doesn't he have to tell you where, so you can plan your trip?"

"I don't want to stay in some half-deserted hotel." Assuming she returned to Washington before the trouble was over, she didn't see why she couldn't stay in the White House.

"What if it's in the Midwest somewhere? You'd fly right past it on your way to Washington."

"That *would* be silly."

"So you're going back, then?"

"You know Dick wants me to settle the business with the house first. I hope you're not trying to get rid of me." And what was the use of rushing back if the White House was partly closed down while Dick was out of town?

"Oh, Pat, you can always do that later. Besides, it might not be such a good time to buy."

"Why not?"

"You might want to see how things go."

Pat turned back to the newspaper, scowling. "I see."

"Anyway, I think he needs you."

"Needs me?" She turned back to look at Helene just as the golden brown toast sprung into the air.

"Sure he does."

"You don't know Dick. He prefers being alone."

"I think he'd feel better knowing you were nearby," Helene said.

"You think so, do you?"

Helene put the toast on two plates and cleaned the crumbs from the counter. "Will you take the girls?"

"I've been thinking about that. But maybe this whole thing will be over in a few days anyway."

"I don't think so, Buddy." Helene put the plates on the table and again asked the question that had seemingly been on her mind all morning. "Are you sure I shouldn't stock up?"

"I love this jam," Pat said, not looking up.

"Come on, Buddy," Helene said, nodding at the paper. "Don't you see what it says there?"

Of course I see it, silly. It's right here on the front page. WAVE OF BUYING HITS MARKETS. Those women didn't know any better, so of course they were frightened. She'd explained it all to Helene, how Dick had to use dramatic language to rally the nation, and maybe he'd even gone too far because someone could actually get hurt with all those women mobbing the stores, told her there's really nothing to worry about because Dick had already concluded last year with the Berlin Fence crisis that while nuclear weapons make a country look strong, they're just too horrible to actually ever use. She explained what she had realized yesterday talking with that civil defense man, Mr. Quinn, that if anyone in Washington was really serious about possibly using nuclear weapons, they would have taken the necessary precautions a long time ago to protect as many people as possible. And yes, there was some fighting in Cuba, and everyone hoped it would end soon. The important thing was, there was no war here at home.

She looked up at Helene, standing by her chair now, and tried for a reassuring smile. "Oh, honey, don't pay any attention to what those other women are doing."

"Isn't Quinn the one who showed you the fallout shelter yesterday?"

"What about him?"

"He said the president might issue an order closing our stores. That's probably why the markets are so mobbed."

"Quinn said that?" She wondered for a moment how anything she had said to him could have planted this idea in his head.

"It's right here." Helene picked up the paper and began reading aloud. "'Joseph M. Quinn said the president probably would order retail stores closed in the event of war, or declaration of a national emergency.' How am I going to keep food on the table if I can't go to the store, Buddy?"

"Quinn seems like a very nice man but he's just beside himself with worry trying to protect so many people. He's blowing this thing all out of proportion, don't you see?"

Helene stood straight. "The Russians have nuclear missiles in Cuba, for God's sake," adding, in a loud whisper, "that's so close."

"That's why Dick is getting rid of them." She smiled and added, "Now how about some more of that delicious coffee of yours?"

"I don't know," Helene said, growing quiet as she stared at something through the kitchen window. "It just seems a lot more complicated than that."

When Helene returned to the table with the percolator Pat put a hand on her friend's arm and tried for a tone that was reassuring and hinted of a confidence shared. "Dick isn't going to order the stores closed, Helene."

"So you talked about it?"

"You know men don't like to talk about their work. Still, Dick would have said something on the phone if he was going to do that." She added milk to her coffee from a small blue-porcelain pitcher. "Do you have a fellow grind your coffee at the A&P?"

Helene smacked her in the side with her aproned hip and returned to preparing breakfast.

Pat was lighting a cigarette when Helene asked, "How did Dick sound when you talked to him? He must be exhausted."

"He did sound awfully tired—I'm sure he's not getting enough sleep," Pat said, shaking the match and tossing it into the ashtray.

"That man works nonstop, doesn't he?"

"You're telling me, kiddo." Dick had told her in the early years of their marriage that he'd been known as "iron-butt" for the endless hours he spent studying in the library at law school. She suspected—knowing he'd never say it outright—he didn't feel as smart as some of the other boys. He also had to compete against those who'd gotten a head start in life, the other kids, not like themselves, who'd had all the advantages. She saw it for herself only after the war, when Dick was elected to the House. From his first days in Washington he came home for dinner only once or twice a week. Many nights he didn't come home at all. He would work into the early morning hours then curl up on his office couch for a few hours of sleep. In the morning, Rose Mary told her, he'd take a quick breakfast, shave, and go back to work.

No matter that she yelled at him about how he had disappointed his daughters, about the missed vacations and the nights away from home when he was traveling; it only ever got worse, until she stopped waiting up for him and stopped keeping his dinner warm. She stopped yelling. And maybe she stopped caring as much, too.

She took her plate over to the sink, cigarette dangling from the corner of her mouth, and paused a moment to look out the window. An unpremeditated smile lifted her Lucky Strike to horizontal.

"Just leave it in the sink, Buddy. I have a dishwasher now, you know."

"Aren't they wonderful?" She saw Helene reading the newspaper and sensed what was coming. "I hope Dick will buy me one when—"

"Buddy, they're saying there isn't a single fallout shelter in the whole South Bay area."

Opening the dishwasher, "Are these clean ones in here?"

"Yeah, those are clean. How could there not be any shelters anywhere around here? This isn't exactly a poor area."

With a dinner plate in each hand, "Helene! It isn't about money."

Helene looked up from the paper. "What's it about, then?"

"How should I know?" She stacked the plates in the cupboard. "Why don't you stick to reading the society page? Aren't the woman's clubs having their fall fashion shows about now?"

"I still can't believe you're not taking this more seriously, Buddy. It's not just the two of us, you know. We can't just think of ourselves."

Pat watched her daughters playing in the backyard and almost didn't notice the delicate china cup slip from her hand. "Oh, your beautiful cup."

She swept the few pieces into a dustpan and Helene emptied the debris into the trash. By the Tappan range, Helene put her arms around her. Pat touched her free hand to Helene's back.

"I'm sorry, Buddy. I know how much you love Tricia and Julie. It's just that I'm frightened," Helene said, holding her tighter.

She wasn't going to let that happen to her. It would be bad for the girls, and what good would it do Helene to see her that way? And yet she also felt disappointed in herself, for as much as she had tried, and as strong as she had been, she knew how little she'd been able to do to reassure her friend, much less the other women across Los Angeles and in cities all over the nation—women caught in the dark and struggling to understand what was happening in Washington and Havana and Moscow; women just like Helene who didn't know if they should buy every last jug of water and can of soup they could get their hands on at the local mart; women who could not understand why there were only enough fallout shelters for a very few of them; women heavy with guilt for disobeying the advice civil defense authorities had been giving for so long to prepare a safe place in their basements where their families could huddle until the worst of the nuclear fallout had blown away and they could begin cleaning their homes of dust and debris. There was no one they could turn to who truly understood their instinct to protect their families, no one to level with them about what they should do.

This, she understood now, was how she could help, and with that she leaned the broom against the wall and gripped Helene tight.

—∞—

"It's my responsibility to encourage the people of Los Angeles to prepare for their own survival in case of a nuclear attack," Quinn was saying as he held her chair and she gathered her brown-and-white flaring full skirt of mitered stripes toward the center inverted pleat.

"I understand completely, Mr. Quinn. That's your job." On a quick tour Quinn had given her of the city's civil defense offices before they closed for the day, she had seen a number of Negroes sweeping the floors. Now, in the director's cramped office, she'd been seated at a round conference table, where she faced a large assortment of flowers arranged in a tall glass vase on the corner table, which, she knew instinctively, had been rushed into place for her unexpected visit. What actually caught her eye—beyond the stacks of paper on the floor and the Teletype machine's urgent messages piling up in a curlicuing pool of spooled paper and the gray-metal bookshelf overflowing with thick manuals—was a full-page newspaper spread thumb-tacked to the large cork bulletin board hanging on the cinder block wall. From where she was sitting, she could read only the headline, RED ALERT! WHAT IF H-BOMB HITS LOS ANGELES?

"I was just repeating the survival advice the government publishes in millions of pamphlets," Quinn continued.

She wanted to give him a piece of her mind for saying what he had about Dick closing all the stores. Anyone who said that must think her husband was completely insensitive to people's needs. She would never get used to the horrible things people said about him because of his political stands. Bad as that was, none of them had accused Dick of being so crass as to ignore the needs of housewives to keep food on the table for their families.

Instead, she said, "You're a dedicated public servant."

"That's kind of you, Mrs. Nixon, but some of my colleagues have not been as generous in their comments."

"I'm sure they appreciate your hard work, Mr. Quinn."

From Quinn's expression, she could see him trying to make up his mind, probably unable to decide whether she hadn't been reading the newspaper or hadn't been listening, it never having occurred to him, as it sometimes didn't to men these days, that she was just trying to be polite. She hoped he hadn't gotten the wrong idea about her when they talked at the Biltmore yesterday, hadn't misjudged her as one of those women who tried to pretend with all their frank talk that they were no different than the men they worked for. This was the risk these women took, try to pretend you are their equal and they'll want you to solve their problems for them. She had encouraged Quinn to speak his mind and from that he must have concluded he had some kind of license to tell her about his troubles. To her regret she already knew quite enough about the matter, including the criticism Quinn had received for advising housewives to stock up on groceries, in case the president ordered the stores closed. Governor Brown said he hadn't been informed of any possible closing and an official from some emergency planning office in Washington said the federal government might not have the capability to close stores after a nuclear attack anyway.

"I know what I said at the press conference caused a buying spree. But that was my idea. Now thousands of families have an emergency food supply—and not a single person was hurt."

"This is what I wanted to talk to you about, Mr. Quinn." He looked surprised and she hesitated for a moment, hoping he wouldn't be angry at what she was about to say. "I'm in Los Angeles to attend to family business and to spend some time with my friend, Mrs. Drown—perhaps you've made her husband's acquaintance, Mr. Jack Drown, of Rolling Hills?" She continued, without waiting for a response. "So you see, I'd like to find some way to help, while I'm here. If you'd have me, that is." With a slight tilt of the head she smiled and girded herself for his response.

He didn't say anything right away so she kept smiling.

"Of course, we can use all the volunteers we can get. Maybe you could hand out some of those civil defense pamphlets." He pointed to a dusty stack of thin, pale green booklets in a corner. "There's a big demand for those."

That wasn't what she had in mind, though she wasn't sure herself what exactly she should do, until she remembered reading in the paper how housewives were flooding civil defense offices with inquires. How wonderful if she could talk to them directly. She was sure she'd be able to settle them down.

"That sounds lovely," she said. "Now, are you getting many phone calls?"

"You bet we are. Yesterday alone we logged more than a thousand calls. As soon as we put down the phone, it rings again."

"So many? Perhaps I could help answer the phones then. I used to answer the calls that came into my husband's office when he was in the Congress, you see. So I have some experience in that line. Perhaps I can calm some nerves, woman to woman, if you know what I mean, Mr. Quinn."

"A woman's voice can certainly be comforting." He looked away, then continued, "But what we're trying for in this office is to convey authority. I'm sure you understand."

"I see," she said, no longer smiling.

Quinn gave a nervous cough. "Of course, we'd have to train you in what to tell folks."

"Do you really think that's necessary, Mr. Quinn? Why, I'll just tell them that there's really nothing to worry about, to go on caring for their families. I'd like to use my maiden name, Miss Ryan, so as not to cause any fuss."

"May I show you something, Mrs. Nixon?" he asked, standing.

The tacked-up newspaper article, she could see now, was from March 1961. Above the headline was a large map of the Los Angeles area. An illustrator at the *Los Angeles Times* had drawn four circles of increasing size on the map, target style. The bull's-eye was over downtown—Vernon and Vermont avenues—and was labeled: FIREBALL.

"Did you say you were staying in Rolling Hills?"

"Why yes, that's right."

"That's right about here, in South Bay," he said, pointing at the general area of Helene's house. "As you can see, that's just outside this circle here." His finger traced the circumference of the third circle to the twelve o'clock position, where it said, LIGHT DAMAGE. "Don't let that label fool you. Drapes, beds, wooden furniture, papers, all upholstery—everything in the Drown house that can burn will instantly erupt into flame. The whole house will be engulfed within minutes, along with all the other buildings in town."

"That would be awful, but I believe the Drowns have a fire department call box on the sidewalk not two doors from their home. I'll have to tell Helene to pull that at the very first sign of trouble."

Quinn looked at her with a stern expression. "There won't be a fire department, Mrs. Nixon." Brightening a bit, he tapped the map a couple times and said, "Now this is a pretty good article here, but it's based on a number of assumptions and things could turn out quite different."

As Quinn talked she studied another of the article's drawings. It showed a man and a woman and their two children, one an infant, in a blast shelter three feet underground. Outside, their house had a few holes in its roof, some broken windows, a tree was down in the yard, and a black rain, labeled RADIOACTIVE FALL OUT, descended in irregular clumps from a black sky. The sheltered family had a fourteen-day food supply, a battery radio, and a storage battery. There was a young boy in the artist's sketch and he appeared bored. She made a mental note to advise mothers to be sure to pack board games.

"Personally, I think the Soviets are more likely to aim at our seaport than they are our urban core. Now, on this map that would be right about here," he said, pointing at an area at about five o'clock on the outermost circle.

"Mr. Quinn, I really don't think this is necessary."

"In that case, you'd be within what this article—and I think this part is pretty accurate—what it calls..." He took his reading glasses out of his pocket and slid his finger down the columns of text. "Here it is. 'And behind the thermal radiation storms the shock front hurled outward at many times the speed of sound like an invisible tidal wave. Roofs collapse and crash down through upper stories. Walls crack wide and tremble perilously and fires torch everywhere, gutting the wreckage in a smother of smoke.'"

"What good can an article like this possibly do? They're just trying to scare people so they can sell more newspapers."

"A scared population is a prepared population, I'm afraid. But I'm not interested in sowing panic, Mrs. Nixon. I've decided not to talk publicly about how unprepared the nation is for nuclear conflict."

"Well, that's wonderful. Now I hope you'll also tell the people who call your office that there's really no danger."

Quinn chuckled and said, "Well, I'm sure you know more about the world situation than I do all the way out here in California, Mrs. Nixon. I've only ever been to the White House with my family on one of those public tours."

She didn't know any more about this business with Cuba than Quinn. Still, she was the kind of woman who could think for herself and it seemed to her that anyone who thought about this for a moment had to conclude that Dick wouldn't put the country in a position where it was threatened with these terrible weapons, with so few shelters for people to hide in.

Quinn took off his glasses. "Shelters are part of the story," he said. "There's also medical care. As horrible as it is to contemplate, many tens of thousands of people in the Los Angeles area—maybe even hundreds of thousands—will have life threatening injuries, if there is an attack from the Soviet Union. But there will be no way for them to be treated."

"Well, I know the California Hospital downtown is adding a whole new wing and will be able to treat many more people than it can today. I was there for the dedication just a few days ago."

"The thing of it is, Mrs. Nixon, that hospital won't exist anymore, and neither will the doctors. A local medical group just sent me a booklet with the names of eight thousand doctors. But how many of them will survive? And of those that do, how would I contact them?"

A lightness in her stomach competed with her determination. "Kind of like the fire department?"

"Exactly. I'm also concerned about food distribution after an emergency. Federal warehouses only have supplies for about 4 million people."

Vanquishing her queasiness, she said, "Well, that should be quite sufficient."

"That's 4 million for the entire nation, not just Los Angeles."

Her gloved hands formed discrete fists. "Mr. Quinn. Don't you think all of this just goes to show that we don't need to worry about any of this foolishness?"

"I'm afraid I don't understand."

"How could we go to war with the Russians if we're as unprepared as you say?"

"But we have gone to war with the Russians, Mrs. Nixon."

Chapter 9

Tuesday, October 23, 1962

RICHARD NIXON TOOK OFF HIS suit jacket and folded it neatly across his arm, having decided to take one more lap around the reservoir after lunch; he didn't want to look like he had worked up a sweat. After he went around again it would be time to meet Finch and Radford in the special room where Mount Weather had its advanced television conferencing equipment for a call with the Joint Chiefs at Site R in Pennsylvania. The Pentagon probably wanted to adjust the number of forces going in to Cuba. He'd ask enough questions to show them how carefully he'd been studying the briefing materials on the invasion and how deeply he'd thought about the issues. He'd take enjoyment from their surprise—hide it though they might try—at the preparation he had done and at his intellectual sophistication and ability to consider these matters on their level, or above, just like the graduates of those elite schools. Then he would give them what they wanted. If he made any objection and something went wrong, they'd blame him.

The driver held his jacket low enough for him to easily slip his arms through the sleeves. During the ride in the backseat of the humming electric cart he went through his mental checklist, picturing the ideas he had jotted down earlier on a yellow legal pad, the many threads and threats he was monitoring, from the items at the bottom that included managing the ongoing sideshow at the United Nations and pacifying the limp-wristed among the Europeans begging him to cancel the invasion, up to the strategy section on top, where he needed to stay focused on what the hell Khrushchev might do about his ruined missile base in Cuba, with his soldiers' blood soon to be running in the streets of Havana, and the imminent deposing of the Latin revolutionary comrade the Soviets had so vigorously vowed to defend.

The guard at the entrance to the secure conference room was just saluting when Finch ran up and blocked the door. "Some of the Chiefs," Finch said, pulling him aside, "want you to do something preemptive—attack the Soviets before they can attack us. Lemnitzer's pushing it, but this was LeMay's idea."

He shoved Finch into the wall and yelled, "How the hell could you let those shit-ass cocksuckers do this to me? It's a goddamn set up," he said, scowling with squinted eyes. Turning quickly, he walked away, heading down a long corridor with exposed pipes lining the ceiling that stretched far into the distance. He slapped the soles of his shiny black Jarmans hard against the tile floor and strode toward the vanishing point, until Sherwood pulled up beside him in a cart. "Can I take you to your office, Mr. President?"

"Take me outside," he said, climbing in. For the first time since arriving at Mount Weather on Sunday he felt a wave of cabin fever. In the back seat he let his arms go limp at his sides and his head slump against the headrest.

"I'll swing by your rooms first to get you a coat. It's awfully cold up there."

Instead of getting angry at Finch, Radford was the one who deserved to be balled out, Nixon thought, as Sherwood made a U-turn, tires screeching against the floor. He'd warned Raddy when the Soviets raised the alert level of their rocket forces to make sure LeMay and the other Chiefs didn't use that as a pretext to lobby for a first strike.

More than Finch or Radford, he was angry with himself, for he should have expected no less from LeMay. It was a moment the general had been planning for, ever since the Rosenbergs handed over our secrets for the Soviets to explode their first A-bomb. LeMay thought the United States should never have allowed the Soviets to build those nuclear weapons in the first place, then wanted to stop them before they advanced to the more powerful H-bomb; LeMay's desire to eliminate the Communist threat only strengthened as the Soviet arsenal grew. If we don't act, there will inevitably be a nuclear showdown, LeMay had predicted.

The discovery of Soviet missiles in Cuba had proven the general right, of course, and from their first meetings to discuss how the United States would respond the general had been straining at the leash.

"The Russian bear has always been eager to stick his paw in Latin American waters," LeMay had said. "Now that we've got him in a trap, let's take his leg off right up to his testicles." LeMay had started to put his cigar back in his mouth. "On second thought, let's take off his testicles, too."

Nixon had leaned forward to see LeMay across the other men seated at the long Cabinet Room table that day and should have known then and there, the president realized now, that LeMay would eventually convince the rest of the Joint Chiefs to join in presenting a formal proposal to do just that by simultaneously destroying all the Soviet Union's nuclear bombers and missiles.

"We can eliminate the Russian nuclear capacity without any significant danger to ourselves," LeMay argued at one of those early meetings. "We'll intercept any of their bombers that are airborne before they even get close to our property," the general added, describing how an F-106 interceptor jet could fire a Genie air-to-air nuclear missile at a formation of Soviet bombers to blast them all out of the sky with a single atomic explosion. LeMay paused to light another cigar with his Zippo and puffed the smoke across the table. Finally he asked, "When do you think you'll be giving that order, Mr. President?"

He should have fired LeMay on the spot, Nixon realized now. Finch or Gates could have been sent to do the dirty work. Some jobs, though, a president had to do himself, or not do at all, and confronting the general could have provoked the kind of angry response he'd learned as a boy to avoid. Just thinking of it now he could hear his father yelling, red faced, and see him unbuckling his belt, this time for him instead of his brothers, who usually caught the blows. They hadn't learned as he had—even if he slipped up this time—not to do anything to anger the old man, or at least not to get caught.

Rumors had circulated for years about LeMay, long before anyone could imagine Khrushchev risking atomic war over a tiny island in the Caribbean. The general had apparently talked of personally launching a nuclear attack, if there were signs the Soviets were preparing to use their missiles, and there wasn't time to wait for a presidential authorization.

It was the one thing that had concerned him about the general and before approving an extension of his term as Air Force Chief of Staff he had Gates get LeMay's promise not to go off half-cocked. And since the start of the Cuban crisis he'd made sure there was always an open telephone line with the Joint Chiefs; he need only pick up the special phone without the dial. In any event, it would have taken more than unsubstantiated rumors to deny Curtis the top job, given his stellar record, and Nixon suspected the post would have gone to LeMay in a Kennedy administration, too.

LeMay wasn't the only high-ranking military man with an itchy trigger finger; what set him apart was his standing as the senior Air Force officer, putting him in a unique position to squeeze. Although many a man, put off by the Air Force veteran's gruffness, made the mistake of dismissing LeMay, he had respected the general's toughness from the time they first met, at Arthur Godfrey's farm, in '57. Curtis simply said what plenty of others in the military believed and were too polite to talk about openly. They all pretty much agreed that a nuclear weapon was just another tool in the arsenal and foresaw occasions when it would be the most efficient choice, its use in the next war inevitable.

On a late-night plane ride during the '60 campaign, Radford had told him about a meeting in '54 with the other Chiefs to discuss the possibility of using nuclear weapons to save the French position in Vietnam. Toward the end of the session, one of the generals said, "You could take all day to drop a bomb, make sure you put it in the right place, and clean those commies out of there; the band could play the *Marseillaise* and the French could come marching out in great shape."

LeMay liked to make the point in more personal terms, saying he didn't see much difference between being killed with a rusty knife or a nuclear bomb, except the A-bomb might be a less painful way to go.

Nixon got out of the cart and followed Sherwood into an elevator, where the thought of LeMay and his cigar made him long for fresh air. The elevator opened inside a small cinder block building. Sherwood walked ahead to hold the door.

The president turned up the collar on his dark-gray coat, glad to be outside despite the afternoon's strong chill wind, instead of listening to Curtis make himself out to be a bigger foe of the Communists than Richard Nixon himself. He'd worked too hard, and for too long, to build up his Communist-fighting credentials to let that happen. The air was clear and dry, with giant blue and white cumulus clouds gliding between the rolling Virginia mountains in shades of gold, red, brown, and green, the sun poking in between to spotlight the farms in the valleys below.

He ignored the two-tone Apache Carryall driving by slowly on the narrow service road and walked head down, leather-gloved hands in his coat pockets. LeMay and the other Chiefs, like everyone else, had heard him say again and again that his goal was to free the Soviet Union from Communism and in so doing, he knew, he had emboldened them to think missiles and bombers could achieve what he imagined would come one day through peaceful competition between two competing systems of thought, one that made its people stand in long lines for bread and another that allowed ordinary housewives to have their own automatic washers and driers. He had made it plain, on the rare occasions when they asked, that the marketplace of ideas, not war, would cause Communism to collapse. Otherwise, he had allowed them to imagine what they would.

It sounded to him like footsteps coming up quickly from behind. He turned to see if anyone was there. What are you doing here, Buddy? She gave a sly smile and said, I came to see if you're still alive. That's just what she would say, he thought. Let's go for a walk, Dick. I know a nice way to go, he heard her say, as she took his hand.

They expect me to live up to the things I've said, but they're taking it the wrong way, he told her as she led him onto a spur road. The Joint Chiefs were not the only ones who read into your speeches what they wanted to hear, she said. I know that, he thought, but it never made any difference, as long as they knew I stood firmly against Communism. It makes a difference now, she said. You made yourself into someone who would do almost anything to achieve his ends to get ahead in his career and now that's come back to haunt you. Her words led him to think how different he was from Eisenhower, who spoke with moderation, letting Foster and his low-road vice president threaten America's enemies with destruction. When it came time to stand up to Communist aggression—when the Soviets invaded Hungary—Ike did nothing in response, and yet avoided looking as though he'd gone back on his word. Eisenhower used you and Foster to look tougher than he was, Pat said. Now maybe you can use Eisenhower for cover. Come on, she said, let's take this path up ahead.

"The Chiefs insisted that you can't wait much longer before making a decision, Mr. President." From the way Raddy was describing it, the conference call earlier in the afternoon with LeMay and the other members of the Joint Chiefs had been pretty tough. Raddy wouldn't say it, but he figured they'd put up a pretty big stink about the president not being on the line. Fuck them. He wasn't going to look like the weak sister. He could have gotten on the call and played the madman role for them, acting as though he was capable of anything. LeMay probably would have made some remark about how it had taken him so long to get on board.

Radford pointed at the aluminum-framed roll-up chalkboard that had been wheeled into the president's office and talked about the Joint Chiefs' plan to eliminate the Soviet threat, explaining the advantages of a first strike as he moved the rubber tip of the long wooden pointer from one bullet-pointed option to the next.

Even though Radford had hung up his uniform five years ago to become a civilian, the former admiral retained the disconcerting ability of military men to dispassionately discuss plans that would lead to suffering on a scale not even Hiroshima survivors could fully appreciate. Military men could no better imagine total destruction than anyone else; still, it was their duty to analyze nuclear devastation and so they retreated from the reality of burning bodies to the comfort of clean calculations. Otherwise, the country's nuclear weapons would have to be put away, with no plans for how or when they might be used.

Listening to Radford's briefing, Nixon thought of Pat's advice atop Mount Weather and decided she had been right about trying to use Eisenhower for political cover—it was a damn good idea—though it would only work if Ike rejected the Chiefs' proposal. He could make it seem as though he agreed in his heart with the proposal for a surprise nuclear attack on the Soviets, but was prudently deferring instead to the nation's most respected and experienced military mind. He'd stop a bloodthirsty plan that would kill millions of innocent people—even if it had been described in bloodless terms—and still look tough. Military men needed a commander in chief they respected and could look up to and he must make them think he was one of them. "This could end the Cold War once and for all," he said, interrupting Radford's presentation.

Finch glanced up from a memorandum he was studying, looking as if he'd missed something important.

"The Chiefs are limiting their offensive to the Soviet nuclear threat so, yes, it would go a long way toward easing the struggle. In time, however, Red China, when they acquire the A-bomb, will want to step up and fill the vacuum," Radford said.

He felt Finch steal a glance at him while rubbing out a spent cigarette on the red CD of the Office of Civil Defense and Mobilization ashtray on the coffee table. Without looking at Bob he knew his chief of staff would be unnerved at the prospect of the president and his national security adviser sounding as though they were seriously considering putting their chips down on a plan to start a nuclear war with the Soviet Union. Bob would just have to wait. You couldn't look like a pussy in front of tough guys like Radford. Bob didn't get that because he could be a damn pussy himself. He put his feet up on the narrow end of the coffee table, matching Finch's posture at the table's opposite end. "What are the odds we'd come through this without more than minor damage?" he asked Radford.

"The Chiefs estimate an 87 percent probability of eliminating the threat before the Soviets are able to launch a retaliatory strike."

Was that supposed to be a reassuring number? If it wasn't 100 percent—and it never would be—how could anyone believe the risk to the United States was worth the benefit of destroying the Soviet Union's nuclear weapons? "In other words, a 13 percent chance that we lose, what, your home town—Chicago?" This was a good chance to drive home the impression that he was the toughest kind of cold-headed SOB, so he showed a smirk, as though recalling that Chicago had gone for Kennedy, though he'd managed to carry the state—barely—with strong Republican support downstate.

"That would be the estimate for the loss of one or more civilian or military targets," Radford said, looking at the president with steely blue eyes.

This was the military man's other trick: Couch madness with neutral words. This way your mind wouldn't conjure up buildings dissolving into tiny particles, along with everyone inside. "The way I see it, they wouldn't settle for hitting one of our bases. Whoever'd be left running things over there—their military would elbow Khrushchev out of the way and be running the show in no time—they'd want at least one of our cities. If one of their bombers got through, how bad would it be?"

"The Pentagon estimate—now this is an average number, based on a single attack on a major U.S. city—would be six hundred thousand casualties, Mr. President."

That would be twice the number of U.S. dead in World War II. From one plane, he thought, and suddenly it was there again, the movie the generals had shown him at the Pentagon after he'd been sworn in. Maybe for Radford the 600,000 was just one of his numbers, nothing personal. He'd always admired tough men like Radford. These were real men who would do anything to succeed. He'd been as tough as any of them when he went after Alger Hiss. It was hand-to-hand combat for his political life. His response to the missiles in Cuba had been tough as well, plenty tough, and exactly what the Chiefs had recommended to preserve United States national security, one absolute imperative he could never shirk. This idea of LeMay's to preemptively attack the Soviet Union was something altogether different, but until Eisenhower was lined up to cover for him, he was happy to play the part. "I'd say this, the Soviets are probably going to want to—this is what I would do—they're going to try and take down the president," he said with a saw-cut motion to his throat. "Decapitation."

"I agree with your analysis that the center of our command and control authority would be high on the enemy's target list. But the Joint Chiefs have concluded the risk to command authority is acceptable, weighed against the value of achieving our objective."

"Eliminating the nuclear threat."

"If we do not avail ourselves of this opportunity, the Chiefs note, then at some undetermined point in the future the potential loss to the United States from a Soviet attack will be substantially greater."

That's right, he thought, but only if there were a war—and if he did his job right, and his successors continued his policy of not making concessions to the Soviets, there wouldn't be a war. The Chiefs wanted him to start World War III now because they considered war inevitable. Well, it wasn't, goddamn it, and he wasn't going to be railroaded by LeMay and the other Chiefs who were willing to bet everything, including his own life, if the Soviets were able to target Mount Weather directly. "It's just a damn crap shoot is all," he said, pointing at Radford's chalkboard and letting more of his true feelings show than he'd intended.

"The situation might be better analogized to a game of blackjack. At the present time we're the dealer."

"Well, I say it's dealing from the bottom of the deck," Finch blurted out. Bob looked unnerved. "You're talking about some kind of preemptive strategy, which this country has never had. Striking out of the blue like that—it'd be like Pearl Harbor in reverse."

"Except that there was a Soviet provocation in this instance," Radford said.

"One commensurate with what the Chiefs are proposing? You'd think they'd dropped an A-bomb on us, the way they're talking," Finch said in a mix of anger and fear.

He let Finch press his case, knowing the Chiefs and perhaps Radford wouldn't put much stock in holding back on an attack out of high morals. And preemption, though not publicly spoken of as a tenet of U.S. foreign policy, had never been taken off the table. Before the Cuba crisis he had, after all, been studying a proposal to bomb nuclear facilities in Red China to keep Mao from acquiring atomic weapons. With Finch sounding scared, he couldn't side with Bob. For now he had to sound strong and hope Pat had showed him a way out.

As soon as Radford and Finch left, the president had Rose Mary place a call to Eisenhower. The former president, when he finally came on the line, was angry to hear that the Joint Chiefs wanted to take advantage of the missile base in Cuba to launch a pre-emptive strike against the Soviets.

"I urge you, Dick, in the strongest possible terms, this isn't something you ought to give serious consideration to."

He had the old man's blessing and Pat's plan was going to work, even if the bastard still didn't see him as fit to be president. Otherwise Ike wouldn't slip in to calling him by his first name, no matter that he extended his former boss the respect he deserved, and no doubt expected, by always referring to him as Mr. President. It wasn't as though he could call the former president Ike, and Eisenhower knew it. He knew what Eisenhower had thought of his vice president. Dick just isn't ready for the top job, hasn't matured enough as vice president. Even when he took over temporarily after the boss's brushes with death and got universally high marks for his restrained and careful conduct, Ike didn't change his tune. In eight years of serving together, Ike had never said it to his face, of course; there were plenty of other ways a president had to let his vice president know he did not have his boss's blessing.

"LeMay seems to be the one who put this idea forward," he told Eisenhower, who didn't sound surprised. Ike said he had enormous respect for LeMay's carpet-bombing campaign against Japan during World War II. No one could deny LeMay's brilliance in planning and carrying out those raids. The trouble was, LeMay somehow didn't understand that strategic nuclear weapons weren't just bigger, better bombs—that was true of the small tactical nuclear weapons, not the multi-megaton bombs, carried in the bays of B-52s and atop giant missiles, that could eliminate Moscow. LeMay didn't understand that the old rules might not always apply with these modern weapons, or he was simply calloused to human suffering. That LeMay could propose unleashing such horrible destruction on half the world before a single enemy shot had been fired, behaving as though the Soviet Union had attacked the U.S. with nuclear arms—it could be grounds for forcing him into retirement, if it weren't for his distinguished record.

Nixon made the case, as well as his lawyerly and rhetorical skills allowed, for implementing the Chiefs' recommendation to put a quick end to the Cold War. This way he could appear to be won over by Ike's response, rather than lapping up a handout.

Maybe that would nudge the old man in the direction of thinking he was capable at more than the dirty, political jobs Ike had given him as vice president, dirty jobs Eisenhower wouldn't stoop to himself, like publicly criticizing Joe McCarthy when it was clear the senator had gone too far. Instead, the old bastard made it clear, without saying it outright, that his former vice president was almost as brutal minded as LeMay, but without those vindicating war medals on his chest.

Before going, Eisenhower urged him once more to stick with the bomb-and-invade plan as they had discussed it in earlier calls and reject the Chiefs' advice.

"I'm afraid it would haunt you for all your days, my boy," Eisenhower said.

Was weighing the destruction of the Communist world with the Joint Chiefs of Staff boys' work? Maybe Eisenhower thought he wasn't able to think this through for himself. A boy couldn't. If he were a man, would he chart his own course, independent of what Eisenhower said? Was he really going his own way if he independently arrived at the same conclusion as Eisenhower?

For now he would swallow hard at playing errand boy again and carry Ike's message back to Radford, who he'd have inform the Joint Chiefs: proposal denied. Along the way he would let it slip out—make it appear it was just slipping out—that Eisenhower was on his side on this one and hope some of the great general's credibility on military decisions would shield him from scorn.

—∞∞∞—

Rose Mary had placed the note on his desk while he was on the phone with Eisenhower. Director Dulles had called. The matter concerned the secretary of state; it was important, but not of critical urgency.

"As you know, Mr. President, Jack believes the Soviets are likely to target our Jupiter missiles in Turkey as a response to our invasion of Cuba. Since yesterday, when you and I talked about Jack's proposal, he has brought this up with me a number of times. What are your thoughts on that matter?"

"This is what I told Jack. Oh, and by the way he thinks we'd have to respond to a Soviet strike on the Jupiters with an attack on a Soviet installation somewhere. That could easily spiral out of control, you see? I planted the idea with him that maybe we wouldn't have to respond, uh, you know—militarily."

"Those missiles were obsolete the day they went in."

"That's what I said."

"Putting aside the issue of the invasion, I wonder if we might be able to swing a deal with the Jupiters that would lessen the chance of a Soviet escalation."

"Offer to dismantle them, is that what you mean?" If it was, his satisfaction with Dulles the other day had been too quick. Suddenly, he felt resentful of Allie, who he could imagine sitting in a big office with picture windows while he was trapped in this damp mine shaft of a shelter.

"Right."

"And in return we get what? A promise that the Soviets won't up the ante?"

"I think we'd all rest easier knowing this thing is going to be contained to Cuba."

"Why should the U.S. make concessions to Soviet aggression? I'll say this, I think it would be seen as tantamount to appeasement."

"Only if the deal were public, sir. If no one's the wiser, it will look like a win across the board for you—a president who eliminated the missile threat, went to the root of the problem—that's Castro—and kept Moscow in check."

"A private agreement to remove the missiles at a later date, is that what you mean?" The Joint Chiefs, he was sure, would object to removing the Jupiters. His opposition to LeMay's plan to attack the Soviet Union was already weakening his credibility in their eyes. Trading away their missiles in Turkey would further undermine his command authority. And yet he understood there was no choice for him but to go along, if it took the possibility of Soviet retaliation off the table. He promised himself he would work hard in the coming years to regain the military's respect. For now, all he could do was spread the idea that he had agreed reluctantly to McCloy's idea.

———∞———

After debating through the evening, the Presidium remained divided on the implications of Nixon's departure from Washington and his military preparations, with those urging caution holding a slim majority; it was then Castro's letter arrived.

Khrushchev read it aloud. "'Danger facing all of mankind is so great that Soviet Union must in no circumstances permit creation of conditions that will allow imperialists to carry out first atomic strike against U.S.S.R.'"

"Castro agrees Nixon is planning first strike," Malinovsky said. "He is very familiar with way Americans think. We should believe what he says."

"If you would all shut up, I would like to continue." The room quieted and Khrushchev read again from the letter. "'Now that imperialists have begun to carry out their barbaric, illegal, and immoral attack on Cuba, this is time to liquidate such danger forever through legal right of self-defense. However harsh and terrible such decision is, there is no other way out, in my opinion.'"

Khrushchev smoothed out the pages on the table as though rolling pie dough, barely able to keep from tearing the letter into the largest number of possible pieces. Castro could go to hell. Because the Americans have attacked Cuba, the Soviet Union must go to war against the U.S., Castro was saying, content to see everyone burn in the same ash pile.

Khrushchev waved the letter above his head and did not hide his anger when he spoke. "Americans are not so foolish to launch first strike on our homeland with no warning—whatever Castro thinks he knows! And we will not sacrifice our revolution as homage to Cuba's," he said, letting the letter flutter to the floor from his outstretched hand. Even Americans stupid enough to think they can survive a nuclear war need something they can construe as a provocation to justify attacking the Soviet Union, he insisted, just as they used our missiles as an excuse to attack Cuba.

The greatest danger they faced now—and this is where they must focus their most serious attention, he told them—is the Americans finding such an excuse when they invade and their ships and troops came under fire from our nuclear artillery. It will be of no importance to them that Soviet troops have no other means of defense. Rather than accept the inevitability of the Cuban revolution, or respond proportionately and with restraint, Pentagon warmongers may use the skirmish to justify the war they've wanted to fight all along, while they still possess a superior nuclear force.

There was no alternative, Khrushchev told the Presidium, except to eliminate the provocation. They could not allow Pliyev to use the Lunas and FKRs for self-defense.

The consequences would be grim. Soviet and Cuban soldiers would die fighting or give up in surrender; either way, the revolution would be lost, handing an unparalleled victory to the capitalists and imposing a singular defeat on the Soviet Union. The tide of Communist revolutions they had looked forward to in Latin America would be stopped. Chairman Mao would be thrilled to see him humiliated and would use this setback to advance the Chinese philosophy of violently overthrowing imperialist regimes, without regard to nuclear war, over his own quest for peaceful coexistence.

As criminal as those events would be, they would not be the end of the world. "If we do not take this regrettable action, we will find ourselves face to face with danger of nuclear catastrophe," he told the Presidium, "with possible result of destroying human race. To save world, we must retreat. Another day has begun," he said, pointing to the clock on the wall. "Hour is late. Still, I ask you to consult and debate whether you are in agreement with this kind of decision."

Chapter 10

Wednesday, October 24, 1962

H ELENE WAS SO SWEET TO GO next door to the neighbor's to use their phone so early in the morning, Pat thought, climbing the stairs to wait in the guest bedroom. The White House operator who phoned ahead to check if she was available said to expect the president's call sometime within the next half hour; she couldn't let him get a busy signal.

That he was calling at all seemed to her to be a minor miracle. She hoped it didn't have anything to do with Cuba, though she almost wouldn't mind if it meant there was a way she could help with something important to him. What that would be, she wouldn't think about and honestly would not be able to imagine anyway. What she most wanted was a sign that he once again needed something only she could provide by being with him, wherever he was.

Even so, as she reached to answer the phone she couldn't help feeling angry with her husband for not calling sooner and for not having told her he was evacuating. Part of her wanted to ask where he was hiding, to dig in to him with the foul implication that he'd run away. Not that she believed he had left Washington because he was scared, or even because it was necessary; she understood he had evacuated because it was part of the game he was playing with the Soviets to determine which would get to control Cuba. Still, she wanted him to know she was angry.

But that would mean giving in to her anger and she was too strong for that. It would also make it more difficult for Dick to admit he needed her help. From the time she'd been young, she had proudly put anger and desire aside for what she needed most and so today, as on so many other occasions, she was prepared to play her part. "I don't suppose you can tell me where you are?" she asked, knowing he couldn't.

"Nope." His wife had every reason to be angry with him for not calling her back, but she seemed to be acting conciliatory today. Ordinarily, he would be suspicious of her motives. Today, for reasons he did not fully understand, he wanted to believe the best. "I'm sorry I couldn't call you earlier," he said.

"I understand. You probably couldn't tell me what was going to happen, anyway."

"Afraid not."

"So where are you then?" It was her duty to be concerned.

Here it comes, he thought. She's not going to let go. Well, he wasn't about to play her game. "I want you to stay in California with the girls until this is over."

"I certainly have no interest in joining you in your shelter— wherever the hell it is," she said, already regretting her instinctive expression of exasperation and disappointment with a husband who could not hear his wife's concern, who only heard a nag, and would only make it harder for her to do what she increasingly realized in her heart she must.

Her words made him happy again—he wouldn't have to bother with her nagging at Mount Weather—but for a small feeling creeping up on him that Pat sounded different today, a change that he translated and rearranged until it became a fear that she might have less patience next time for taking the stage, and playing her role, when he needed a wife at his side. Or she might not insist that he press on, the next time he needed to prove his anger and frustration by threatening to quit. "This is no place for women—no high heels allowed here, that's one thing," he said. After a pause he added, in a low voice, "It could use your decorator's touch."

Was he saying there was work for her there, maybe even, in his own way, that he might need her there—or that she was forbidden to go? "I'll never catch up on answering my letters if I don't get back soon," she said.

The trick was to keep her in California but not preclude the possibility of her joining him under any circumstances. He had opened the door a crack and that was enough. "Now, about San Clemente—"

"I don't see why I can't go back and stay in the White House." Wherever the shelter was, it would probably be easier to get there from Washington, in case he changed his mind.

"It should be obvious," he said, suspicious she was testing to see if he'd say something about her safety she could interpret as caring for her welfare. She was always looking for a sign and, despite his instinctive concern for her, something kept him from giving in to her demands to show it. How could she really think he would let any harm come to her? Could she believe he was that callous? The idea almost made him want to hurt her.

She felt a weightlessness in her stomach and for a second she could see Quinn pointing to the *Los Angeles Times* graphic. "You mean Washington could be...?" She couldn't say it. Oh, of course he didn't mean it that way. She smoothed her skirt, confident she'd already answered her own unfinished question. By now she should know better than to take Dick seriously. He was just pretending there was a danger.

"Anything's possible," he said, calculating how his words would upset her—and keep her away.

Yes, she was sure now. He wanted her to believe he was keeping her in California out of concern for her safety, not to close on the house. She was so silly to ever question his motives. "I toured a civil defense shelter in Los Angeles on Monday." You see, Dick, I'm doing my part, being a good First Lady.

"I approved it." Maybe he shouldn't have told her but he enjoyed bringing her down a notch.

"What do you mean?"

"The civil defense office out there called and said your secretary had contacted them." Just as he had hoped, her visit had received national coverage and helped reinforce the White House line that the nation was prepared.

"They didn't tell me that." Next time she spoke with Quinn she would give him a piece of her mind for going behind her back.

"Why should they?" Usually the White House set up the First Lady's appearances, so it made sense the CD office in Los Angeles would call for clearance, but they had agreed to let Pat think she was doing it all on her own. "Anyway, I said it was okay."

"That was very kind of you." He wouldn't let her do anything on her own; she was always being watched and managed.

"It shows there's plenty you can do out there till this is over. You can help calm down the women." He doubted anyone could accomplish that.

"I've been saying there's nothing for them to worry about." She didn't see why she needed to be in Los Angeles to do that. "If the shelter where you are really has a television studio, I could give interviews from there. I could show our family is pulling together, just like everyone else's."

Finch and Klein would love that, though it wouldn't be a complete family picture without Julie and Tricia. "What about the girls? It would be very educational for them here."

"Oh, honey, I don't think a shelter—well, I guess I really don't know anything about what's it like where you are. Helene thinks you're at a big hotel in the mountains."

"Ha! It's no hotel. I'll just say this, it's very utilitarian here. Only the basics."

"It doesn't sound like a proper place for children then."

"Would Helene mind taking care of them?"

"I'm sure she'd be more than happy to."

Once again he felt her suckering him into something he hadn't wanted. It was part of some grand equation with her. To retain the flexibility to put her aside and go on with his business when he had no need for her, but have her act happy to play her part when her name was called—for that he sometimes needed to throw her a bone. "If you really think you can do more good from here, then I'll make the arrangements to fly you out."

"I'm ready to do whatever you need me for, Dick," she said and held the line as he conferred with someone in his office. When he came back on the phone he said it was possible for a Military Air Transport Service plane to take her back early that afternoon, if she could be ready. She would stay overnight at Camp David and in the morning a helicopter would bring her to the shelter where he was staying, which she realized now couldn't be too far from Washington. In the meantime, she could get in touch with J.B. to have whatever clothes and other items she wanted sent separately. She tried to ask why she couldn't stay in the White House overnight; he just said that's how it had to be.

"I want to emphasize, it isn't anything like what you're used to."

"I'm sure I've experienced worse."

As a miner's daughter, he knew she had. "All right, Buddy. I'll see you tomorrow then. Give my love to the girls." He hung up the phone and made a note on his yellow pad to order the immediate installation at Mount Weather of the same windows and curtains he'd seen at the shelter under the Greenbrier.

"Helene! Helene!" she said with girlish excitement, skipping down the stairs in her billowing teal blue sailor dress. "I'm going!" The two friends embraced and twirled around.

"The shelter, you're going to the shelter?"

"I can't wait to see what it's like!"

—————∞∞∞—————

Gray automobile taillights extend as far as the camera can see along the interstate highway, four usually lonely lanes divided by a verdant median recently cut through farm and forest. Now families are packing up the Ford, the Chevy, and the Chrysler with whatever will fit, taking the mementos they can't bear to leave behind, and doing their best to decide what they'll need for the uncertain future ahead. There they go, the television announcer says. See how everyone's waving so long from the windows? Those who have decided to stay behind, mom and dad and the kids on the lawn—there they are, waving back, brave smiles, ready to move into the basement bomb shelter when word comes over the transistor radio junior is keeping to his ear, listening for the sharp warning he's heard so many times in practice drills. When they hear that familiar sound, everyone will take shelter immediately. There's the freeway again. It looks like these folks may have a long wait in front of them. Luckily, most have come prepared, with games for the kids and plenty of healthy snacks, the announcer says. Before too long they'll arrive at their journey's end a safe distance from the city, the lively metropolis having become a dangerous bull's-eye for the Communist's missiles and bombers, to wait out the tense international crisis with friends or relatives in the safety and tranquility of small-town U.S.A. Others are looking a little uncertain of their ultimate destination—but there's mom to the rescue again! She's got a map from the friendly Mobil station unfolded across her lap and is already hard at work plotting a course for this village or that. Wherever their path takes them,

she's sure little Bobby and Mary will quickly make new friends.
Maybe an older couple with an extra room or two in their house
will welcome them to stay until they can safely return home. Of
course we know mom needn't worry her pretty little head. In small
communities all across the land, everyone is pitching in and work-
ing together to put out the welcome mat for their fellow citizens
from the big city over the hill. At a time like this everyone knows
to put aside their differences, the city slicker with his shiny shoes
and the farm hand with a long blade of wheat in his mouth shaking
hands across the pasture fence.

"After we talked on the phone, I called the networks right
away," press secretary Herb Klein said, pointing at the Philco
Briefcase Portable television that had been set up on a table in
the small room adjacent to the president's Mount Weather office.
"Said we needed something to balance the news programs—
something that certainly didn't include footage of the looting
or men pushing stalled cars off highway embankments, which
just, you know, causes more panic. They were hesitant at first,
so I used your idea—said they'd have to consider how we'd react
when their broadcast licenses came up for renewal."

"You've got to be tough with them, Herb—I know you don't
always agree with that." Nixon stood beside Klein, facing the TV,
one arm resting atop a tall green file cabinet. "Let's see if we can
get that TV special made into a newsreel for the movie theaters."

"Already working on it, boss," Klein said, putting a hand
through his thick black hair.

"The looting should die down once the National Guard
soldiers take up their positions. Do we know who the trouble
makers are?" From what the president had seen on television
earlier in the day, most of the rioters were Negroes. "It's a race
thing, isn't it?"

"Been pretty much confined to areas where people may not
have cars or enough money to get a train out of town." Klein

paused as a woman on the television asked her friend why the air smelled so fresh in the powder room. *Was the window open? It isn't an open window, her friend answered, it's Glade air freshener.* "Had to send Marjorie and the kids to stay with relatives out of town," Klein said. "Wanted to let you know."

What did Herb want to hear? That there was no need for precautions? Aides and advisers at Mount Weather had been telling him stories of family members leaving Washington since he'd arrived at the shelter and most of the time he did not know how to answer. If he were honest, he would say he felt the same way those leaving for safer ground must feel, uprooted and afraid of being unable to return. Despite the reams of information he received he didn't know much more than they whether Washington would continue its slow Southern ways or was destined to become a once-upon-a-time capital for tomorrow's children to imagine. His comfort was knowing that he and Khrushchev had the ability to prevent war; his fear was understanding that either of them might make a fatal mistake. If he were honest he would also tell Herb that he found it all too easy to imagine the unimaginable. So instead, he said, "You know how these fellows in the press think, Herb. All they care about is getting their story, and the more sensational the better."

Klein looked at the linoleum for a moment, then said, "Reporters aren't as compliant as they used to be. The designers of this place didn't understand that, I suppose." Klein patted the concrete wall. "What the heck? Did they really think a president could go on indefinitely pretending he was at the White House and the press would go along?"

They would if they cared about the country. But Herb used to be one of them, a reporter first at the *Alhambra Post-Advocate*, then the *San Diego Union*, and that's where his loyalties remained. "They've got a similar set up in the television studio at the Greenbrier shelter—have you seen it?—a big backdrop of the

Capitol on the wall to make it look like the members are still on the Hill."

Klein unbuttoned his dark blue suit jacket and put his hands in his pants pockets. "Didn't even know the congressional shelter existed till a few days ago—this one either. Guess they couldn't imagine how things would play out in an actual emergency when they were designing these places."

"So, the White House reporters, they're—where are they now?"

"Newspoint—another government shelter, here in Virginia. We've got direct communications between High Point and Newspoint, and with Low Point. The rest of the press that wants to cover this, they're out there."

"Where's that?" Nixon asked, idly turning the combination lock on the top drawer of the file cabinet to appear casual.

"Low Point's in Battle Creek, Michigan."

They watched the TV in silence as a man standing in front of a school adjusted his fedora before leaning toward the reporter's big microphone. "Attendance is off about 50 percent, I'd say."

"You said it clearly on the videotape we put out—the networks keep replaying it—you're in a secure facility so you can command the armed forces more effectively and will soon be back at the White House. Things would be much worse if you hadn't put that statement out," Klein said. "On TV, folks see you're in charge."

He knew what Herb was thinking and didn't like it. "You think something more from the president would help, is that it?"

"Yes, sir."

"Even though my announcement was on TV just the other day?"

"If you answered some of the reporters' questions—I'm doing what I can, but if you talk with them it'll give the impression that—"

"That the situation is under control, no need to panic—that kind of thing?"

"Would sure help. We're getting calls from local officials from all over saying we have to do something to keep people off the roads."

"From the looks of it," he said, twisting his body like a golfer teeing off, swinging his arm toward the television, "it's too late for that."

"Would still help." Klein glanced at the Simplex clock on the wall above the television. Just then, the long hand jumped forward three minutes, to 1:12 p.m. "We could call a press conference for this evening. The reporters at Newspoint and Low Point would be able to see and hear you and you'd be able to see them and hear their questions. We have the capability to send your image out live to all three networks. No president's ever done that before, given a live press conference, but it would be the quickest thing."

Klein looked at him with desperate eyes he'd never seen before. Usually he resisted Herb's urgings to hold more press conferences, which had always been done with cameras there to make a recording that the White House could clean up before sending it to the networks. "I'd need time to get ready, Herb. Those bastards'll try to lynch me with their shit-ass questions."

During the '60 campaign he had tried to make it seem as though he liked the press boys, share a drink and make a dirty joke, keep the temper down. Near the end of the race he discovered that some of the reporters—Bill Lawrence from the *New York Times* was one of the worst—had formed a conspiracy to try and get Kennedy elected and told Herb that was it, no more press conferences. It wasn't till the campaign was over that Bryce Harlow, who wrote speeches for Ike, told him just how right he'd been about Lawrence. At a campaign stop in Nashville, Lawrence had boasted to Harlow about how he'd lied in a story he'd just filed on the airport rally there. The local police chief told Lawrence that 15,000 had come out to see Nixon and that 5,000 had attended a rally earlier at the airport for Kennedy. Lawrence said flat out—with pride—that he'd filed a story reporting that 10,000 came to see Nixon and 15,000 had come to see Kennedy.

"If I do it," he told Klein, "I don't want Lawrence there. Make sure he's still on our blacklist." Lawrence left the *Times* after the election to become White House correspondent for A.B.C. and had asked repeatedly for a one-on-one interview. He'd made Herb turn down each request. No matter how many re-takes they gave him to get his answers right, Lawrence would find a way to make him look like an ass.

Even without Lawrence present, he didn't like the idea of holding a press conference. He could probably come up with 150 or 200 questions they might throw at him and each had to be written out, along with some different ways he could go at it, and he'd have to choose the best answer. The study and memorizing would take a full day or more and he already had dozens of calls lined up with heads of state angry he hadn't taken their views into consideration before making his decision on Cuba, instead of just sending an envoy to brief them on what they could see by then was a fait accompli; telephone calls with congressional leaders; a briefing on the presentation that had been made to the United Nations; and a call to Pawley to thank him for finally agreeing to back Kohly to head the new Cuban government.

On the television, a housewife, head in hands, was looking at an empty grocery-store shelf, scheming, the announcer said, about how she would whip up a scrumptious dinner for her family without most of the items on the crumpled shopping list clutched to her chest.

"You can't talk sense to females like that," he said, nodding at the screen.

"It's mostly the men we want to reach anyway," Klein said. "They listen to the news and make the decisions, so I would say you should direct your answers to the average man, just the way you always do."

"Yeah, I'll think about it. Now put it on A.B.C. See if Lawrence is on."

"FKR and Luna regiments are prepared to fire. Nuclear warheads have been mated," Pliyev told Castro as the two men entered the bunker. "Americans will be here soon."

"The imperialists have decided upon this war—a war of choice, not of necessity—and they must suffer its consequences," Castro said, walking backwards to face Pliyev. "The responsibility is theirs, for the harm they have inflicted with their bombs, their illegal occupation of Guantanamo, and their many acts of sabotage."

Inside the control room, the map they had used earlier in the day was still on the table. Pliyev pointed to a spot in western Cuba, near Mariel. "FKR regiment here has forty warheads with eight launchers. This is where we believe Americans will try to come ashore. Other FKR regiment is here, with an equal number of warheads and launchers," the general said, pointing to Mayari´, near the eastern end of the island. "These weapons will deliver blow to U.S. naval base at Guantanamo."

Castro studied the map. He pointed to a small town near Guantanamo and said, "My brother is at Mayari´ now. Raúl is very interested in watching as the illegal American occupation there is eliminated."

"These are three locations of Luna regiments," Pliyev said, pointing to two places near Havana and another near Remedios. "Each has four warheads."

Castro lit a long cigar and breathed deeply. "Why did you bring so many fewer Lunas than you have FKRs?"

"This is because our FKRs are much more powerful."

"I would like to join with the people of La Panchita," Castro said, pointing to a town on the northern coast, "and together climb to the hills where we would have a good view and together there we can celebrate our great victory over the Yankees."

"It will be something to witness. How high is it, this place? Do you know?"

"Not precisely. More than 100 meters, perhaps."

Pliyev used the slide rule holding down a corner of the map to calculate his answer. "Horizon will be about 40 kilometers away, so you would see most of action from there. You would see many mushroom clouds rising into sky."

"And underneath each will be thousands of dead American soldiers," Castro said, relishing the thought.

"Smaller clouds, by shore, will be from Lunas. These weapons are well designed for neutralizing concentrations of landing troops. Far off shore, closer to horizon, you would see mushroom clouds from FKRs. You've probably seen picture of cloud rising above Hiroshima when Americans dropped atomic bomb. Well, each FKR will produce comparable explosion. We will target FKRs at their aircraft carriers and other large ships."

Castro rolled his cigar between two fingers. "At the same time the Americans will feel our sting at home," he said. "I have sent agents to the United States and they are under orders to plant bombs that will give Nixon more regrets about his perfidy."

"What are their targets?"

"The Empire State Building, the symbol of capitalist machismo—we will blow a big hole in the middle and, with luck, the top will fall over. That will be a great sight. Another team has been sent to the Pentagon to show we can land a blow to the heart of the American military machine and we hope to kill many of the generals responsible for attacking our revolution."

"Excellent."

"We will also plant a bomb in the Holland Tunnel—this will disrupt all transportation in New York City—and another bomb at the New York Federal Reserve Bank Building to upset the capitalist banking system. We will attack American decadence too. Theatres in New York will explode with our bombs. This is Operation Boomerang and agents began infiltrating into the Unites States at the beginning of this year, so they are well prepared. We have also placed agents throughout Latin America with *Defensa Activa Revolucionaria* to bomb American installations and corporations in these countries. When we are done, the world will see that what Chairman Mao said was true, that America is a paper tiger."

"Let us hope so. Khrushchev has made comment on Mao's words. He told me, 'this paper tiger has nuclear teeth'."

"You do not think that Nikita is afraid of the Americans, do you?"

"Premier does not want nuclear war. He understands that neither side would win."

Castro's puzzlement was palpable. "And yet he has given you orders to use tactical nuclear weapons against the Americans, has he not?"

"Yes, but these are very small compared to warheads atop our missiles. FKRs and Lunas are nothing more than very powerful artillery. They are to be used on battlefield, not to destroy enemy's cities, so they can safely be used without risking nuclear war. Obviously, Nikita believes this or he would not have given me orders he has."

An aide handed the general a note.

"What does it say?" Castro asked.

"It is good that we received our final orders from Moscow. Americans have bombed our communications ship, moored offshore. We are on our own now."

Secretary McCloy crossed the president's office with his customary long strides and sat next to the CIA director, the two older men facing the young commander in chief across his Special Facility desk. "Mr. President," McCloy said, putting one hand on Dulles's back, leaving the director to juggle a fat handful of the secretary's chocolate drops, "when Allie here called me this morning to say his staff believed that air inspection wouldn't be a viable option, he mentioned seeking some further clarification, if I'm not mistaken."

President Nixon looked at Dulles, silently asking if the director had once again betrayed him.

"Ah, that's right," Dulles said, adjusting his rimless glasses below his high forehead. "I broadened the net a bit, if you will. On something this important I believe in getting confirmation from as many sources as possible."

This time he'd stop him, goddamn it, Nixon thought. He leaned across his desk toward Dulles, scowling. "They all agree," he nearly shouted, "that's what you said—Allie called me, Jack, and gave me the disappointing news." He turned with a smile to McCloy, who looked to Dulles with an arched left eyebrow.

Dulles stroked his mustache, as white as the remaining hair on his head, then said, "That's precisely what I was going to say, Jack—I'm afraid they're unanimous that it's a no-go, for just the reasons we discussed."

McCloy paused for a moment, then said, "From what I'm hearing, I suspect the matter is settled, then," McCloy said, eyes downturned. "That's extremely unfortunate."

"Yeah, so I want our cable back to Moscow to lay down a hard line," Nixon said to the two men, though really speaking only to McCloy now. "I want to be clear about this thing, we're putting all our chips on the table. That's one thing," he said, ticking it off with a press of right index finger against left. "Second, we aren't folding." The right index finger now ticked the left middle. "We respond with force at the first sign of Soviet aggression. The greatest mistake we can make, and you know I feel this strongly, gentlemen, is to show the slightest sign of weakness. Now, Jack, I want you to start drafting something as soon as we're done here."

"I have some of my people here with me, so—"

"I'll have Rose Mary find you an office with a typewriter and then we'll meet again when you have something for me."

"I wonder if I might offer a suggestion, first," Dulles said.

President Nixon, confident now the director would follow their plan, watched Dulles draw on his pipe and wondered if it was helping Allie to keep from grinning. "What's that?"

Turning to McCloy, Dulles said, "The president told me, of course, about the compound nature of your initial negotiation proposal, if I may put it that way."

"Yup, yup. A promise of Cuban sovereignty and an offer to dismantle the Jupiters."

"I've been wondering if the Soviets might just agree to a peaceful conclusion to this affair—no retaliation in Berlin or Turkey, nothing of that sort—if we simply offer to dismantle the Jupiters in Turkey in the months after we've occupied Cuba."

"Absolutely not," Nixon said, playing the part as he and Dulles had rehearsed it. "I won't be a party to appeasement—which is exactly what that would be. We'd be buying their cooperation—and who's to say they'd live up to the bargain? Khrushchev promised to send his transport ships and subs back to port, but there's been no change in course."

"I can see how that would be a legitimate concern, Mr. President," McCloy said. "In any event," he added, turning to Dulles, "I'm afraid the Soviets will insist we also allow Castro to stay in power."

"Perhaps it's the spy in me, Mr. President, but what if we were to limit knowledge of the arrangement to just those who needed to know?"

"Well..." The president leaned his chair back and slowly released the air from his cheeks, as he'd seen de Gaulle do. "I'm against it on principle, I want that to be clear. But if the two of you are convinced this is something we ought to try, because, you see, I respect your thoughts on this thing, well... What do you think, Jack?"

"I'm skeptical, I must say. But I imagine there'd be no harm in putting the offer out."

"I feel it is our obligation to explore every avenue that increases the chance we'll be able to bring this dreadful episode to a peaceful conclusion," Dulles said.

"I'd have to agree with that," McCloy said.

"I'll say this, Jack. In our cable back to Moscow I want it to be clear," Nixon said, making a horizontal underscore in the air with his finger, "that if Khrushchev rejects this offer, and chooses force instead, there'll be hell to pay."

"Yes, sir," McCloy said, looking blankly at the United States flag.

"Good. Now how long—in your estimate—how long before we'd get a reply?"

"If it goes out by noon, say, it'll be received 12 hours later. Then, of course, they'd have to chew over their response," McCloy said. "Add another 12 hours to transmit it to Washington, so I wouldn't expect we would see anything come in before Thursday evening or maybe early Friday. That'll be cutting it mighty close."

McCloy excused himself to provide his staff guidance to begin crafting a draft cable back to Moscow. In the lull, Dulles stretched out his legs, revealing his slippered feet. There was nothing the president could think of or wanted to say about the director's gout; it was personal and of no interest. Instead, he now anticipated asking McCloy about the secretary's televised confrontation the day before at the United Nations Security Council with the Soviet ambassador to the U.N., Valerian Zorin.

Nixon began before McCloy could sit again. "On the U.N. thing, Jack, I wanted to say this, you really gave Zorin the one-two."

"You got a chance to see it then on the television set?" McCloy asked.

"Yes, and I'll tell you this: Zorin had a lot of nerve saying we made up the whole missile thing just to have an excuse to attack Cuba." His eyes moved back and forth between Dulles and McCloy as he made a mental check of his own facial expressions. He didn't want anything to give away what he was thinking. Thoughts of Operation Northwoods must have been going through Allie's mind now as well. The director returned a look of uncertainty about whether to tell Jack of the work of which they were both so proud.

"Missiles in Cuba? If we'd tried to fabricate something like that to use as a pretext for invasion, nobody would have believed it," Dulles said.

"Certainly not without the U-2 surveillance photos your agency took to prove the missiles were real," McCloy said.

Nixon cut in before Allie could offer the CIA's expertise with doctored photography, which the director had put to good use in preparing for the Northwoods plot. "Who else has come out against us at the U.N., Jack, I mean outside the Communist block? Is it the Swedes? Well, who cares? Who else?"

"Other than the Security Council, there's—"

"If they're not in the Security Council, who gives a rat's ass? Taiwan hasn't given us any trouble on the Council, have they?"

"No, sir."

"I didn't think so. Now I talked to de Gaulle yesterday and he couldn't have been more supportive. You talked to him, too, didn't you, Jack?"

"Yes, sir. He was very encouraging."

"Well, I'll say this, if we have de Gaulle in our corner, there can't be any doubt whatsoever that we're on the right path here. Isn't that right?"

"Absolutely," Dulles said, gesturing with his pipe for emphasis.

"On the other hand, if some of these pipsqueak countries at the U.N. want to run around yapping at our feet, what the hell. I mean, let them, you know? I don't give a shit," he said, emphasizing his last words to come across as angry. Jack was one of those eastern Republicans who trusted in institutions like the U.N. to solve disputes among nations and so he'd frozen him out of most policy-making in his administration, relying instead on his national security adviser and the rest of the national security staff in the White House. He wasn't willing to go so far as some of his Republican friends, who urged him to pull out of the U.N. altogether; neither was he ready to entrust the national security of the United States to a bunch of foreigners.

"Some of them secretly support us, but they can't come out publicly and say it," Dulles said.

"Some of our Latin American friends fall into that category," McCloy said. "They have to say, for public consumption, that the U.S. invasion is heavy handed."

"Those are the worst kind," Nixon said. "They don't have the balls—they have a good word for it that they use down there, cojones, so let me just put it this way—they don't have the cojones to stand up for what they believe in. I say they'll get theirs when the time is right."

"You'll see how loud they scream when we cut their aid," Dulles said, tugging on the vest under his suit-jacket.

"That's the first thing I'm going to do when this is all over. The U.N., well, I guess it was the right place to show that we'd caught the Soviets red handed. But we're in this fight by ourselves. Hell, you boys know that as well as anyone."

McCloy stretched out his legs and, rubbing one shin against the other, began a long explanation of the important role the U.N. could play in mediating disputes between nations. It was the old Rockefeller Republican line that he figured he would have to listen to when he nominated Jack to head the State Department. McCloy spiced up the telling with his own tortured anecdotes that almost made him worth listening to, until you felt you couldn't listen any longer.

Dulles was apparently equally eager to change the subject. "Now that you're back from New York, Jack, will you be a prisoner here of the president's for the duration?"

The president didn't like the way Allie made it sound as if he were the warden of this basalt cave. "Jack's free, as he has been, to come and go as he pleases, same as you, Allie. But if either of you feel the need for a more solid roof over your head"—he shot them both a quick smile—"there's room available at the inn," he said. "The rules here say the private rooms are for the president, the Cabinet, and Supreme Court. But since so few of them are here, I can have them put you in private rooms. Now for me, well they goddamn forced me to come out here—you know that."

"At our current state of military readiness, my understanding was that the White House Evacuation Plan would kick in straight off," Dulles said.

"Nope, I nixed the WHEP—wanted to keep it low key, you see, just move the critical White House staff out here—Finch, Radford, a few others." To avoid stirring up attention, he had ordered the selected evacuees to be driven to Mount Weather at staggered times, overriding long-standing evacuation protocol calling for them to gather at pre-designated assembly points in Washington where helicopters could land. "I called Lyndon and the other leaders in the Congress about this too. Since most of the members are in their districts, it was just a precaution, but I said there's no need for them to relocate to their alternate site under the Greenbrier. And I brought up the issue of avoiding unnecessary panic."

McCloy asked, "Just out of curiosity, were any of the members asking to go to the Greenbrier?"

"McCormick made the point that he didn't think members who had family in Washington would agree to go to the congressional shelter, anyway. Of course, there are only a couple people on the Hill who even know about the facility out there at this point."

"I know some members of the Cabinet felt the same way about coming here—they just wouldn't leave their family behind," McCloy said, pulling himself up straight. "I certainly put myself in that camp. We understand the risk we're taking but we feel that at a time like this it's important to stay together as a family and since High Point can't accommodate families, we're putting our faith in God."

Was McCloy trying to run him down for not having Pat and the girls with him? He had made the right decision, then, in agreeing to let Pat come and needed to let Jack know the news. First, he wanted to show an accommodating side. "We've made all the arrangements, should you change your mind, to move your dependents out of the city, that goes for all the Cabinet members and of course for you, Allie, and some of the others. But I understand your decision, Jack, and I know you share those feelings," he said, nodding in Dulles's direction. "Some of the Cabinet members have phoned me and said they'll fly out here at a moment's notice for a Cabinet meeting and are staying near a telephone but they can't move here and leave their families behind," he said, gesturing toward McCloy. "Since I haven't implemented the WHEP, as I said, that's fine. They have that luxury. Well, I don't." I'm the prisoner here, he wanted to say.

"Thank you for the offer, Mr. President," Dulles said. "It's a very impressive facility, if I do say. Very impressive."

"It can't compare with your new setup at Langley," Nixon said, adjusting the penholder on his desk. The location Allie handpicked for the CIA's headquarters, which had been the director's baby from the time he started pushing the idea almost 10 years ago, until the official opening in May, was miles from Washington and surrounded by forests. Most people at Allie's level in government tried to flaunt the rule that all new head-quarters had to be at least twenty miles from the Zero Milestone on the Ellipse to survive a nuclear attack on Washington and built their new offices as close to the White House as possible. The new CIA building was neither far enough from Washington to escape harm, nor close enough for immediate access to the White House.

"It isn't often a man gets to design his own office," Dulles said. "Come on out when this business is over and we'll give you a proper show."

"It's a deal," the president said, looking away from Dulles, bored already at the prospect. He fingered the knot of his black-and-blue-striped tie, checking that it was centered against the top button of his starched white shirt. "I haven't told you fellows this yet, but I persuaded Pat to join me here—she arrives tomorrow morning—though she would have preferred to extend her vacation in California."

"Will Julie and Tricia also be coming?" Dulles asked.

"Uh, no. Pat wanted to bring them, but I said—because I've seen what it's like here and she hasn't—so I said, absolutely not."

"I hope I'm not speaking out of turn, Mr. President, but some of the men—I'm sure you're aware of this—but some of the men are convinced this isn't going to end well," McCloy said.

Dulles showed a sly smile, with one eyebrow raised to ask permission. Nixon nodded and Dulles said to McCloy, "They don't know about the president's Madman Theory, Jack." The director briefly explained the idea. "Of course, Khrushchev isn't the only one who knows now that the president is working from Mount Weather and whatnot so, of course, they too have been fooled into thinking the U.S. is gearing up for the End of Days."

McCloy looked as though he'd become lost in a thicket. When his eyes focused again he said, "There's one part of this I'm not quite sure I understand."

"Yeah," Nixon said, bracing himself.

"Putting myself in Khrushchev's shoes for a moment, I might think to myself, well, if President Nixon is crazy enough to start World War III, I should strike first so I can eliminate as much of the U.S. nuclear capability as possible before the onslaught comes," McCloy said, rubbing his palms along his thighs.

The movie images from the president's Pentagon briefing on the power of nuclear weapons were playing now behind McCloy as the secretary elaborated Khrushchev's case. Like lost memories, they came back for an instant and were gone again. And when they were gone his conviction returned.

"This is how Khrushchev sees it," the president told McCloy. "However many of our bombers and planes he can destroy in a first strike, it won't be enough to save the Soviet Union from a devastating blow in return. The better bet for Khrushchev is to just send his angry cable and lodge his protest at the U.N., without doing anything that might push me over the edge."

"Never has so much ridden on one man's bet," McCloy said, shaking his head. "If it did come to that—God help us—I'm afraid I would not be strong enough to bear the burden that would be upon your shoulders, Mr. President," McCloy said, hands folded in prayer.

"Do you mean, to pull the trigger?" Dulles asked with a shudder of head and shoulders. "I know I couldn't," he added, drawing again on his pipe.

Nixon adopted an impassive expression to look for them and feel for himself like he'd have the guts McCloy and Dulles lacked, wondering if a person would truly have to be mad to order a full-scale nuclear war, or if that would come later, when millions lay dead.

For now, the president chose an indirect play to win the sympathy of his colleagues and appear selfless. "You know who it would be toughest on, don't you? I've been thinking a lot about this since coming out here and you shouldn't be concerned about me. It would be those boys in the planes, the bomber pilots. And those poor fellows down in those silos we have now, and in the submarines. They're the ones who'll have to push the button to let the bombs fly. They'll have to live with that awful realization for the rest of their lives."

"Good point," McCloy said. "Though I understand the pilots of the planes that dropped the atom bombs on Japan are quite proud of their role in ending the war, to this day."

"They're the real heroes," Nixon said. "They actually saved tens of thousands of American lives. Hell, they might have shipped me over there to help with the invasion of Japan, since I was already stationed in the Pacific. That was clearly a case where dropping the bomb was the right thing to do."

"The only way you could live with yourself, I would think, would be knowing your action was the single way to prevent a larger catastrophe," Dulles said.

Nixon didn't know if Dulles was referring to the pilots and missile silo operators, or the president; he preferred to think it was about himself. "The only circumstances in which any president would use nuclear weapons, of course, would be if the Communists used them first," Nixon said. "Except to defend Berlin, of course, and in a few other circumstances where we just don't have the conventional forces to match the Soviets. But in that case we're talking about those small A-bombs we have in the field. Those are a different matter."

"The tactical nuclear weapons," Dulles said.

"Yeah, and those aren't an issue with the Cuba situation," Nixon added.

"That's right. Arthur Lundahl—you both know Arthur from his many briefings—it was his group that first spotted the missiles, you know—well, he and I were discussing the most recent intelligence on this on the flight out here. Now that we're on the subject, I'd like to bring him in for a second—the man's a walking encyclopedia," Dulles said, referring to the head of the CIA's National Photographic Interpretation Center and the foremost expert on interpreting pictures from the U-2 spy plane.

Dulles returned with Lundahl, talking to him quietly as they walked to the president's desk.

"Mr. President, Secretary McCloy," Lundahl said, standing at the side of the president's desk. "The Soviets have a variety of tactical nuclear weapons. Two that are representative are the FKR, with a range of 110 miles." Lundahl noticed the yardstick he'd left on the easel with the map of Cuba after an earlier briefing and decided to demonstrate the FKR's range. Choosing a hypothetical launch point at the center of the island, he positioned the yardstick's other end on Florida, illustrating how the weapon could reach much of the waters between the United States and Cuba. "The FKRs can carry a fourteen-kiloton warhead."

"That's about the size of the A-bombs we dropped on Japan—just to put that in context," McCloy said, looking up at Lundahl.

"That's right, Mr. Secretary. I know you were closely involved in those events."

"Just an advisory role," McCloy said. "But please go on."

"The other weapon I was going to mention has a smaller yield. That's the FROG, short for Free Rocket Over Ground. The Soviets call them Lunas. Range is twenty miles," he said, moving his finger down the ruler to a spot on the Cuban shore, "with a two-kiloton warhead. As the director has mentioned, we've seen no evidence of either Lunas or FKRs in Cuba," Lundahl said.

"Do our troops coming ashore have these kinds of things?" Nixon asked, looking to Dulles, who remained standing.

"Tom Gates says they're not—that they're not needed," Dulles answered. "All our intelligence confirms that the Soviet technicians in Cuba didn't come prepared to put up much of a fight. We can assume they didn't think they'd be found out, much less that they'd be fending off an American invasion. The Soviets are there to get their long-range ballistic missiles—the MRBMs and IRBMs—all set up. That's the one bit of good news in this whole damn mess."

"All right, now look here," Nixon said. "I want you to keep a close eye out, Lundahl. If you spot any of those damned things, I want to know right away."

———— ∞ ————

After a long discussion into the early hours of the morning, with many side meetings and adjournments, the Presidium agreed to send a cable to Pliyev rescinding his authority to defend the revolution with Lunas and FKRs. "It is categorically confirmed," they wrote, "that it is forbidden to use nuclear weapons from missiles, FKRs, and Lunas, without approval from Moscow. Confirm receipt."

Chapter 11

Thursday, October 25, 1962

ITTING A CUSHION AWAY from her husband on the leather couch in the vestibule of the three-story building deep inside the Blue Ridge Mountains, Pat could see down the long corridor to the front door, where two Navy ensigns stood guard. She absentmindedly rubbed her fingers against her watch, sensing it would become the only way to know the difference here between night and day. That most important distinction had apparently already slipped from her husband's grasp, judging from the bags under his bloodshot eyes, his pale skin, and his haggard look. She stole a glance at him again—he looked worse than she'd ever seen him—and decided to keep her concern to herself, rather than get off on the wrong foot.

"When you get settled they'll give you a tour," the president told his wife, hoping to get this greeting over with as quickly as possible and return to work. "It's something to see," he said in a flat voice. "All right?" She had that look he had seen many times, her special mixture of exasperation and acceptance. He thought he also detected the smallest bit of excitement. Pat was always ready for an adventure.

"This place could do with a woman's touch," she said, examining the government-issue furniture that seemed to resemble the type used to outfit the offices and antechambers of senior government officials.

"Feel free to order some new things."

"Well," she said with a sigh, "I have a lot of unpacking to do before I can even think about that. Since you wouldn't tell me how long we'd be staying here, I had to give Mr. West instructions to send quite a bit."

"Someone can do that for—"

"Oh, you know me, Dick, I'd rather do it myself."

"Our living quarters are actually quite nice, considering that—"

"That we're in a cave?"

He decided to show a big smile and give a short laugh, hoping it might be contagious. "Well, I meant compared to some of the quarters the others have to put up with here."

"I'll bet we have a better view from our window too," she said, smiling genuinely.

———⊗⊗⊗———

The trunks and suitcases sat open, each on its own stand, and there were neat stacks of wooden hangers on adjacent tables. The doors to two gray metal clothes lockers stood open, a small stool by one; her garment bags had been hung in one, Dick's in the other.

The two beds by the far wall were narrowly spaced and the sitting area to the right was just large enough to accommodate a single club chair.

Damn him, she thought, smiling, when she saw the window. He must have known. The snow-capped mountains beyond the pasture were higher than any in Virginia, the scene painted to look more like Mount Rainier, in Washington state, than the rolling Shenandoah hills outside. And yet the colors were a pleasant match with the royal blue curtains, set against off-white wallpaper with a repeating presidential-seal pattern.

The wall covering was heavy-handed. Still, for the little time she would be at the shelter, she could live with it. The beds were another matter, she thought, hand in front of her mouth.

No matter how hard Dick tried to be quiet when he got up in the middle of the night to work, she could almost never get back to sleep. When he'd started his habit of speaking notes into a Dictograph, she hadn't been able to put up with it any longer. At the White House their rooms adjoined across a hall, by the Yellow Room.

"Is everything satisfactory, ma'am?"

She didn't recognize the young woman, a brunette with fair skin, as one of the staff from the White House, the real White House. "Yes, thank you."

The young woman looked about the room. "Hasn't anyone unpacked your suitcases yet?"

The view from the window may not have been of Virginia, but this girl was, judging by her Southern accent. She wondered if she'd have time enough in the shelter to instruct her not to speak unnecessarily, as she'd done with the White House servants.

"What's your name, dear?"

"I'm Mary," she said, and curtsied.

"Mary, I don't suppose you know if there are any spare bedrooms?"

"We haven't never had so many beds made up before, never. Will there be someone coming who isn't on the list we got?"

"Check if there are any spare bedrooms, Mary. And that'll be all."

"Yes, ma'am."

"Wait, there's one other thing. I'd like to have a television."

"You won't get much of a signal in here. Only a few areas are set up for television, ma'am. They have a wire straight up to the top of the mountain where there's the biggest antenna you ever did see."

Pat sighed and asked, "And what areas might those be?"

"The president's office, the radio and television studio, and the War Room, I believe."

With Mary gone she took off her mink beret and white gloves before carefully unwrapping the tissue paper from the silver paperweight in the shape of a dog. As she held it in her hands she could see the disappointment on Dick's face the day he told her about King. Before leaving to fight overseas during the war, he'd given his dog to his parents. They felt the Irish setter needed a place to run free and had loaned him to a dairy farmer they knew. When Dick returned home from the Pacific he learned the farmer had given King to another family, which had since relocated. Dick hadn't been able to find them, or his dog.

All that was left was this paperweight he had given her as a gift in '39, knowing she loved the dog as much as he. He'd asked the jeweler in Los Angeles where he bought it to oxidize the silver, giving it the same red color as King's coat. She had always kept it by her bed, until they moved into the White House and she put the dog on his desk in the Oval Office one day when he was away, not long after the inauguration. There the figure glistened in the sunlight from the room's thick windowpanes. Here, under florescent tubes, it was a dull red.

Curled up on the bedspread, still in her pink silk A-line skirt and overblouse, she held the figure in both hands against her chest and heard Dick say again that coming here was only a precaution. Something about playing a role to fool Khrushchev. She didn't understand that part, but he refused to explain, something else she didn't need to know, he said. It didn't make sense, what little he told her, and she still couldn't stop thinking of those maps in Mr. Quinn's civil defense office in Los Angeles.

⎯⎯⎯∞∞∞⎯⎯⎯

"Special Facility construction was completed four years ago, ma'am," the Navy lieutenant said as the tram slowed to a stop.

That explained why everything here looked so modern. Of all the underground buildings she'd seen—they'd toured about a dozen, which was only about half the complex—the most impressive had been the War Room, where Navy officers sat in what looked like a theatre behind large desks with all kinds of space-age television screens with more buttons and dials and switches than they probably knew what to do with. All the men faced a wall with yet more TV screens, except these were much bigger than anything she'd ever imagined. They were more like glass movie screens and they showed maps and lots of numbers. The Iconorama, they called it. Luckily, the desks were on tiers at different heights, so the men could all get a good view. She knew the lines that went out in all directions from the North Pole were for longitude and that all the horizontal crossing lines were for latitude. She just smiled as they explained this. All over the maps were circles with numbers inside. There were even more numbers in rows and columns in different spots on the map and more on the wall to the right of one of the maps. They didn't tell her what those were for.

"What do the red lights on that map show?" she asked, pointing to a twelve-foot-tall wall map of the United States. "That's the Bomb Alarm System, Mrs. Nixon," an officer explained. "Those lights you see are connected to sensors on top of telephone poles in ninety-nine locations around the country. As soon as they detect the intense heat of a nuclear blast, a signal travels along the telephone wires and almost immediately the corresponding bulb on this map here will light up."

In the drawing she'd seen at Mr. Quinn's office, all the telephone poles had been snapped in two and she wondered if that would be a problem. "What will they think of next?" she said with a smile.

Riding to their next stop, the lieutenant pointed at the ceiling. "Overhead are iron bolts that go eight to ten feet into the rock—twenty-one thousand of them in all." Her guide was particularly proud of the building where he showed her the indoor driving range for golf enthusiasts. There were also machines men used to strengthen their muscles, Ping-Pong tables, and other diversions to take their minds off the grim surroundings. This was all after they toured the hospital and from there went to the cafeteria building, which looked large enough to hold most everyone at one time and where, she was told, the food was delicious. She said she was sure it was.

At the radio and television studio she could almost picture Dick sitting at the replica of his Oval Office desk. And the windows and curtains behind his desk, well, of course, none of it was real. They told her the studio set up was useful because it gave the people watching at home a familiar feeling that would set them at ease. Whatever he said here would zip right out to the broadcast networks and right into living rooms in all parts of the country, just like a long-distance phone call.

"I understand you get good television reception here."

A civilian technician showed her into a freestanding booth where one of the screens, set among dozens of buttons and levers, was tuned to A.B.C. White House correspondent Bill Lawrence was seated at a desk, the network news logo behind him on the wall to his right.

She looked up at the technician and asked, "Would it be a problem if I just sat here for a few minutes, alone?"

"Not at all, Mrs. Nixon."

Lawrence was narrating videotaped scenes of near panic as motorists formed long lines at gas stations and housewives mobbed grocery stores. "Scenes like these, filmed earlier today in Philadelphia, have been playing out all across our nation ever since the revelation that President Nixon had abandon... had left the White House for a secure government facility whose location is still very much a mystery to the American people, as well as to news reporters," Lawrence said.

Though she had begun following the news on television and in the newspapers while still at Helene's, seeing these reports now, after having toured much of Mount Weather, she began to wonder if she might have been too quick to dismiss the public frenzy as an overreaction. Unlike the inadequate civil defense preparations she'd seen in Los Angeles, and those she'd read about elsewhere, what she'd seen so far of the shelter made it clear that the government had, indeed, gone to extraordinary lengths to prepare for a nuclear war.

"This will be our last stop this afternoon," the lieutenant said, holding her hand as she stepped off the tram. "Usually the V.I.P.s I escort say they've seen enough after the first one or two buildings. You're the first to take the entire tour. I imagine you're pretty tired by now."

"Oh, no," she said, smiling, as he opened the large steel door for her. "I've got plenty of energy and I'm enjoying it immensely."

"This is one of the dormitories, Mrs. Nixon." The room was filled with metal bunk beds with four-rung ladders at the foot. Below each mattress was one metal drawer. Sets of two metal lockers stood between every two bunks. The bed frames and the lockers were painted a dull yellow.

"How many people can Mount Weather accommodate?"

"We're currently set up for a maximum of one thousand— there are three other dormitories like this one, one of which is for the females. There are also private rooms for members of the Cabinet, the Supreme Court, and the president, of course."

"You didn't mention the vice president."

"The president and the vice president are not permitted to shelter in the same location. But Mr. and Mrs. Lodge could occupy the president's quarters, should President Nixon be relocated to

Looking Glass—that's the president's national emergency air-borne command post—or to the national emergency command post afloat—that would be a ship, ma'am."

"So this isn't the only place where the president can go in a, well"—she might as well call it what it was, she decided—"in a war?"

"Yes, ma'am. There are contingencies where it might not be safe for the president to be on land anymore. And he'd be able to give his orders to the military commanders from either of those emergency command posts."

If there was still more she didn't know about the government's preparations for going to war with the Soviets, and as they left the dormitory now she suspected there most likely was quite a bit, she'd seen and heard enough to know she owed Helene an apology for denying what now seemed so undeniable.

On her tour she had passed the many people who staffed Mount Weather, seeing them in every tunnel and building, a small army preparing for the worst. At least some of them were lucky enough to work outside, where they could breathe.

She had toured the top of the mountain, a pedestrian encampment much like those she had seen in her visits to military bases, except everywhere you looked here you could see large antennas that she was told convey vital information to and from the communications equipment inside the mountain. A small village unto itself, it had bus service between buildings that housed a cafeteria serving three meals a day, a convenience store, sleeping facilities, and offices, all of it encircled by the forest that spread over and across the rolling mountainside to the horizon. When she said she missed the fresh air, her escort agreed to try and make arrangements for her to be escorted out each morning for a walk. Barring unforeseen circumstances, he said. The outdoor facility could support the underground installation indefinitely, he added. "Until the balloon goes up, that is."

"You send up some type of weather balloon? Is that necessary?"

"Actually, this *was* initially a weather facility. They sent up weather balloons from here."

"It is awfully windy," she said, one hand holding her head to keep her light blue scarf from blowing off. "Is that why they call it Mount Weather?"

"Yes, ma'am. I was using military slang, again, I guess. These days, the balloon going up refers to the initiation of hostilities with the enemy. At that point the Protected Facility—that's what we call the underground area—becomes self-sufficient."

"Do you worry that it might come to that, lieutenant?" She hoped he would say no, though she was prepared now for the truth.

"We train for it every day and pray every night that it'll never come. We've never been as close as we are now to making the facility self-sufficient, Mrs. Nixon. I mean, this is the first time the president has come here, other than for an exercise."

"Tonight I'll also say a prayer," she said, letting him help her back into the Chevy Carryall truck, where she was glad to be protected from the wind. "Now you were saying something about a balloon, I believe."

"Oh, yes," the lieutenant said, looking at her in the rear view mirror. "When the balloon goes up, everyone up here goes inside and we button-up. The air will last for 72 hours."

She couldn't tell whether her escort thought that would be sufficient time. From the little she had learned about nuclear fallout at the civil defense office in Los Angeles, she wasn't sure if 72 hours would be long enough for the air to be safe again.

"After that," the lieutenant added, "we have to open the vents."

———⊗∞⊗———

"Excuse me, ma'am."

The First Lady looked up from her correspondence and wondered how long Mary had been standing there, by the table where she was working.

"There is another room available. Shall I pack your things?" Mary must have sensed her surprise, quickly adding, "Many of the people on our list have not checked in yet."

"Do you know who?"

"Members of the president's Cabinet, ma'am, and the Supreme Court."

She took a long drag on her cigarette. When she spoke, white tobacco smoke enveloped her words. "That's odd."

"I know I wouldn't if I was them."

"Don't be silly." Silly that Mary could imagine herself one of them, yes, but she meant that of course Mary would come, in that absurd circumstance. "It's their responsibility to come."

"I just couldn't leave my family behind like that."

"Whatever do you mean?"

Mary stammered and said, "The president's family, of course, the president can bring his—"

"And the others?"

"None of the men are permitted to bring their families, ma'am," Mary said, without any visible emotion.

The long corridors had felt almost empty of civilian life, no children, of course, but almost no women either, except for a few in uniform, and few men in business suits. They must all be in another building, she'd figured, and was thinking it would be grand to get all the wives together for a social. "No other wives?"

"No, ma'am."

Mary's attitude toward working—maybe she slept here, too—at a shelter standing ready to close its vents to the radioactive fallout of nuclear war did not seem that different from the young lieutenant's; each was content to let their responsibilities distract them from their reality.

"That will be all for now, Mary," she said, thinking with another draw on her cigarette that the girl's matter-of-fact attitude disguised an inner strength she hadn't given her credit for. Her White House secretary, Isabelle Shelton, hadn't shown the same resolve. Stopping briefly at the White House before boarding a helicopter for the trip to Mount Weather—defying Dick's directions so she could retrieve King from the Oval Office herself—she tried to convince Isabelle to come with her. Isabelle believed the danger was real and wanted to stay with her family. "I might never see them again," Isabelle had yelled over the roar of the helicopter and through her tears before turning and running back to the East Wing.

She was sure the no-families policy had been dreamed up by some bureaucrat without the foresight to imagine the consequences of asking government officials to leave their loved ones behind. Until now, she hadn't known what her own job might be at Mount Weather; perhaps, if she presented the facts to Dick, she could persuade him to have the rule changed.

———∞∞———

"Well, I got the grand tour this afternoon and..."

She waited to see if her husband would look up from his dinner when she failed to go on. He concentrated on his hamburger.

She tried to think of something shocking she could say to get his attention. Maybe her escort had shown her something she wasn't supposed to see, though she didn't know what that would be. Even if there was something she wasn't supposed to know, bringing it up now, she thought, watching him drink his pineapple milkshake from a straw, would only make him mad, and what would that accomplish?

The small, featureless room, furnished only with the small mahogany table where they ate, remained quiet until, finally, she said, "I talked to the girls."

He put his glass down on the edge of the placemat and looked at her from across the table. "How are they?"

She told him how Julie and Tricia had been crying when she left and about the uncertainty she'd seen in their faces. He promised to call them; it wouldn't be long now and they'd all be together again, he'd say. They talked of the Drowns, as well, and Dick said Jack had been a great help to him before retuning to California Wednesday to be with Helene and Maureen.

She reached across the table to steady his glass. "Do you remember when we were still living in California, not long after we were married, and the four of us went to that nightclub in Los Angeles?" They were all sitting around a little table, everyone laughing, unaware the world was on the verge of war. "What was the name of that place?"

"It was called Earl Carroll's," he said, spreading his hands apart in front of him to frame the big sign out front. "I remember we hesitated about the expense." The thought brought a smile to his face. "That $2.50 cover charge seemed awfully stiff. Times sure do change."

She was surprised Dick could remember the club's name—they hadn't talked about that place in 20 years—but she was sure he'd remember their slogan, "Through these doors pass the most beautiful girls in the world," and everything else about that night. "Do you remember the garters? What about all those girls' legs sticking up in the air? How many garters did you throw to win that bottle of champagne—can you remember?"

At first she thought his face was red with embarrassment. When he turned back to his dinner she saw his furrowed brow, eyebrows brought close, and cursed herself.

After a long silence he spoke without looking up from his plate. "I told you I didn't want to talk about that." How could she not know that men didn't want to talk with their wives about half-naked women?

She was sure he'd never told her not to bring up the subject. "I'm sorry, Dick, I just forgot," she said, putting her hand on his fist. She wanted to tell him more about her trip to Los Angeles and the house in San Clemente, she even wanted to try telling him about Quinn getting into hot water for saying the president might order stores to close down.

When he pulled his hand back she said, "The girls can't wait to come home."

"I hope you didn't tell them where we—"

"Of course I didn't."

"I don't want them to know where we are—under any circumstances. They're too young to understand, both of them," he said.

His eyes seemed softer now.

"By the way, Jack Sherwood said you asked about being able to walk outside. I gave the okay, but you'll have to stay in the secure area," he said, making a mental note to call Jack right away to say it was alright. "Maybe I'll join you up there," he said, trying an appeasing smile.

She knew from his expression that he wouldn't. "That would be lovely. But if you have any free time maybe you should use it to get some rest. You sure look like you could use it."

He quickly drank the rest of his coffee and got up from the table. "I've got to get back to work."

The CIA director pushed across the president's desk an aerial photo taken on a low-level reconnaissance flight over Cuba the day before. "Now compare that to this earlier photo," Dulles said, sliding over another picture. "This is the same area, San Diego de los Baños, but the second photograph was taken before the bombing began."

Lundahl, sitting to Dulles's right, handed the president a large magnifying glass. "The San Diego de los Baños site had eight missiles," said Lundahl. Though a few years younger than the president, his hair had already gone gray. "There's no evidence of the missiles now."

As the president looked through the magnifying glass, moving it up and down, Dulles reached into a crowded pocket of his Harris tweed jacket, pulling out a pipe, a tobacco pouch and his engraved lighter. When Nixon looked up, the older man's craggy face stared at him from behind a plume of fragrant white smoke the color of the director's hair.

"LeMay and his boys really chewed the place up," Dulles said. "I'm sure ol' Curtis is singing a happy tune," he added with a ho-ho laugh and a twinkle in his eye. As Allie concluded his analysis of the damage done on the ground by the air strikes against Cuba, the director seemed to rise above the fray; describing events unparalleled and dangerous, he bowed but briefly to the gravity of war initiated against the nation's nuclear enemy, sounding almost jolly at the military success.

It was the first time Nixon could remember hearing Dulles laugh since the missiles had been discovered. He shared Dulles's sense of relief that the bombing was effective, if not the director's high spirits—not with air losses continuing to be high, and not until the Marines landed tomorrow and were able to overcome Soviet and Cuban defenses, and only after he was convinced Khrushchev would not retaliate in Berlin or Turkey.

"What about their defenses against invasion, Allie? Have the reconnaissance flights picked up anything new on that?"

Dulles used both arms to lift himself out of his chair. Standing by the map of Cuba, he pointed to the primary landing site for the Marines on the northern coast, twelve miles east of Havana. "They're continuing to work on beach fortifications here and elsewhere—every time we hit them from the air they rebuild—but it doesn't stack up to much."

"You mean because—"

"With the overwhelming manpower and materiel superiority of the U.S. Navy that we're about to put ashore, Mr. President, it'll be a cakewalk."

After telling Lundahl he needed to speak to the president alone, Dulles eased himself back into his chair and described a small fight that had broken out among members of the '61 CIA-sponsored invasion force that had landed at Trinidad. After more than a year in the mountains, they were now staging sabotage missions against transportation sites and government buildings. Some of the men had gotten into a brawl over who would head the new government in Havana. Many of them supported Kohly; others were bitterly opposed. "Pawley has a lot of influence with the men and once he stands up for Kohly there won't be any more of that nastiness," Dulles told the president. "I talked to Pawley today and I believe we'll soon get what we're looking for."

"Shit—this better not...are they going to be able to all fight on the same side tomorrow? If they screw up we'll lose the advantage of attacking from two sides."

"Pawley's working on it now. I'll check in with him when we're through and get back to you."

"What is it, Bob?" he asked as Finch handed him a note. He unfolded it and read the answer for himself. The Soviet submarines and transport ships the Navy was tracking had all turned around in the Caribbean and were heading home. He stood and clapped his hands. "Hooray! They're running away," he said shaking hands with Dulles and Finch.

"So, it seems the promise Khrushchev made in his cable was sincere after all," Dulles said, returning a vigorous handshake, without fully sharing the president's excitement. "I suspect there was a delay getting the order out from Moscow to those boats, then additional time was required for our surveillance to pick up the movements."

Still wanting to celebrate, the president motioned toward the liquor decanters on a side table and offered Dulles and Finch a drink. There were no takers, so he decided to abstain as well, for now, returning to his seat behind his desk. "We're not out of the woods completely, boys, remember that. I was going to ask you about Berlin. What are your fellows picking up?"

"All quiet on the Eastern front, Mr. President," Dulles said, unfolding a pocketknife he kept in his suit and using it to scrape the bowl of his London-made Peterson Premier pipe.

"That's because I scared the shit out of Khrushchev by going underground and moving to DEFCON 2," he told Dulles. He could feel Khrushchev's respect for his toughness and could almost hear the cursing in Moscow. "Of course I'm not going to do anything, you know that."

"Naturally."

"But he doesn't know that—that's the thing. Nixon's got his finger on the nuclear button and there's no telling what he might do. He's a *madman*." You see, Allie? I'm just as smart as any of your spy agency's spooks.

"Very crafty of you indeed, sir. And very sane, I might add. There's a real logic to it."

If the logic held, the Soviets would continue to be cowed into sitting on their hands and watching Cuba go down the toilet out of fear of a final vaporizing flash of blinding light that would bring their great Communist experiment to a sudden, blazing conclusion. The president smiled to himself: That crazy Richard Nixon, he's capable of anything.

It was after three o'clock in the afternoon when Dulles left. With a small opening in his schedule before he was to talk by phone with Secretary Gates, he called for Sherwood. After five days underground he was beginning to lose his usually keen sense of when he needed to get outside if he was to go for a walk while there was still at least some sun left in the sky. Maybe being at a high altitude would buy him some more daylight.

Riding in the electric cart he almost immediately fell asleep reading. He woke quickly, though, and for a few minutes resumed reviewing a report from the American embassy in Moscow. Ambassador Beam, who had been warning of an almost certain Soviet military response to the American invasion, was now guardedly optimistic the Kremlin would agree to forego any military action in exchange for the U.S. dismantling the Jupiters. He was asleep again when he felt Sherwood's hand on his shoulder.

"Going up," Sherwood said, holding the elevator door. "Lingerie on five."

"Yeah, stop there. I'll get something for my dead-ass wife," he said, laughing. Over the years that Sherwood had been assigned to protect him, starting when he was vice president, the agent had heard the joke plenty of times about the man who makes love to his wife four times in a day and through the night. In the morning, when she's finally had enough, the man calls her a dead-ass. By now, it was enough just to repeat the punch line.

The water fountain he was looking for was by the door and, leaning over, he swallowed the Benzedrine pill he'd been hiding in his left hand. Outside, he estimated the temperature to be in the low thirties and there was a strong wind. He pulled down on his fedora and tightened the charcoal-colored wool scarf inside the double-breasted cashmere coat he brought today. Short, open pipes sprouted from the neatly mowed grass on both sides of the service road and under a looming billboard from the Office of Civil Defense and Mobilization, with its reminder of where workers should turn their radio dial in the event of an emergency. He drew in a deep breath that smelled of pine.

This time he knew the sound was real. "I thought you took your walks in the mornings," he said.

"An informer told me you might be out here, so I thought I'd surprise you—and take you up on your offer of a walk together. Come on, there's something I want to show you," she said, taking his hand.

————— ✺ —————

The note in Khrushchev's trembling hand fluttered as though there was a breeze blowing through the meeting room. Bombs from American planes, it said, had destroyed the Soviet communications ship moored off Cuba that had been used to transmit messages between Moscow and Havana. The order to Pliyev rescinding his authority to use tactical nuclear weapons against American invaders may have come too late. It was impossible to know if it had been received.

This, Khrushchev decided, left him with two unpalatable choices. Preparing for the worst, and assuming the message had not been received, he could preempt an American attack on the Soviet Union, which he believed would follow the use of Lunas and FKRs against U.S. forces, by initiating a Soviet nuclear strike.

Whether or not the message had been received, he could, alternatively, try again to scare Nixon out of invading, escalating from the vague threats in his first cable to a limited military action, such as bombing American missiles in Turkey, or closing off American access to West Berlin. Even if he only stalled the Cuban invasion, it might buy enough time to find another way to deliver the Kremlin's orders to Pliyev.

Malinovsky stood to suggest a third alternative. He agreed wholeheartedly with the premier: The Americans were violating international law by destroying the missiles sent to protect Cuba, he told his colleagues, letting his voice show his anger at this injustice, and the Soviet Union had every right to destroy the similar American missiles threatening them from Turkey.

"Even imbecilic Nixon must accept this logic! And yet, we are peace-loving nation," he continued, now in a conciliatory tone. "And so, let us tell Nixon we are willing to make concession so we might avert escalation of present hostilities that could be difficult for either side to halt. We concede to allow capitalist's missiles to remain in Turkey. In exchange for this concession we will ask Nixon to make concession of his own," he said. "This is only fair. We will ask Nixon to cancel plans for invading Cuba."

"And what if Americans do not accept your proposal? I think they will toss it in trash can," Khrushchev said in wonderment at his defense minister's deaf political ear.

Malinovsky stopped short his explanation of how the Turkish missiles would be destroyed if Nixon refused the offer when a young military aide crossed the room toward Khrushchev with a large blue envelope for the premier. Inside was a cable from President Nixon.

There was silence in the Presidium meeting room as Khrushchev read the cable aloud. The Americans were offering a deal of their own. If the Soviet Union pledged to refrain from military action elsewhere in response to the invasion of Cuba, within six months time the Americans would dismantle their missiles in Turkey.

As he read these words, Khrushchev let go of any remaining hope of saving the Cuban revolution. As dear to his heart as the revolution was, he could not protect Castro, not with Nixon determined to match any military response with further escalation. In other circumstances he would have sneered at the prospect of sacrificing the revolution to eliminate the Turkish missiles, no matter that the threat from those weapons haunted him from the day they were announced. Today he had no choice.

"Americans," Malinovsky blurted out, "want us to accept takeover of Cuba as fait accompli. Are we ready to give up revolution this easily?"

"Loss of Cuba is *already* fait accompli," Khrushchev yelled, unsure if Malinovsky wanted to go to war to save Cuba. "It is our responsibility to people of our great nation to see to it that Caribbean affair ends in Caribbean, not with loss of U.S.S.R."

"And if General Pliyev did not receive orders, what will happen," Malinovsky asked, "when Americans see mushroom cloud rise from where troops used to stand and their aircraft carriers at bottom of sea? Perhaps then we will not need to concern ourselves any longer with Turkish missiles—because Americans will use them to retaliate and Moscow will be big pile of stinking rubble!"

Khrushchev had asked himself this question over and over and did not yet have a satisfactory answer, but as he talked through a problem an answer often came to him. It helped to talk while walking in the quiet woods. Instead, he paced the room. "To buy time we will make counteroffer."

"There is not time for more schemes, Mr. Premier."

"Shut up and listen. Nixon wants guarantee we will not retaliate with military in Berlin or Turkey. So we will demand same terms. Both sides agree not to extend fight beyond Caribbean. He cannot refuse."

"Americans will not suffer our use of nuclear weapons and lay down like tired dog."

"I think Americans do not know about Lunas and FKRs in Cuba. That is only reason they would not mention them in their cable."

"If United States has not seen them from their airplanes, they will soon find out what they have failed to observe and will respond—like mad dog."

Khrushchev turned and walked in the other direction, hands clenched behind his back, head down. "If they have pledged before world to act with restraint beyond Caribbean, this will be factor." It was a slim reed, he knew.

"If we have broken our pledge, why should Americans—"

"No—precise language of agreement states Soviet Union will not respond to American aggression against Cuba with use of military force beyond boundaries of Cuba. Of course, we cannot ask Cubans to surrender and lay down their arms. Americans will accept this."

"FKRs and Lunas are not Cuban weapons."

"All Soviet arms in Cuba are for defense of revolution. This is what we have always said."

"Premier is dreaming of solution. His dream will become nightmare and end with American missiles."

"Then shut your mouth and get on airplane right now for Havana and tell Pliyev yourself that he cannot use nuclear weapons."

Chapter 12

Friday, October 26, 1962

"SECRETARY McCLOY IS ON THE LINE for you from Washington," Rose Mary told the president, after apologizing for waking him. "He says it's urgent."

"Mr. President, the Soviets have put a message out over Radio Moscow that answers our cable."

Still in his pajamas, President Nixon sat up against the headboard. "Over the damn radio?"

"The quickest way to communicate. They've accepted, with a condition."

"Damn it, Jack, we have to deny we made the offer. The Jupiter deal only works if no one knows about it. Khrushchev is out of his damn mind to answer like that!"

"He didn't mention the Jupiters, sir, so we're okay on that front. But Soviet acceptance is contingent on our pledging to take no further hostile action subsequent to our invasion."

"Why the hell would we?"

"Precisely."

"Does he think I'm crazy?" Or maybe Khrushchev thinks I can't control the Pentagon, he thought. "Or that I'm not in charge? Bastard."

"The public nature of the Soviet response makes it difficult for us to decline the terms."

"Why the hell would we? We've eliminated the missiles, we, uh, land on the island and verify that we've got them all," Nixon said, smiling, "and we don't have to risk that the Soviets will escalate this damn thing. I know a thing or two about deal making and let me tell you, this is a hell of a deal."

"I suggest, sir, that we find a method to get our response to Moscow without going through normal channels, in the interest of time."

"We have too many damn radio stations—the Soviets can't be monitoring them all. Unless we issue—"

"A press release, yes, and ask that it be read on the air. Most undiplomatic, I must say, but I don't see any other alternative."

"All right, I want you to get to work on that so we can put it on the air right away."

———— ∞ ————

Breakfast provided his wife one of her few opportunities during the day to corner him and so he quickly ate his corned beef hash and poached eggs while he finished reading a memo from McCloy about Communist China's invasion into India. He was thinking of Prime Minister Nehru's gall in continuing to support China's membership in the United Nations, despite the fighting between the two countries, when almost against his own will he looked up to see if Pat would catch him before he finished his furtive meal. When he turned back to McCloy's memo it was Pat he was thinking of still and the walk they had taken yesterday. Reluctantly, he had accepted her hand and soon she was showing him a path through the woods. She pulled him along, trying to make him run, looking young again and in that moment Beam's report and all the rest of it receded and he could see, as he hadn't for many years, the woman he had fallen in love with in Whittier who wanted no more than to help him succeed.

He had justified each sacrifice she'd made in the name of his work. Only in this way had he been able to make it to the center of the arena, where he had always longed to be. He made it there because he had been willing to arrive alone, with Pat remaining in the stands with the others to cheer him on. She didn't understand her place there; without being called for she wanted to run out onto the field to back him up. On their walk in the woods he'd been no more able than he'd been in the past to explain. But at least he had tried.

They talked as well of how she had arranged a room for herself and he heard out her complaints about his use of the bedside Dictaphone, as though that were the only reason for their long-established routine of separate bedrooms. They said nothing of not having slept together as man and wife for probably a year now. Without the possibility of sex there was no point for him in putting up with her fussing about, filling the room with her silent discontent, and no point for her in being kept awake as he dictated his notes, and so he had agreed amicably to her arrangements.

"Good morning, Dick," Pat said, aligning the white linen napkin on her lap. When Mary told her the president had been spotted on his way to breakfast she had finished making up her hair and face and walked as quickly as she could to their dining room.

"Glad you could join me," he said, collecting his papers.

She wouldn't have much time so she dispensed with small talk, which Dick never liked, anyway. "There's something we didn't have time to talk about yesterday, before you had to go."

"All right."

"Is it really true that the men aren't allowed to bring their families to stay with them here?"

"Yeah." He put his briefcase in his lap, ready to leave.

"Why is that, do you think?" She hoped this would work better for now than telling him directly what she thought. He didn't always react well when she gave her opinions on such things.

The policy had been set during the prior administration, without his involvement, and he had never given it any thought until Sunday. Now that he was here, he could see the shelter had not been designed with families in mind. And yet it was apparent, with Mount Weather in active service for the first time, that the policy could be dangerously counterproductive. If it should ever be necessary for a future president to order a full-scale government evacuation so that vital operations might continue in the event Washington was destroyed, Mount Weather's no-family policy could sink the entire endeavor, should officials refuse to relocate to the shelter. Perhaps he'd have his staff do an analysis of the options for changing the policy as part of an overall review of Mount Weather operations after things got back to normal. For now, though, it was not something he needed to concern himself with and so he told Pat, "Arrangements can be made for Cabinet members' families to leave Washington, if that's what they want."

When he refused to answer her questions directly, she felt he was hiding something, probably because she had a good point to make. "But why can't they all be together here?"

This was becoming just the sort of conversation he dreaded, the kind of thing he tried to use as an example with Pat yesterday. Of course, she wouldn't understand why he would take issue with her questions now any more than she could fathom the examples he had used Thursday. "This isn't a social club, Buddy. There's important work that has to get done and families would just get in the way."

That comment, she knew, had been directed at her and she couldn't help herself. "Like me, you mean? I get in the way?"

"We discussed this yesterday," he said, standing now and ready for the opening that would let him escape, if he didn't just turn and leave as she was speaking.

Yesterday they had talked more directly than they had in years and Dick had seemed at one point to understand her desire to help, but it was clear now that nothing had changed. "That's what you said, that I get in your way."

"I said 'sometimes.' But this has nothing to do with the shelter."

"You're right, I guess. I'm in your way no matter where we are," she said, watching Dick's gaze grow more distant with each word.

Talking with her was as pointless as sleeping in the same bed. If he wasn't so tired and could think more clearly, if he hadn't stayed in his office past midnight before dressing for bed and working there until four this morning, re-writing a statement to be released today explaining again why the partial government relocation was purely precautionary, fine tuning Bill Safire's attempts to find the best compromise between truth and reassurance, if his mind wasn't full of all that awaited him, maybe he could make some sense of what she was saying.

She watched him turn abruptly and leave.

"It proves what I've been saying all along—they've got no defense," the president said, releasing his fist at shoulder height and letting go with a half-speed, I've-been-out-there-on-the-field-roughing-it-up-with-the-other-boys-don't-forget air punch.

Dulles waited for the president to sit. "Blanda and Tittle are both great quarterbacks," Dulles said, sighing as he settled his large behind into the sofa opposite the president. He took a pair of slippers from his valise and began untying his shoes. "Hope you don't mind."

"This is how I see it," Nixon said, preoccupied with his favorite distraction until some word reached him on the progress of the invasion, now in its second hour. He leaned over the coffee table and began to draw a diagram of the teams on his yellow legal pad. He was thinking the CIA director wasn't a football fan and that he had to explain the intricacies of the game to him and that maybe if he did Dulles would develop more of an interest, when suddenly, feeling the excitement of a new idea, he looked from the pad to Dulles to the drop ceiling and back to his diagram, delighting at the thought, imagining himself telling Allie about it, wondering at the reaction and smiling to himself in anticipation. "Yelberton Abraham Tittle. If I had a Jew boy name like that, I'd sure as hell pass myself off as Y.A. Tittle, too."

"I didn't think people of the Jewish persuasion played much football."

"Most of the Jewish fellows don't have the guts for it," he said as he resumed drawing his diagram. He turned the pad around and pointed his pencil at Dulles, who leaned in for a closer look. "Here's my point. The Redskins' defense is—"

Dulles rose from his seat to greet Radford who brushed by the director's outstretched hand to face the president. Dulles didn't seem to have a clue; Nixon saw it plain as day.

"I was just handed this report," Radford said, holding out a sheaf of papers. "Between approximately 0830 and 0930 hours today the Soviets fired three tactical nuclear devices—most likely FKRs—at our carrier force off the coast of Cuba. The Enterprise, the Independence, the Essex and the Randolph have been lost, sir. In the same time frame Guantanamo was targeted with nuclear artillery, believed also to be FKRs. No damage assessment for the base is available at this time but we must assume the loss is complete or nearly complete. The 1st Marine Division and

2nd Marine Division coming ashore at Tarara were in or near the blast zone of two atomic devices, estimated at two-kilotons each—Luna class. Casualties are extensive. There have also been reports of atomic blasts at three airfields where paratroopers from the 82nd and 101st Airborne Divisions were being dropped. The SecDef and JCS are preparing a full presidential brief to commence at 1115 hours in the War Room."

Nixon squeezed the pencil in his fist, plunged the sharp graphite point into the leather upholstery, and lunged out of his seat for the tackle. Radford held him back by his arms as spit-mixed rage, learned from his father, rained on Dulles.

Just yesterday Dulles had assured him that Russian troops on the island were not equipped with tactical nuclear weapons, neither Lunas nor FKRs. The only nuclear weapons in Cuba were warheads for the missiles that could reach the U.S., and those that could be dropped from airplanes—missiles and planes destroyed in our bombing runs.

Safe in Radford's firm restraint he could see a fireball glowing within a great gray chimney of a cloud, billowing high up into the blue sky, first one then another, below each he saw heaving seas radiating for miles in bull's-eye circles. This time the movie was real.

The briefing began at 1125 hours when the Army Signal Agency successfully established phone-video communications with Site R.

"The targeting alternatives available to you, sir, are set forth as part of the Single Integrated Operational Plan." General Lemnitzer's husky voice boomed from the speakers. "Once you have provided your authorization the Joint Chiefs will designate the Alert Hour."

The president leaned toward the microphone on the large conference table. "I think we need to include here—for the record, you understand—non-nuclear options as well. And, of course, we will understand these do not constitute your recommendations, general. So if you wouldn't mind just going ahead and laying those all out for us, then."

Half of Lemnitzer's bright orange face was visible on the phone-television screen in the War Room. "As you know, Mr. President, it has been long-standing policy that an atomic attack upon the United States, or its military forces, will automatically trigger a U.S. atomic response."

"Now when you say automatic, what does that mean, exactly, general?"

"That the plan is fully implemented immediately upon your authorization."

"Which brings us back to the integrated plan—is that what you're saying?"

"Yes, sir. The Single Integrated Operational Plan for the optimum employment of the U.S. atomic delivery forces."

"The general's right, sir." On the television, Lemnitzer was looking to his left. The voice coming through the speaker over the Red Line Network from Site R's Alternate Joint War Room belonged to Defense Secretary Gates. "Under present circumstances, the department is standing by for your order to invoke SIOP-63."

The screen was blank for a moment. When the picture returned it held a black and white image of Gates staring directly into the camera. The defense secretary carefully explained how B-47 and B-52 bombers, Atlas and Titan missiles, and Polaris submarines had been readied and were awaiting the president's order to deliver their nuclear payloads against the Single Integrated Operational Plan's recently updated list for the new fiscal year of 3,742 pre-assigned targets—military bases, industrial centers, and cities in the Soviet Union, China, North Korea, and Eastern Europe, a full-scale retaliatory response using almost every strategic nuclear weapon in the United States arsenal to eliminate the Communist threat.

"In other words, we're gonna bomb the living shit out of 'em," LeMay said, his stark image flickering between black and white and color.

Despite the seventy miles that separated the nuclear war combat operations center inside Raven Rock mountain, by Waynesboro, Pennsylvania, and the alternative White House inside Mount Weather, the advanced teleconferencing system allowed the president not only to see the men in the Site R War Room. He could also understand what they were thinking.

There was nothing worse than a weak president, except a president whose weakness brought military defeat. It wasn't only the men at Site R who believed that. He had long held to the same belief. The Chiefs were thinking that if he'd approved their earlier plan for a preemptive response against the Soviets, our forces invading Cuba would not have been lost. He wasn't so sure. Short of dropping A-bombs on Cuba, the Russian soldiers there would still have defended themselves the only way they could, by hitting us with their nuclear-armed Lunas and FKRs.

And yet hitting first—why hadn't he seen it before?—would have made all the difference. You'd have been in the arena fighting with all you had. Then, if you'd gotten a bloody nose in Cuba, it would show 'em you're a man—pick yourself up and keep on fighting. There's honor in that. Instead, you allowed it to happen. You were weak. You put down your guard. You were goddamn soft—Richard Nixon, who knows better than any man how the soft always lose. Offering to trade the Jupiters for peace made you look soft, too, at least to Khrushchev—and a lot of good that did. And then he suckered you into publicly pledging to stop all hostilities with the invasion. He kicked the table leg then kicked it again. The other men sitting nearby looked at him, startled, some with fear in their eyes, before turning back to the screen or their papers.

"How long will it take you to get ramped up to implement the SIOP, General Lemnitzer?"

"We've begun clearing the civilian airspace and SAC has started scrambling its bombers—those that weren't already airborne, following standard operating procedure. The sooner you provide authorization, sir, the better. The danger in delay is what the Soviets might do in the interregnum."

"In Cuba?"

"No. Following your directive suspending Operation Scabbards there has been no evidence indicating additional Soviet aggression in that theatre."

"The SIOP decision is our priority now."

"Agreed, sir."

"The danger of delay, then, is what?"

"If I were in the Kremlin right now, Mr. President, I'd know what's about to come over the horizon and I'd want to get the drop on it."

"You're saying they could strike first?"

"Yes, sir."

"Wouldn't it take them some amount of time to ready their forces?"

"More time than we require, actually. That's right."

"Are there other preparations you can get started on in the meantime?"

"Yes, sir. And if we knew the Alert Hour in advance, SAC bombers could be scheduled to reach their positive control turn-around points in time to receive their go codes."

"What if the Alert Hour was tomorrow morning at seven o'clock?"

Lemnitzer, Gates and LeMay spoke into one another's ears, examined flight charts and looked at the thick watches on their wrists.

"0700 hours, yes, sir," Lemnitzer said.

"Put everything in place so you can implement the SIOP on my order," President Nixon said, staring into the space somewhere between Gates and Lemnitzer.

— ⚙ —

Six men in white shirts and narrow ties leaning over the circular conference table in the president's office cleared a space in the middle among the maps, charts, and emergency plans and a Signal Agency officer set down the secure phone. McCloy and Hall, recently arrived from Washington, discussed a draft declaration of war; Gates, who had flown to Mount Weather from Site R, talked with Radford about identifying and destroying Luna and FKR installations in Cuba.

President Nixon was in the sitting-area armchair he favored, a legal pad full of notes on his lap, the telephone at his ear, talking on an internal line with Finch. Bebe was on the couch nearby. Returning to his office from the War Room, the president had spent the last two hours meeting with members of his Cabinet and a few of the other administration officials arriving at Mount Weather and had spoken on the phone with those who'd traveled to the homes of friends and family in small towns and out-of-the-way cities. He talked with heads of state in European and Asian capitals and the vice president at the Camp David shelter. The White House switchboard tracked down and connected him with the congressional leadership, scattered about the nation, so he could seek their advice and tell them he was calling the House and Senate into emergency session at their shelter under the Greenbrier. He took and made calls to a few friends and some of the Republican Party's retired stalwarts, governors Stassen and Dewey and President Hoover among them; he even put in a call to Kennedy, who advised a tit-for-tat response with tactical nuclear weapons against Soviet ships in the Havana harbor and any concentrations of Soviet troops on the island.

"Who's going to give Ike his background briefing before I get on the phone with him, Bob? Is it Radford...? McCloy? Even better...yeah, go ahead and set up the call. No later than 3:45. And I don't want to be put on hold again, goddamn it. This time I want you to keep him waiting for a few minutes, then I'll come on the line." Bebe gave a thumbs-up.

His most stalwart supporters were expecting him to follow through on the plans and strategies and promises put in place during the Eisenhower years. We had committed ourselves as a nation to unleashing the full might of our arsenal in response to the Soviet Union's use of nuclear weapons. "There's no turning back now," Goldwater told him.

The phone was heavy in her hand and the line noisier than she anticipated. "I was looking forward to talking to the girls. I miss them so much. I wish they were here." She could see them sitting on the bedroom floor next to her now, playing one of their board games, laughing.

"If I had known you were going to call this morning, I wouldn't have—"

"There's no need to apologize, Helene. I'm sure they're having a good time at the park with Maureen. Tell them mommy called and sent her love."

"I will. Tricia's so adorable—she wanted to know if you left Checkers alone in the White House."

She let the dead air between them speak for itself.

"Buddy, are you still there? You don't understand. Dick's evacuation from Washington is all over the television now. I didn't tell them."

"Well, what's done is done. I don't know what you can tell her about the dog. They wouldn't let me bring her to the shelter."

"I'll think of something—I'll tell her there are lots of nice people taking good care of Checkers at the White House and you'll all be back home soon."

"We'd better be—I'll tell you that, kiddo."

"I'm sure you're eager to get back to Washington, but how's the hotel?"

"It isn't a hotel, but I can't say anything else." She wanted to tell Helene all about this place, from the little village on top of the mountain to the war room deep inside. "I'm under strict orders not to talk about it. But I'll tell you one thing. The women aren't—"

Once again, a man's voice from a loudspeaker outside her room issued some kind of order. These intrusions had started up after breakfast and she was beginning to find them quite annoying.

"I'm sorry, I didn't hear you, Buddy."

"I was saying women are only allowed to wear flat shoes."

"What kind of place would have a rule like that?"

Now an alarm was going off in the hallway again. She started to tell Helene she'd have to call her back, but as she spoke the noise seemed to pass by. She took a cigarette from the silver tray on the side table and held it between her lips for the blue flame from the matching lighter.

"How many other wives are there?" Helene's voice sounded far away.

"You won't believe this, but there aren't any. The men aren't allowed to bring them, or their children."

"They're expected to leave their families behind?"

"That's probably why most of them haven't come."

"I know you think this is all going to blow over, Buddy, but can't you see?"

Even with Helene, who she so wanted to buck up, it was hard to act optimistic, having seen the preparations being made at Mount Weather, knowing as well of the other facilities that had been constructed in an arc around Washington to keep the government operating after a nuclear war. All of it had convinced her that Dick's evacuation from Washington was much more than a political maneuver. She had been waiting to tell Helene and this was the time.

"I know."

"What?"

"I'm sorry I didn't take your concerns more seriously, Helene." Or Quinn's, she might have said. Or those of the families she heard about in California who obviously felt so afraid and powerless, not knowing if they should stay or flee, unsure whether the life they knew and the country they loved would survive. Awakened to the danger now, she too had that sense, when she wasn't able to turn her mind away, that the present moment might be the last.

She tried to explain it to Helene as best she could, without saying more than she was allowed about Mount Weather. They talked of precautions and safeguards, always returning to what was best for the children. Should Helene and Jack pack their car and leave Los Angeles? Where would they go? What about the rest of their families? Maybe they could organize a convoy. If they stayed, did any of the neighbors have a shelter?

"Jack said Dick told him to make advance arrangements with the best equipped shelter in the area to set aside room for the three of us, your girls, his brothers and his mother. Do you think that would be the Subway Building shelter?"

"Helene, do you know if Jack called Dick's brothers and mother to tell them about the arrangements?"

"I don't know, Buddy. I could ask. But I'm sure it's just Dick being caring and super cautious. From the charts in the newspaper, Los Angeles is actually one of the safer places to be."

She didn't know if Helene was trying to make her feel better now. "Then why are the roads crowded with people leaving?"

Helene hesitated. Finally she said, "You know how people always overact to things."

"Oh, Helene, I don't know what to think anymore."

The line was silent. Then Helene asked, "Is Dick getting enough rest?"

"Oh, dear, he looks awful. He's hardly slept at all since we got here."

"Hmmm."

"He's..."

"What?"

"Oh, I'm sure it's nothing."

"Make him get some rest."

"I will. I've seen him like this before." He'd gone without sleep for days during the Berlin crisis, too, and he'd pulled through that all right. "He's under a great deal of pressure, as you can imagine."

"I know what that means."

"I don't think he's overdoing it."

"Men do need a drink at times like these."

"I'm sure you're right."

"To calm his nerves."

"Do you think?"

"Well, keep an eye on him, Buddy."

"And you keep an eye on Jack."

"I think Jack's keeping an eye on the babysitter, if you know what I mean."

"Oh, you're such a—"

"Wait a second, Buddy... Jack's insisting there's something on the television I have to see. God, I've never seen him like this. Talk to you later, hon."

She tried to say good-bye, but it was too late. She lit another cigarette and picked up the phone again. "Mary, this is Mrs. Nixon. Bring me the bar menu, please."

Bob's voice came over the intercom on the side table to say
Eisenhower was on the line. Bob must have been standing by
Rose Mary at her desk, outside his office. "President Eisenhower
has been on hold for ten minutes now. Do you want me to keep
him a bit longer or—"

"Put him through, Bob. I think the old man got the point."

There were never many pleasantries when he talked to
Eisenhower and there were none today. The former president
launched right in, rambling regrets about the Soviet nuclear attack
and how history had taken a sharp turn for the worse. Making
Eisenhower wait this time seemed to have made a difference. As
they discussed the details of the attack on Guantanamo and U.S.
ships off Cuba it seemed to him that his predecessor sounded
more respectful than during earlier calls. The former president
sounded more sad than angry, almost as though he had been
expecting the attack. Eisenhower said the U.S. had gone the
extra mile by offering to dismantle the Jupiters and assured him
there was nothing more he could have done to prevent what happened, since there had been no intelligence indicating the Soviet
soldiers on the island had been equipped with tactical nuclear
weapons. They discussed the reasons why the U-2 spy planes
had not spotted the installations, agreeing that their small size
made them easy to camouflage and that the bombing runs had
made surveillance flights more difficult. Even if we had known
they were there, some would likely have survived, Eisenhower
told him. Nixon asked if Eisenhower believed the Soviet radio
message had been a trap to get the United States on record as
pledged to ending hostilities with the invasion. Eisenhower said
the Soviet's use of nuclear weapons changed everything, that the
world would not hold the U.S. to its pledge and that Khrushchev
was a fool not to know this.

Soon they were on to the question consuming the thoughts of all who were privy to the Soviet attack. Eisenhower reiterated his oft-stated belief that once a president committed to a military operation, he had no choice except to see it through and in war with the Soviets we always knew we'd have to use nuclear weapons. "It's just the thing I always feared on my watch and I made sure it never came to this," Eisenhower said. "Now you have the responsibility for the policy to carry out what Foster and I put in place to massively retaliate. We really left you no choice but the SIOP."

If he understood these convolutions, Eisenhower was telling him he'd failed in his most critical responsibility, where the former president had not. And it was as though Eisenhower was taking the decision about what to do next out of his hands, that Eisenhower and Foster had decided years ago, with nothing left for him now but to be a good boy and follow their script. Ike wouldn't live the rest of his life having given an order causing 100 million deaths, wouldn't suffer the poison and hatred that would follow all-out war. Nixon's the one they'll go after. And this time they won't settle until they have his head. He would stand in front of the cameras with Eisenhower at his side, the old man giving his full endorsement, and still the tough questions would be for him to answer. People are saying you overreacted, Mr. President. They're saying too many innocent lives were lost, that you could have ordered a more limited response. Eisenhower would explain how anything less than a full-scale retaliatory response would destroy the deterrent effect of our weapons, all but inviting another, more devastating nuclear attack from the Soviets or, someday, from Red China. The reporters would write the former president's words in their notebooks and in the next day's papers they'd once again give Nixon the shaft. Herb Block would draw him this time as—he didn't know what—a baby killer?

When he put down the phone, Bebe poured him more Scotch.

"Eisenhower says there's really no choice. I have to respond with the SIOP. You're not supposed to know about it, but what the hell. It's the military's plan for retaliation against the Communists, if they attack us—with their nuclear weapons. We hit them with everything we've got."

"Jesus."

"I want to spare the Poles."

"They love you there."

He looked over the order one last time for changing the military alert status and added his signature. "Here you go," he said handing it to Radford, standing by his chair. "Tell Gates I want everything kept tied down tight till he hears from me," he said, looking up. "I don't want LeMay, or anyone else, going off half-cocked till I give the word. Then they can go."

Radford said something and handed him back his yellow legal pad. The noise from the other side of the concrete-walled room made it difficult to hear. He saw Radford looking at Bebe and said, "It's okay, he's cleared."

"Sir, our forces have no experience with this—moving to DEFCON 1."

"Haven't trained for it. Is that it?" he asked, examining his hands.

"It puts us on a hair trigger, with a commensurate risk of accident or—"

He pounded the table with his fist. "Goddamn it, no accidents. That's an order."

When Radford had left he held up his glass for Bebe and thought again about Eisenhower's advice. If he didn't go along with Ike and the JCS, the Soviets would spread their sick ideology all through the Far East and Latin America, knowing the U.S. does not follow through on promises to defend its interests.

"I can't let that happen. I mean, I can't put our security at risk like that."

"By...?"

"Our base will hang with us on this one, Bebe. Don't you think?" He didn't want an answer and Bebe knew better than to respond. "The president didn't have any choice except to strike back with overwhelming force," he said, slapping fist against palm. "That'll be our line. Once the Russians crossed that threshold and started using nuclear weapons against us, who could say if they'd keep escalating. You never lose by being too tough."

"You've always won by being tough."

He used the legal pad in his lap for backing and signed the papers activating the White House Evacuation Plan and the Defense Department's Joint Emergency Evacuation Plan.

"This one is to activate the sites in the Federal Relocation Arc," Finch said, handing him another sheaf.

He just wasn't as sure what being too tough meant now that nuclear weapons were being used. Maybe dropping one big one is enough to go down as the toughest motherfucker ever. One H-bomb on Moscow could change the game completely, maybe scare Russia and China into some kind of peaceful cooperation agreement with the U.S. Or drop one of those small A-bombs, Hiroshima size, on Havana, like Kennedy said. It had always been easy for him to make these calculations. Now, nothing seemed to add up. He learned his lessons from history and here he sat with no history to read, with every parallel from the past ill-suited to the new world that dawned with the burning balls of light rising over Cuba this morning.

"Herb Klein will be here in a few minutes, Mr. President," Finch yelled above the din from the conference table, the telephone receiver to his chest. "We need to talk about when you'll go on television and he has a draft statement for you to look at that he's ready to put on the wire."

"So where the hell is Safire—do we know?"

Finch said a couple words into the phone and hung up. "Bill called in earlier—said he can't leave his wife."

"Damned newlyweds. All they wanna do is get laid."

"He's still at home, if you want to call him," Finch said, standing halfway between the conference table and the sitting area.

"Hell, it isn't like he can work from home. We're not gonna send a damn helicopter to pick up his copy."

"No, sir," Finch said, re-joining the men around the table.

"Safire was there in Moscow when I stood up to Khrushchev, before the election," he said to Bebe in a quieter voice. "But not now. Fuck him—I can write my own damn press release."

"You showed you were interested in peace when you were in Moscow."

"Hell, I still am—interested, I mean," he said, making notes to himself as he talked. "We offered Khrushchev a deal on this Cuba thing—I insisted on it. I said we had to do everything possible to work for a peaceful outcome." He never got the credit he deserved for his efforts to avoid war; shaving a little off the top for a bit more recognition was only fair. "Khrushchev wasn't interested in peace," Nixon said.

Bebe brought him the memos Finch had stacked in neat piles on his desk. He read some of them and made more notes on his pad. Instead of going down in the history books as one of the great presidents, he'd been set up to be reviled through the ages. A Quaker no less; mother wouldn't approve. He signed his initials and handed the paper to Bebe. "Give this to Bob."

For the first time he almost wished Kennedy had won the election. Yet he knew he was the one destined to be sitting in the president's chair when fate brought the world to the brink. This way his enemies would get their goddamn poetic justice.

"I'm the one who has to take the knocks when things go to hell. But I don't mind. I'm used to it."

"You never let crap like that get to you."

"Goddamn right." Otherwise he'd be a coward like McCloy and Hall over there, who were afraid to take risks. When the chips were down they became small men without balls who played it safe. "I never believed in taking the easy way out, you know that." Cowards were always trying to minimize their losses, politically and on the world stage. Instead they minimized their gains. The gutless leaders who played it safe were not the ones history honored. What more evidence did anyone need than Chamberlain's attempt to get his so-called peace in our time by appeasing the Nazis? Peace never comes cheap. "Sometimes you have to stand your goddamn ground," he said, again pounding his palm. You have to be ready to throw down all your chips. "No one will ever accuse Nixon of being gutless."

"No one ever could," Bebe said.

"You know what's tempting? To just say, 'the hell with it,' and throw in the towel." What point was there any more? His only choices were to become the madman he threatened to be or be vilified—maybe impeached—for leading the nation to a humiliating defeat, he thought, his hand covering his eyes.

If Pat had let him give in when all seemed lost during the Fund Crisis in '52, if she hadn't encouraged him to gamble everything to clear his name on that theatre stage in Los Angeles with her at his side, the empty seats in front and the nation at home, watching, he would have lost his place on Ike's ticket, received the blame for the inevitable Republican loss to follow, and never would have had a chance to become president. He showed them all that Nixon is not a quitter. At the same time he showed he could stand up to Eisenhower, to the extent any man could. The cards, letters, and phone calls that flooded in after he went off the air that night in Los Angeles left the general little choice ultimately but to keep Richard Nixon as his running mate, no matter how angry Ike might have been about having the decision taken out of his hands. Ever since that confrontation he had tiptoed politely around Eisenhower, agreeing without a word of dissent to take the low road politically so Eisenhower could stay above the fray.

Now, ten years later, the tables were turned and it was he, Richard Nixon, who had to decide whether to chart his own course—as Eisenhower had strangely advised him about his fate on the reelection ticket in '56, when any fool knew that as vice president he obviously wanted another four years in the White House—and reject the general's expectation that he would implement the SIOP, or once more do as he was told.

Finch left through the door to Rose Mary's office, returning a minute later with the Army major who carried the football. Nixon nodded to Bebe, who excused himself, and invited his chief of staff and the major to sit nearby on the couch. The officer put the satchel on the floor and removed a binder. "These are the Emergency Action Papers," Finch said, ash falling from the cigarette in his nervous hand. "Radford—he's been called to the War Room—Raddy said it was time to show them to you. I think maybe—I hope—maybe it won't be necessary to sign them."

Chapter 13

Friday, October 26, to Saturday, October 27, 1962

S HE WAITED UNTIL BEBE LEFT TO CRY. She cried so she didn't have to think, so she could feel angry that Dick had let this happen, so she could feel pity for the young men who had lost their lives doing what was right, so she could feel the burden Dick felt and she cried so she would not have to think about what might happen next. And then, for some of the same reasons, she stopped.

In the bathroom of the presidential suite she leaned close to the mirror and, with short strokes, guided the eyeliner pencil from the inner corner of one eye across the upper eyelid, precisely along the eyelash roots. Dick would immediately demand to know how she had found out. She'd say Helene had told her. She looked at her Hamilton white gold watch—it was eight thirty in the evening—and calculated a plausible time for their call, in case Dick asked. The Soviet nuclear attack against our poor soldiers and sailors must have been on the news not long after they talked. Helene would be hysterical, though surely not in front of the girls. The best thing would be to make sure the girls knew nothing about it. She'd tell Dick people were terribly afraid of what would happen next and were starting to panic, people like Helene and Jack. Dick, with his responsibilities, didn't have that luxury, so maybe he didn't understand.

Or maybe she should not let on that she knew at all.

Bebe had said the military men who were advising Dick had a good plan that would put an end to the fighting and were asking for his approval. There would be a war, but it would be short, shorter than any war in history. Bebe had said there would be many Communists killed. There was really not much danger to the U.S., he said. Dick had made sure to keep the country strong and now that was going to pay dividends.

Bebe mentioned that Dick had placed a long-distance phone call earlier this afternoon to Eisenhower. That was probably just a courtesy on Dick's part. If Dick had asked her, she'd have said, now that you're president, you don't ever have to talk to that man again and maybe she would remind him how the Eisenhowers had never shown any obligation to be polite to the second family. Sometimes it even seemed Dick looked up to the old man, even now that he'd won the office on his own, fair and square and without much help from Ike. When it came to foreign affairs, Dick still seemed to have a hard time making important decisions without consulting the former president. She didn't know how much he was still taking his lead from the general when the two of them talked. What she was sure of was that he would have to stand his ground with the former president eventually. Until then, he would not be a truly great president in his own right. He was capable of that, if he would trust his own instincts and be willing to make an important decision in world affairs without Eisenhower's blessing.

"Get Admiral Radford on the line, Rose Mary," the president said into the intercom on his desk. Watching the men talking around the table across the room he thought for a moment of his office in the White House, longing to return there while also realizing that his own decisions might make such a homecoming impossible. Depending upon the course he charted in the coming hours, the military-style construction of Mount Weather, and the similarly designed outposts built to ensure continuity of government in the aftermath of nuclear war, could be his home for the remainder of his time as president.

The first of the Emergency Action Papers the Army major had shown him this afternoon had been a proclamation declaring a national state of emergency. Like the others in the satchel it had been prepared in advance as part of Mobilization Plan C for the president's signature upon initiation of thermonuclear war. As he read the order that would suspend the writ of habeas corpus for 60 days he thought again of his predecessor of a century ago. Those who accused Lincoln of violating the constitution for abrogating that basic right of the accused didn't understand what a president might be required to do to keep the country together as its cities burned. If the Nixon haters said the same of him, he could at least take some pride in being compared with a giant.

Finch, his voice breaking, had directed his attention to the prepared public statement among the papers "to be used in the event of general war," Bob said. Above the line awaiting his signature it read, "I have also taken action for which the legal basis may be uncertain but which were required in my judgment, by the urgency of the situation. I am convinced that the Congress, had it been able to function, would immediately have made the authority for those actions specific." Whomever had written this, he thought, had a great deal of faith in the willingness of Congress to go along with the president, or—as Safire would say—chutzpah.

He had never seen the Emergency Action Papers before, though from the moment he'd been sworn in they'd always been at hand, carried, along with the SIOP, by the major sitting beside him who had opened the satchel, or one of the others who shared the duty. Some of the documents established emergency agencies—the

National Food Agency, the National Transport Agency, the National Housing Agency, and the Office of Censorship—with sweeping powers to set prices, seize property, and detain citizens. The Office of Civil and Defense Mobilization could command the "voluntary and involuntary services of all persons, except members of the armed forces, and move such persons to places where such services are needed." His signature on another document would order the Declaration of Independence and the Constitution removed from Washington. There were orders for increasing the size of the armed forces and for embargoing non-essential postal deliveries. To preserve "the public safety and order," a declaration of martial law had been prepared. Another assured "that commercial stocks in the hands of retailers will automatically be available to local governments to supplement local stockpiles." The latter was tantamount, it seemed to him, to ordering stores closed. Finally, a request to Congress asked for a declaration of war "to ratify my actions and thereby remove any doubt as to their legal basis."

Foster used to tell him that constraining Soviet aggression not only required the U.S. to prepare to fight a nuclear war; the U.S. must intend to follow through on its plans. If only he could talk it through with Foster, the two together now, after the first shot had been fired, when nothing was the same. Did he have a moral commitment, he would ask, to implement the SIOP, even if its real purpose was not to fight a war but to prevent one? Was there sense in following through on a bluff, if a bluff is what it had been? He looked at his hands, as though examining a hand of cards; it was up to him to decide if he would sweep the table with a royal flush, or fold.

Pulling a clean legal pad from a desk drawer, he made his preliminary notes: *The Decision. October 26, 1962. 8:10 p.m.,* he wrote. Under that: *Surrender or war* and on another line: *MORE CHOICES.* He underlined the capital letters twice.

"What if we start small?" he asked when Radford came on the line. "Some of the congressional leaders I've been talking to have been asking about this." There was no reason to discredit the idea by mentioning Kennedy's name.

"A response in kind?"

"What about that? Give back as good as we got. Some small A-bombs on Cuban targets—military targets."

"It's a high-risk strategy—you're aware of that, I'm sure, Mr. President—it risks all-out Soviet retaliation."

"But it isn't as high, I mean, not as high risk as shooting off everything we have."

"We leave ourselves open."

"Open to what comes next."

"Yes, sir. We run the risk that the Soviet Union will respond in force against U.S. targets."

"Yep, whereas—"

"Whereas the SIOP has been designed to minimize that risk."

"I see. But not totally, I mean it doesn't totally eliminate the risk."

"No, it doesn't. A limited number of Soviet nuclear forces could survive the attack and succeed in penetrating our defenses."

"On the other hand, if we have a limited response—play it out—would Khrushchev go to general war? Is that it?"

"His military may not give him any choice."

"I feel a bit that way myself, Raddy."

"The SIOP does provide you some flexibility, sir. These options are in your briefing book."

"The way I read it, the SIOP is designed for execution as a whole."

"That is correct. Notwithstanding that, some flexibility is built in to the plan by design and some is inherent in the mechanism for control of forces committed to the plan."

"Part of that doesn't apply here, am I right? I mean the part about executing the plan either in retaliation or as a preemptive strike. This isn't preemptive. Too late for that. So that part's moot."

"Yes, sir. But strikes can also be withheld against targets in any or all of the satellites, except for defensive targets."

"I was very warmly received in Poland, you know. Some of those same people who came out to greet me, they'll, well, they'll perish."

"It is possible for you to direct withholding strikes against all targets in the satellites, providing the commanders have sufficient notice in advance of E-Hour to alter their existing plans."

"I wouldn't think we'd have that much time."

"No, sir. We don't."

"So we have to include the Poles and all the rest who weren't involved in this Cuba situation."

"Due to the positive control we have over our nuclear bomber forces, you—"

"I can—"

"LeMay's bombers, SAC bombers, have orders to return to base unless they receive a positive coded message—their go codes—to proceed on to their targets."

"Turn back the ones going to Poland, save those folks and so forth. Not just them, of course, but is that it?"

"You may direct that attacks be withheld against any specific category of targets. For example, you may order that no direct attacks be made on cities."

"But the briefing materials say, as I read them, not to go that route."

"I believe it emphasizes that any decision you make to execute only a portion of the entire plan, which is designed for execution as a whole—that excluding categories of targets would run the risk that our unused forces do not survive and that the task essential to our national survival might not be fulfilled."

"So what you're saying is, this holding back on some of the SIOP targets—that involves the same kind of risk we run if we respond in kind, with one or two small ones, the kind they hit us with in Cuba?"

"In so far as both scenarios increase the likelihood that Soviet nuclear forces will successfully reach targets in the U.S., yes, sir."

"I take it, Raddy, that you don't believe Khrushchev will be scared off by a response in kind."

"The danger is that he won't, sir."

"If he thinks I won't stop there, with a single punch, that I'm going to hit him with every damn thing we have"—like some madman, he cursed to himself—"then he would have a good reason to hit us with everything he's got, cause if he waits he'll get knocked flat."

"You could say that, yes."

"That would be the same reasoning we're using. Use 'em or lose 'em."

<hr>

As soon as the telephone console light went out on the internal line to Radford, Rose Mary started across the room. Usually she talked to him through the intercom and he braced himself for more bad news.

She spoke in a low voice so the men still working at the other end of the room would not hear. "Pat is here," she said.

"Now?"

"I told her you were dealing with something very important, but she's very determined to see you."

He pulled back the white French cuff covering the gold face of his Waltham watch. He'd been on the phone with Radford for more than a half hour. "Tell her I can't see her now."

"Maybe it has something to do with the girls—she wouldn't say."

"Oh, for Christ's sake." He looked over Rose Mary's shoulder at the men at the table. "All right, but only for a few minutes. And tell them," he said with a nod of his head, "that I need to meet with someone alone."

Rose Mary smiled and gently squeezed his arm.

"Take them out through the other door, would you?"

When Rose Mary returned with the First Lady, the two were speaking seriously together, with none of the lighthearted banter they usually exchanged. The president opened a drawer in the bureau behind his desk, turning his back to the women and pretending to look for something in lieu of whatever the appropriate response might be.

Rose Mary touched the First Lady's forearm before turning to leave. "I appreciate your kind words, Pat."

He listened for Rose Mary's steps toward her office; when he judged her a few feet short of the door he turned to face his wife. "What a nice surprise," he said, without smiling.

She knew he didn't expect her to take his words at face value. Nor did he want her to respond to his irony, even with Rose gone. She knew what he was thinking and he knew her reaction; they didn't need to speak about it. Most times it was more comfortable this way for her as well. Not today.

"Like hell it is," she said.

He slammed his shoe against the tall leather back of his desk chair, sending it spinning.

"Is this about the girls?"

"No, they're fine." It took all her strength not to tell him how worried she was about them, and everyone else, to not cry again and to pretend, for now, that she was aware only of some incalculable risk of nuclear war, and that she knew nothing about what Bebe had described.

"Then sit for a minute so Rose doesn't think I threw you out, then get the hell out. I don't have time for you."

Hardly moving, she slowly lowered herself into one of the straight-back chairs against the wall, folding her hands in her lap.

Retrieving his chair, he didn't know whether he wanted to slap her or slink away—whatever would send her back to her room and abort the confrontation she seemed to want. "All right, you can go now. Tell Rose we had a nice chat and the President is holding up well," he said, looking at his papers.

"You look like you could use some sleep," she said. "Your eyes are puffy."

She must have barged in to his office to plead for him to let her go back to Washington, though he'd thought since yesterday that she had become more content here. If going back to Washington was out of the question before, it was impossible now. Or maybe she wanted to go to California to see the girls. "Go ahead and go to California—I think that's a great idea. Give the girls my love." He could be working now if she weren't here. It had been a mistake to bring her here in the first place.

She would rather be with her children now in California than here. Going there now, at such a dangerous time, was another matter and she was hurt that Dick would allow her to travel. "Tricia can't understand how you could leave Checkers alone in the White House."

The water glass he'd been holding a second before shattered against the hard wall. "Goddamn it!" He slammed his desk, again and again. "She knows"—slam—"we're"—slam—"not"—slam—"there?"

"The evacuation is all over the television, Dick. Helene said it was impossible to keep it a secret."

"Why don't they just turn the damn thing off? Now go on," he said, waiving his hand, "I have a call coming up and I can't have you here."

"Is it with Eisenhower? Well, you give *him* my love," she said, resisting the impulse to massage the back of her neck, afraid to show any sign of weakness.

Her smirk, so redundant with her sarcasm, angered him as much as her impudence. She wasn't the one who had to suck up to the old man for eight years—or ten, if he was being honest and counting the two years he'd been president.

"I know what you're thinking," she said. "Well, I had to put on a show too—every time I went to the White House or saw him in public. But you had it much worse. I guess you can just let it wash over you."

This was one thing they still had in common, he thought, trying not to let her dig get to him. "He's a great man, Buddy, and we wouldn't be where we are today without him."

"We should be so lucky," she said, grabbing a White House matchbook from a side table to light her cigarette.

When she tried to get under his skin this way, he thought, it was best to control his anger more and not engage with her. "You've been cooped up in this shelter for too long, that's all," he told her. She was the one person who understood how Eisenhower had brought them their deepest sorrows and their greatest joys. "For all the grief he's put us through, I still value his advice."

"Is that why you called him? So he could tell you how to get out of the mess we're in?" She held her Lucky Strikes breath for a moment, waiting to see if he would continue to accept this kind of talk, or catch her hint that she knew what had happened.

He slammed his desk again, using it this time to signal her to back off. He should have predicted before his last call to Eisenhower that the old man would not approve of anything less than the SIOP's all-out retaliatory response. And he should have known the old man would not approve of him if he did anything less. If he rejected the JCS plan to implement the SIOP, Eisenhower's lack of faith in him would be borne out, assuming Gettysburg survived, which it probably would. Ike no doubt had a first-class shelter out there. If he could reach an agreement with Khrushchev to call it even after a proportionate U.S. attack on a Soviet military target, Eisenhower would say Nixon hadn't fulfilled his obligation. There was no telling what the senile old bastard would say—probably that he knew all along his boy hadn't sufficiently matured to effectively carry out his presidential responsibilities. Pat would never understand any of it.

"For one thing," he said, "regular calls at a time of international crisis are a courtesy a former president expects."

She blew smoke out of the corner of her mouth, determined to make him engage, or throw her out. "So whatever he tells you to do, that's what you do? As if you didn't have the guts to go your own way." She didn't know what advice Eisenhower had given Dick and she didn't believe it mattered. Her faith was in her husband to do the right thing, if only she could convince him to decide for himself right from wrong.

"I'll do whatever I think is right for the country." It was a rote response that he began yelling before his wife's note of encouragement rang through. "You don't understand, Pat." Giving the order the JCS wanted—that would take guts. She didn't understand the decision they were waiting for, of course. What she understood from her own grievances with Eisenhower, and had somehow helped him understand, was how to put the old bastard to use for his own ends. And so he was inclined now to listen to her, as he rarely did. Ten years ago she showed him he had the strength to stand up to Eisenhower and fight to keep his place on the Republican ticket. Now he would need her again if he should contradict Eisenhower's expertise, to say nothing of overriding the recommendation of the Joint Chiefs of Staff. "I don't know if I can do it, Pat."

She smiled and reached into her purse, slipping King in her closed hand as she stood to meet her husband, coming toward her now.

—◦◦◦—

"There isn't any legal basis for it, Mr. President, either martial law or suspending habeas corpus," Hall said, shaking his head, his second chin following a half-step behind. "You'd be subjecting yourself to impeachment, for heaven's sake."

President Nixon tried to imagine impeachment proceedings in the congressional shelter beneath the Greenbrier, picturing the chamber where the Senate would meet, with its movie theatre seats in place of wooden desks; he was unable to remember if a picture of Lincoln or Eisenhower had been mounted in the hall. "These Emergency Action Papers would only be signed, Len, if we...hell." He shook his head and looked away. If he couldn't say it out loud, what hope was there that he or Len or anyone else could comprehend the horror that would make these orders necessary?

"What about you, Jack?" he asked, without looking at McCloy or the other men, some standing, some in chairs scattered haphazardly around the conference table in his office.

"That's my feeling as well, Mr. President," McCloy said, pausing respectfully before taking the last ham sandwich from the food cart that had been wheeled in hours earlier.

"There are reports that looting is widespread now in many cities—Chicago, Philadelphia, New York, Washington, Los Angeles, and elsewhere. Roads are completely jammed—there's nothing moving, and there are reports of more shootings on the highways, vigilantism, and so on," Klein said, pointing to locations on a large United States map taped to the wall. "You've got to go on television to reassure people. Things have only gotten worse since your last statement."

He could go on television and say there's no need to panic, that there's no risk of war—everyone please go home. Then, if he approved the SIOP—or maybe even if he didn't—they'd be sitting ducks for Soviet missiles and bombers. The spontaneous exodus that was happening in cities across the country, as confused and dangerous as it was, might save many lives. Apart from encouraging the holdouts to make the roads more crowded still, a government-ordered evacuation would only put an official stamp on what people were smart enough to do for themselves. "When would we actually order evacuations?" the president asked the 54-year-old crew-cut director of the Office of Civil and Defense Mobilization, Leo Hoegh, an Eisenhower appointee he'd reappointed.

"If a Yellow Alert is sounded, Mr. President, people will hear their sirens—a steady blare—and they'll be instructed on CONELRAD radio to take shelter. Over the last year or so we've pretty much abandoned the policy of evacuating the cities," Hoegh said, a defeated look in his eyes.

"When would you put that signal out?"

"That alert would be reserved until a Communist attack is considered imminent," the former Iowa governor answered.

Was an attack imminent? That's what the JCS seemed to believe. "I'd say this, people have had time to leave if they want to and I say, let 'em go," he concluded with a sweep of his arm. "They have a right to make up their own minds about how they're going to handle this damn thing. That's what you've got to understand with this crappy situation—and it is a crappy situation—I'll be the first to stand up here and admit it."

"Damn crappy, sir," Hoegh said, bushy eyebrows lowered over closed eyes.

"Now what the hell are we doing about all our vital records in Washington? Leo?"

Hoegh looked at the president. "Each agency has a duplicate set of its most important papers at its alternative site. Thank God for that."

Finch, who had been waiting for an opening, slid a typewritten sheet of names across the table. "This is our most up-to-date list of who's been evacuated to Mount Weather."

Seeing that none of the Supreme Court justices had arrived, the president asked Finch if this was still true. When Bob said it was, he couldn't help thinking of the historic opportunity he could have to shape the court with new appointments, even as he felt ashamed at having the thought.

"Now, Len, I want you to take a look at the rest of these emergency orders. Then we'll talk some more."

"And Tom, I want you to put every man you have on those rescue operations off Cuba and I don't give a damn about the risks. Now get going on that."

"The radiation levels are still very high," Gates responded, "and the DEFCON-1 alert has us at such a high tempo that—"

"I don't care!"

"We'll do everything we possibly can," Gates said.

Dulles moved a photo across the conference table with his index finger.

The president looked down at the black-and-white image. "What the hell is it?"

Dulles pointed to a small dot. "Lundahl says it's an FKR—maybe the one that hit Guantanamo."

"That asshole doesn't know shit," he said, thinking as much of Allie as the photo interpreter. "What else?" For the first time in hours, no one around the conference table immediately spoke.

"Why don't you take a break for a few minutes, Mr. President," Radford suggested.

———ରରରୋ———

"Able to get some sleep, were you?" he asked when Bebe returned to his place on the couch.

"Took a walk outside. Fucking cold up there this time of night."

"Yeah. Went for a walk with Pat there the other day. Damn cold even with the sun out," he said. And then she came to my office this evening. I can't tell you what happened there but she doesn't always get the credit she deserves for knowing what it means to have guts. "She came to see me after all this shit hit the fan."

"Came here to your office?"

"Threw her out, of course. On her dead ass," he said with a smirk. Before she left he had talked with her about all that had happened, about the path history had sent him down to carry out the plans of the giants on whose shoulders he stood; they also talked more about Eisenhower, who, he told her, had advised him to stand firm.

"She shouldn't be interrupting you at a time like that, but she had no way of knowing."

"I taught her a lesson." Lessons can go both ways though. Who else but Pat had such faith that he was a good man who had the guts to do the right thing? If only he knew what that was.

Others seemed so sure—Eisenhower certainly was. On his legal pad he'd broken it down further and, looking over those notes now, he found it hard to be optimistic about the future if he were to once again buck the Chiefs' recommendation and, this time, his former boss's advice.

The generals had shown him a study not long ago saying that even though we had many more missiles than the Soviets, by the end of the decade they would be able to completely destroy the civilian and military leadership in the U.S. with a nuclear strike, rendering us incapable of retaliation. It also seemed clear that what Khrushchev was trying to pull off in Cuba was just a first taste of what we could expect from the Soviets in the years to come, as they worked to spread their influence around the globe. He had thought the Eastern Hemisphere—our own god-damn backyard—would be last on Moscow's list, and yet here Khrushchev was already, trying to establish a military base to threaten the U.S. and its neighbors.

If he did what they expected of him, the dust would settle on a different world. The Cold War would be over, Communism defeated. It would finally be possible for democracy to spread unchecked. People everywhere would have the same opportunities for a middle-class life that every person in the U.S. enjoyed. Countries that once found our standard of living unimaginable might themselves achieve unprecedented prosperity. In the process, we would supply them with washing machines and refrigerators and automobiles, growing immeasurably richer ourselves, and the threat of confrontation, which darkened every American's natural optimism each time the air-raid siren wailed, or the gazette landed on the porch with news of yet another Soviet first in space technology, would finally be lifted.

Pat said that whatever he did, she'd stand behind him. But he knew, without her having to say it, that she expected him to find his way down a different road.

The boardwalk by the Black Sea was wide enough for father and son to walk side by side, keeping close. Together they breathed the sweet mix of sea and forest. "Be quiet so I can think," the premier told Sergei. Under the bright sun, the small gravel stones on the beach collided, one against another, as the water came gently in and, after a quiet moment, as it went noisily out.

Khrushchev pointed toward the watery horizon. "They could be here in few minutes," he told his son. Whenever he handed visitors his binoculars and told them to look across the sea to Turkey, they claimed to see nothing but water. He'd grab the glasses back and look for himself. There they were, American nuclear missiles aimed right at him.

"Is Nixon crazy, father? I think he'd have to be to go back on his word and start World War III. You defended Cuba only way you could."

"Until few days ago, I considered him worthless piece of horse shit, but smart man and sane man. When he began preparing to fight nuclear war with us I questioned myself. He was still worthless horse shit, I said. But sane man does not risk death of 70 million of his citizens to prove political point about tiny island. That is why I decided I must allow Americans to cut off head of great Cuban revolution." Khrushchev angrily jabbed a finger at his eyes. "But I have brain in my head—nothing can justify destruction of both our countries! Maybe Nixon took very big shit and his brain came out his ass."

"What will you do, father?"

"I told Malinovsky to ready his nuclear forces. When we return to dacha I will call him on high-frequency line and give him orders."

They walked along again in silence until Sergei asked, "Might not Americans decide to have small response, more in keeping with scale of their own losses?"

"That is what you or I would do, son. But we are not madmen."

Chapter 14

Saturday, October 27, 1962

I T WAS WINDY AGAIN ATOP Mount Weather, even without the churning, turbine-driven blades of the dimly-illuminated Sea King helicopter waiting on the landing pad, ARMY spelled out in large white letters on the tail boom. Hesitating imperceptibly in his forward stride, the president reached for his suit jacket pocket, holding in his fist the small, oxidized figure, as he quickly mounted the four fold-out steps to climb aboard.

In the short time it took to fly from High Point to Washington, the sun rose just enough to make the city sparkle, and he could clearly make out what he had come to see.

It was not yet five in the morning when he had called to order Marine One to be readied. He had been unable to sleep much more than an hour, after having stayed up most of the night with Bebe, reading some history and again going over his notes, speaking into the Dictaphone, composing memos for Rose to transcribe, all of it in preparation for later this morning, when he would pick up the phone without the dial and announce his decision.

Following his instructions, the helicopter made slow loops around the Washington, Jefferson, and Lincoln memorials, the Capitol building, and, coming into view now, the White House, small and dark by comparison. "Tell the pilot I want to take another loop around," he told the military aide sitting at his side.

The helicopter banked over the Fourteenth Street bridge, flew the short distance up the Potomac River to Georgetown, then headed south toward the State Department. As the pilot flew over the National Mall toward the Capitol, he saw what had been and what might be. "Heaps of smoking ruin," a British soldier had written of what remained the morning after his troops had set the city ablaze, 145 years ago. He could not remember from what he had read last night if Washington had been evacuated then. If LeMay's forces allowed but one Soviet bomber to penetrate our defenses it would no doubt be sent here to drop its nuclear payload. History, he had learned, moves in cycles. Again a soldier, this time a Soviet pilot circling back over the city, would watch a raging firestorm and again, in time, the city would be rebuilt. Chicago and San Francisco once stood in ruins and were now some of the nation's finest; Nagasaki and Hiroshima thrived. And yet, as he looked down on his life as it had been—all the avenues spread out below that he'd so often and so urgently traveled, along Constitution, back and forth on Pennsylvania, across Independence, along all these streets, from the Capitol out to the farm in the distance of Whittaker Chambers, from the White House to Mount Weather, to all the places where he had helped in ways large and small to bring history to this point—he longed to return to the city passing beneath him to take up his place again in the Oval Office, returning to nothing less than the familiar struggle against America's adversaries in Moscow, Peiping, Hanoi, and the other capitals of the Communist world. He had spoken from every corner of the country as a candidate, a congressman, a senator, vice president, and president about defeating Communism. He had spoken of war, it was true; the nation must be ready to fight and strong enough to prevail. He had also spoken of victory achieved in a great struggle of ideas that pitted one system against another and promised transformation without destruction. A week from now he would fly this way again, having made the choice between a horrible victory and a continuing struggle, returning to the city where he had made his life or inspecting the cost of fighting for freedom and on his way to a new future.

———∞∞∞———